DARK RIVER

AVERY JENKINS

Black Rose Writing | Texas

First printing

This is a work of fiction. Names, characters, businesses, places, events, and incidents are either the products of the author's imagination or used in a fictitious manner. Any resemblance to actual persons, living or dead, or actual events is purely coincidental.

ISBN: 978-1-68433-611-1
PUBLISHED BY BLACK ROSE WRITING
www.blackrosewriting.com

Printed in the United States of America
Suggested Retail Price (SRP) $19.95

Dark River is printed in Calluna

*As a planet-friendly publisher, Black Rose Writing does its best to eliminate unnecessary waste to reduce paper usage and energy costs, while never compromising the reading experience. As a result, the final word count vs. page count may not meet common expectations.

To a woman called G

DARK RIVER

PROLOGUE

"Momma told me I can't see you anymore," the girl said. "She's gonna make me go talk to the police."

She brushed her blonde hair aside, put the tiny pipe in her mouth, inhaled and handed it to the man. A slight breeze carried her words out the window with the smoke.

"What do you mean, go to the police?" he asked. "And how does she know about me?"

He put the hash pipe on the console between the two front seats of the car. He didn't smoke, but he always gave her some so she could loosen up a little before they had sex. The first few times she had been pretty nervous. All she'd ever done before was oral sex, she told him. That had been different.

That wasn't what he wanted. Where he'd been, the women had been pretty well used up before they got around to him. He either paid them or they ignored him.

"She doesn't know it's you. She thinks it's another guy, one who's always hanging around with my friends. She wants me to file a statutory rape complaint against him," the girl said. "She says he's too old. It's illegal, she says. I don't really care. I love you." She snuggled up against him in the back seat of the Trans Am.

The breeze, of course, heard all of their words. It heard all words everywhere. From the cries of a child being born to the moans of death and the wailing of the living. The whispers of lovers, the caress of water over rock, the crack of a breaking tree limb, the crash of waves on the shore. Nothing spoke without the wind knowing.

The couple was parked at their usual spot, a landing on the river at the end of a dirt road above the Cauldron, where the river funneled into a tumult of white water. He could see the river over the girl's shoulder, its current running dark and smooth. The first fallen leaves of autumn were scattered across its surface.

She was barely fifteen and he was twenty-three, and he didn't want to go to jail.

He didn't respond to her cuddling and she looked up at him.

"I told her that I'm not seeing anyone, but she's going to know soon, anyway. I'm pregnant," she said. "I'm gonna have your baby." She gave his arm a squeeze. "Isn't that wonderful? We can get a house, somewhere along the river up here, where it's quiet. We can raise our child together."

God, no, he thought to himself. Goddammit.

He had to play this just right, not lose his cool, just stay in control. He used to have that control. All the time, 24/7. Now it was harder to find it.

"No, bunny. It's too soon," he said with a caring that he didn't feel. "We can't do that...yet."

"But I want to," she said. "This is what we wanted! What we both want!"

Her quiet wail was carried by the wind to a crow sitting in a tree above them. Unlike the wind, which conveyed without listening, the crow paid attention. These noises, these words of men, could mean food. The crow sat on its limb above the parking spot because people left scraps behind them. It knew most people who came here left something.

The man shook his head. If the lies he told this girl were the worst of his sins, he would be a saint, he thought.

"We will...soon, bunny," he said. "I just gotta get a few things straightened out. That's all. Before that, we can't really have a baby."

"You want me to...?"

"It's easy. You'll see," he said. "Just make the appointment. I'll give you the money for it and take you there and I'll be in the car waiting for you when you're done. It takes fifteen minutes, that's all."

"I can't do that! It's our baby!" she said and started crying. "I thought you wanted this," she said between sobs.

"I do, bunny, I do. Just . . . we just can't do it now."

"Well I'm not doing that!" she shouted at him.

He slapped her. There was silence.

"Don't ever speak like that to me again," he said.

That was the wrong thing to do, he thought. Not for her, but for him. Then the rage began uncoiling inside him, just like it used to, just like they had always wanted it to, that cold, controlled rage that gave him all the power.

He resisted it, just a little bit, just enough to tell himself later that he had tried...and then he let it go.

He slapped her again. Harder this time. She started crying louder.

"Shut up! Shut up, bitch!"

She tried to put her hands over her face. He grabbed her. And then the snake took over.

The crow, its left eye glittering in reflected moonlight, watched the man as he dragged the girl out of the car. Its claws twitched as she died, not in sorrow nor in joy, but because it was a crow. It paid not to have too firm a grip on a branch, as a crow. The limb it was sitting on let go of one of its yellow leaves.

The crow watched as the man rolled off her. The girl was naked now, lying face down in the dying grass beside the river. She wasn't breathing. The yellow leaf finally slid off the breeze and landed on the girl's back.

The man got up and pulled his pants up.

What a fucking mess, he thought. Stupid bitch. He remembered the first time he had seen her that summer, on the beach by the swimming hole below the dam. She was coming out of the water, in her bikini, those small breasts. She was beginning to develop some real curves, a little pudgy, but right then she was just right, straight blonde hair falling over her shoulders.

He had watched and waited and bided his time until he got a chance to bump into her at the snack bar. His smile, his easy confidence with her, his taut muscles, all worked their charm on the child. He had her phone number and a week later, her virginity.

Well, we met by water, now we part by water, he thought.

He opened the trunk of the Trans Am and found the tire chains. He pulled both of them out, and some rope, and wrapped the chains around the body, tying them in place. He'd throw her in, and that would be it, he thought. By the time they found her, there'd be no evidence of him at all, no evidence that he'd ever been on top of her, driving and punching and choking her into submission, and afterward, oblivion.

They wouldn't even know it was her after the pounding her body would take through the Cauldron.

He started to drag her body into the river and noticed the tattoo on her upper arm. Fucking tat! If that was still on her, the goddamn thing would identify her instantly. Fuck.

He walked back to the Trans Am and pulled the K-Bar knife out of the glove compartment. Thank the gods he always kept it sharp. He tested it against his thumb and then ran it down the dead girl's arm, outlining a six inch slice of skin from shoulder to elbow around the tattoo. He peeled off the skin, carefully, like he was peeling an orange, and threw it far out into the river.

Minutes later the girl was out there too. The river took her in, as it did all things, wrapping her in its cool embrace. Her life's energy, freed from its confines, expanded into the water. The river absorbed these new currents of energy from her, incorporating them into its own currents, easing the body to the rocks and silt below while the release continued of her body's tightly-wound strands of being. Living things paid little attention to the enormous amount of energy it took to keep them from moment to moment, but the river and the earth understood.

From the branch above the crow watched as the man rinsed off his hands and his knife and then sheathed it. He suddenly bent over and threw up once before he climbed into the Trans Am and drove off.

Even then, the crow waited, watching and blinking, one eye glittering in the moonlight, before flying to the ground to see if anything of value had been left. It pecked at a button from the girl's blouse, but it wasn't food, and it wasn't the time of year to be making a nest. The bird flipped it aside. After hopping from spot to spot in the parking area, the crow glanced down at the river and then flew off for the night.

The crow would keep his silence, but the marks of his talons and the wind and the thin track of a body being dragged across the dirt told the story for any with eyes to see.

FRIDAY – CHAPTER 1

"Goddammit," I said to nobody in particular.

I set my boot against the log and pushed it off the splitting stump. It fell on its side with the head of the maul stuck in the log and the handle half-splintered a third of the way up. It looked like somebody had kicked it and had probably broken their shin doing so.

I shook my hands to get the sting out, grabbed the handle, wrenched it off at the break and used the freed end to beat the head back out of the piece of firewood. I dropped the broken handle on the ground and took the head back into the workshop.

The birds had stopped their chatter to stare at a quietly cursing old man. I glared at them and went inside.

I fished around my pile of lumber until I found the spare handle and spun the vise closed around it, pulled a drawknife out, and started paring down the end to fit into the maul. Thin slips of hickory curled up and dropped on my boots.

After ten minutes with the drawknife, I was able to pound the maul's head onto the handle. I flipped it upside down and tapped on the bottom of the handle with a mallet. Each tap drove the head further up the handle until it was where I wanted it. I cut the end even with the head and drove in a wedge.

I swung the maul a few times. Compared to swinging a katana, or even a wooden sword, swinging a maul just feels stupid. But a maul's job isn't all that smart. You're either bashing something with one end or splitting something with the other.

I went back out to finish the firewood. Overhead, clouds were gathering. The weather reports were predicting rain soon, rain and wind. Well, actually they were calling for a full-blown hurricane coming my way. Inland though this town was, we were still expected to catch a major part of the blow. I wanted to finish my winter's firewood before everything got slippery and soaking wet and cold, and I would be standing out here in gloves and boots just making it all that much harder.

I'm not a young man anymore, and I don't see any reason to take the harder path when another will do. I've got nothing left to prove.

The hurricane was pushing unusually warm weather ahead of it, and it was a sweaty eighty-five degrees at the woodpile. Frankly, I thought late September was a little belated for a hurricane in the first place, but as usual nobody was asking me. The world has its own ways, and those ways seem to be changing.

I soon found my groove again, a feeling of being able to sense the cracks and grain in the wood, and I could split a piece into three or sometimes four pieces, with a single blow. It's a nifty trick, and I don't know anyone else who can do that, but it's not exactly a marketable skill.

Hearing the birds starting to chatter in trees behind me, about what I don't know, I lined up the last round on the stump, blasted through it, and let the maul stay stuck, this handle still in one piece. I dried my face on my shirt.

My hands didn't really start griping me until I was stacking the wood and trying to grab the pieces that I used to be able to pick up so easily with one hand. The arthritis weakened my grip or rather, made a stronger grip more painful. I ignored it and slung the split pieces up anyway, stacking them on the last row in the three-sided woodshed.

I was two-thirds of the way done when I glimpsed someone standing at the gate of the short picket fence surrounding my yard. A woman, tall, slender, long gray hair streaked with black pulled back in a ponytail. She was dressed casually, but nicely, in creased jeans and a white sleeveless blouse. There was a tattoo on her right forearm, but I couldn't make out the design. The hell. My home address wasn't something I really advertised.

"If you're making a delivery, just leave it on the front porch," I said. "Unless it's pizza, and I didn't order any."

She smiled. Cool, but not unfriendly.

"And I'd be the best-dressed delivery gal you've seen in a while, wouldn't I?" she said.

I nodded, returning the smile. "You would be at that," I said. "But the shop's not open right now, and as you can see" – I waved at the pile of unstacked wood – "I'm kind of in the middle of things."

"Oh, I didn't come on business," she said. "I'm just here to take a look."

"Can't say I'm surprised," I said. "Which bicep do you want me to flex first?"

She laughed. "Don't get yourself too excited, old man," she said. "I'm looking for a house, not a night on the town. I was hoping to see what this neighborhood was like."

"For starters, it's the only neighborhood in this town," I said. "Not much like . . . " I paused and looked her over. "the Upper East Side."

"Georgetown, DC, actually," she said. "But not a bad guess. So you're used to New Yorkers around here?"

"Not so many of them these days, but I'm okay with that," I said.

"No doubt you are." She rested her arm on the gate. It was a lotus tattoo on her forearm.

"Well," she smiled at me again, and pointed at her face. "My eyes are up here, you know."

"I was just admiring your tattoo."

"Sure you were."

"Unusual to see a tattoo like that on a mature woman," I said.

She raised an eyebrow. "This lotus would be an unusual tattoo to see on anyone," she said. "But I'm not here to trade banter about body art. It's nice to see that the natives here have a sense of humor, though."

"Oh, I'm no native. I only moved here seven years ago, and this is small-town New England. You're not considered a native until the second generation."

"So I've heard," she said. "If you don't mind me asking, where did you live before here?"

I shook my head. "It's a long story," I said. "I doubt that you have the time."

"I have more time than you would think," she said and looked at me sharply, "but less than I would want. So I really should be going."

"Well, down by the lake, there are some nice properties," I said, "but I don't really do real estate. You should talk to an agent."

She nodded slowly. "I should," she said, "but that's not how I do things." She thought for a minute. "Well, thank you for your time. I'd best get moving." She started away from the gate.

"No problem," I said. "By the way, what did you say your name was?"

"I didn't," she said, turned and walked up the driveway.

I watched her. That was odd, I thought. Maybe she had actually come to sell me something. After all, I'm in the business. But then she'd backed off. It happens sometimes. I hated to miss out on a good deal, but if she just up and walked off like that, the thing was probably sketchy to begin with. Maybe an ex-husband's expensive watch, misplaced on the field of battle during the divorce. Or his replica Civil War sword that he'd always claimed was worth a college tuition.

What I really wanted right now was a moon rock from the Apollo missions. I had a client who wanted one. Acquisition and verification would be a bit dicey, but there would be a good profit. I doubted that she had one.

Shaking my head, I went back to stacking the wood. By the time I had finished, the birds had left to get some dinner. It was time for me to do the same. I stepped back and looked at the woodshed. On the right-hand side, the stack slanted outwards as it reached up toward seven feet. It looked like a collapse was imminent, but I had stacked enough lousy piles to know that the wood would hold. Probably.

The clouds were getting thicker as I walked back up to the house, a nothing-special, side-gable colonial that needed a paint job. But it had been the right price, only about a mile from where I had intended to open my shop, and it had a room for a study, where I could sit, read a book and smoke a pipe. Since I live alone, I could probably do that anywhere, but a man reaches a point in life when he really should have a study.

A crow swooped down and perched on a low-hanging branch of my maple tree and looked at me.

"I'm thinking stir-fry. How about you?" I asked. It cocked its head at me and said nothing. I popped open the back door, swollen in the humidity, and started getting dinner ready.

FRIDAY – CHAPTER 2

After dinner, I sat for a couple of hours with a cup of tea and a book. My hands were still aching, and I felt the tiredness in my muscles. My eyelids were beginning to droop. I had one more thing to do before going to sleep. If I didn't do it now, I would end up sawing logs with my mouth open, my eyes closed, and my book in my lap.

I put on a maroon t-shirt and a pair of loose white cotton pants with a drawstring, the bottom half of the uniform favored by those who train in Eastern martial arts. The t-shirt read "Certified Original Parts" and I couldn't argue with that. The pants were well-used, loose and floppy. They felt like pajamas and like I had been born to wear them.

I went into my study and stood in front of the low Chinese scholar's desk, meant to be used while sitting on the floor. The top of the desk was empty, save a candle in each of its three corners and a bowl of ashes in the center. I lit each of the three candles, pulled three sticks of incense out of a drawer and lit each of them with a different candle. I stuck the incense sticks in the holder and sat down with my legs folded underneath me to meditate.

My hands, lightly clasped together, rested on my thighs, and one breath gave way to another. I sank slowly down the layers of consciousness. First I counted the breaths, one per exhalation. After reaching a count of ten, I started over again at one. Then I let go of the counting and followed my breaths as each one entered my lungs and then exited. Soon, the ache in my hands stopped. Or I wasn't aware of it, which amounts to the same thing.

Following the body's breath without counting is often a confusing point in my meditations. This is when images, sounds and sensations arise, all clamoring for my attention, all trying to drag my mind from resting in silent breath on to whatever framed the struggle at hand.

The images can be anything, from friends to cars to bicycles. They can be realistic or cartoons. They can be friendly, annoying or terrifying. Each arouses an emotion in me, or more likely the emotions in me arouse the image. It is so easy right then to let my mind go off on a tangent, thinking about that weird Uber ride in Budapest or that lovely night in the northern mountains under a cold winter moon, hearing the howl of the wolves in the valley below.

Getting past this roadblock takes a little time and concentration, but I am used to it now, and generally don't get stuck. Tonight the image that called was of a river, broad and deep, with a slow moving, strong current in the middle. I struggled to detach myself from it. It was dark and quietly menacing, and I felt that if I turned my back on it, it would attack me.

Attack. Attack, response. Attack, response. I pulled my thought out of the whirlpool of words, found my breath again. And again, the current, pulling me under, but I didn't struggle, not this time.

I let it pull me down, deeper, dark, stillness . . .

Until it was gone. I was gone. Where I breathed was nothing, where I thought was nothing. Nothing breathed, there was only breath. Nothing sat, only breath. No words, no actions, no one to do those things because there was no then and no now. I was not there to breathe. The universe was breathing.

And that was all.

Then, suddenly, another image. A face where there should have been none, becoming clearer and clearer, but gray, and hair twisted around the face, looking at first like a mound of dough. The water's current began pushing it into some shape...a nose, and a chin, not much more than a child. Her eyelids opened and the eyes, gray too, and dead, and then her mouth opened.

She screamed.

I jerked forward at the altar, knocked one of the candles over, and gasped for breath like I had been underwater for a year. I couldn't get enough air. I fell over and now I could feel my heart and it was racing.

Her face was still fixed in front of me, wavering in the current, screaming for help. I couldn't get it out of my vision. I couldn't close my eyes.

I focused on my breath again. My breathing slowed, my heart steadied. Soon I felt the rug underneath me, my legs tingling, coming back to life. The face faded from view. I took one last deep, slow, breath.

I must have been sitting for a long time, I thought. I heard one of my clocks chime. It was midnight. I had been sitting for two hours.

I stood, stiffly, and picked up one candle holder. The other two had burned themselves out. The only light in the room came in through the window from the nearly-full moon, its light dimmed by thick clouds. I found my way to the leather easy chair, sat, and looked toward the barely lit landscape outside.

A light wind moved smaller branches, like arms reaching for something they couldn't see, and eventually my eyes felt too heavy to keep open. I closed them, and with them, all images, for the rest of the night.

SATURDAY – CHAPTER 3

People ask me what I do for a living, and my simple answer is "I sell stuff."

Mostly I try to leave it at that, but if they pester me for more information, I tell them that I sell antiques. Which is partially right, but not entirely. Over the years, I've gotten to know a lot of people in a lot of different places around the world who have quite specific interests. Sometimes these people need to get rid of a thing or two, or they need a thing or two, or somebody dies and I pick up a few things from the estate of the deceased. Then I ask around to see if someone wants it.

What things, specifically, depends. I am a pretty reliable source for various historical books and manuscripts that are frequently hard to get or sometimes flat-out illegal in some countries. I also dabble in mechanical devices, as well as religious artifacts from prehistoric Indo-European and Chinese cultures up to the present day. I don't get stuck on any one thing, I try to flow with the market.

To my credit, I did manage to stay away from beanie babies, and I usually don't buy anything that's stolen. I'm less fastidious about moving things across borders, though. Borders, unlike history, don't really exist. They're only lines drawn in the sand until the next high tide.

I have a shop jammed full of varying types of inventory on the main street of Nemaseck. I named it *Tempo Gardas*, which translates from the original language into "Time's Keep." It's part of a row of brick shops with common walls and has two plate glass display windows, into which I occasionally throw stuff, and wide wooden steps leading to a double-hung front door with broad windows.

Long and narrow, the shop is crowded with obscurities from around the world, and in the back is a short staircase of four steps which leads to the door of my office, which is never closed. It extends from one side of the shop to the other, has four windows that face out the back of the building. I can see the river about a football field away, running through the center of town, smooth and deep.

Truth be told, I sell damn little out of the shop. Like most brick-and-mortar stores that are still in business, the bulk of my sales come through the internet or directly from clients who have contacted me.

The mile walk from my house went easily, considering I had spent the night in a chair. I had drunk my cup of coffee and had had a bowl of rice for breakfast, and then I'd gone out back for forty-five minutes of martial arts practice so I was pretty loosened up by the time I headed out the front door. Even my hands felt better. Like most of the side streets that ran away from the river, the road to my house ran uphill, out of the narrow river valley, and was populated by old Victorian and colonial houses like mine. It was only a long walk, downhill, to my shop.

I glanced up over the open front door at my sign, an arch of black lettering on white, and as I walked in, I saw the soft glow of a computer screen at the side of the room. Its blue light was mostly blocked by a head and an explosion of tangled black curls.

She didn't turn around when I walked in. She just asked, "Did you bring me coffee?"

"No, it's not my turn," I said. "And good morning to you, too, Neveah."

Now she turned around.

"It is too your turn. I brought it yesterday."

"It's never my turn, Nev. I'm the boss, remember?"

"Pfft." She turned back around to her screen again. "We got orders up the ass, you want them to go out today, you gettin' the coffee. I got no time. Also, how the fuck you want me to pack this up?" She gestured to an orrery sitting on the table next to her. "It's too damn big. Can I take it apart or something?"

"Jesus. No. I'll show you what to do after I get the coffee."

Neveah, or Nev as I called her because I could never quite get the breathiness of that second syllable quite right, had showed up on my doorstep four years earlier. Literally. I was going to the shop to open up in the morning, and she was sitting on the steps waiting for me.

"You the guy looking for shop help?" she asked.

"Yeah," I said as I unlocked the door. "Got someone for me?"

"Yeah. Me," She walked in front of me into the shop and looked around. "Damn," she said, "What the hell you sellin?"

"A lot of stuff," I said.

"Looks like junk to me." She walked over to the computer, sat down in front of it and flicked it on. "This is where you need help, it said in the ad."

"I need someone to keep the website together, get inventory online, handle shipping, and man the shop when I'm not here," I said.

She swung around in the chair and looked up at me. She had thick, long, curly black hair that fell to her shoulders, and maroon lipstick. She was wearing jeans and a tank top, and I could see part of a tattoo on her left shoulder. The black ink on her dark skin looked like it was hiding something.

"I can do that," she said. "When do I start?"

"Whoa," I said. "Who the hell are you?"

"Neveah," she said. "Like heaven spelled backwards, but my parents fucked it up and it's spelled wrong."

"You have any experience?"

"Sure," she said. "Used to do web stuff at the 42nd St. Y when they were shorthanded."

"Umm, yeah," I said, "I was looking for something more than that."

Neveah looked at me, and I realized she was sizing me up the same way I was her.

"Maybe I did more" she said. "Maybe I can tell you later, if you hire me. But I'm good." Her eyes wandered around the shop. "And maybe I can get all your bullshit here straightened out."

"It is straightened out."

She laughed, a full-bodied laugh, her hand over her mouth as if she were embarrassed by it.

"Damn, this is *not* straightened out. I mean, look at this shit here." She walked over to one shelf and picked up an old, yellowed meerschaum pipe, dusty from its long life there. "First of all, you gotta throw some of this shit out."

She chucked the pipe over into the wastebasket.

I jumped forward and grabbed the pipe mid-flight.

"Jesus. That's a hundred and fifty year old Al Pache," I said.

"Well, somebody needs to clean the thing up. Looks like shit. You think you gonna sell that looking like that?" She pointed her finger at me. "You need some help here."

I set the pipe down. Carefully. Where it wouldn't get knocked over.

I looked at Neveah. She looked at me. I knew at this point it would be useless to ask her for a resume or for references. This is what I was going to get. Her eyes were steady.

"Where are you living?" I asked.

"First things first," Neveah said. "Gotta get a job, then I get a place. I got a job?"

I shook my head. "Yeah, you got a job," I said. What the hell was I doing? She nodded, serious now.

"By the way," I said, "my name's Asa. Asa Cire" I held out my hand.

She ignored it. "Asa? Hell no, I'm not calling you that. Sounds too much like asshole."

"You can call me Mr. Cire, if you'd like."

"Hell no, I'm not calling you that, either," she said. "And you ain't no Jefe."

She dropped that thought and swung around in the chair to face the computer again.

"Now what's the password here and are you going to get us coffee?"

The memory snapped shut. Neveah was looking at me expectantly.

"Yeah, I'll get us some."

"Well, don't forget the cream," she said. "I may like my men black, but I like my coffee light and sweet."

Jesus.

I turned around and headed out the door.

SATURDAY – CHAPTER 4

Inasmuch as I knew this was going to happen this morning—I *always* get the coffee—I had brought an old and battered bent-stem pipe, tucked in my pocket and pre-packed with 1970s-era Balkan Sobranie tobacco, my favorite blend. You could still find it, if you knew where to look, and I knew where to look. The price was a bit steep, though.

I took a minute to light the pipe before I walked down the street to the coffee shop. Of course, I wasn't actually heading to the coffee shop, at least not at first. I had a different place in mind. I walked a couple of blocks, took a left, and went a few more. I took my time. Balkan Sobranie is not a tobacco to rush your way through.

Nemaseck is an old, post-industrial New England town built next to a river where waterwheels, then coal, then oil powered mills and factories. The river runs north to south, and the town was built on the west side of the river, where the ground sloped smoothly to its banks. From the back of the shops on West St. to the river, the ground is a mowed grassy field with picnic tables scattered across it.

Here the river is wide and sedate and makes for good fishing and boating down to Lake Wenamaug, a once-popular summer resort area.

Instead of Main Street, the founding fathers had quite sensibly named the main road through town West Street, as the west side of the river. Across the river, the east bank is rocky and steep.

Upstream, out of town, the banks on both sides gradually close in until several miles north they narrow to what is called the Cauldron, a steep, waterfall-like run with vertical rock banks where the water crashes and spumes as it spits through earth's funnel.

Above the Cauldron, the river grows calm again, but remains narrow. The current runs faster there than it does below and has too many shallows and rock outcroppings to allow for motorboats. Hemlock and pine grow there, clinging for dear life onto the rocks and acidic soil along the bank.

Still further north, the land gets hillier and rockier still, and even today harbors few houses as the hills gradually turn into mountains.

After the death of the textile business, Nemaseck had a long dry spell and became a backwater town in a backwater county with not much to speak for it. Then wealthy New Yorkers found it and turned it into a summer play place. They bought the old houses, fixed them up and invited their friends for weekends in the country. They bought up the land around the lake, put up small mansions with boat houses and docks and buzzed around the lake with water skis in tow.

The bass fishermen stayed anchored in the bays after that and ventured out only when their sonars told them the fish were on the move.

Business in town changed to adapt to the new clientele. Estate jewelry, high-end clothing and restaurants now dominated West St. where once there were dime stores, grocers and butchers. And, of course, there was pizza, liquor and Chinese food, the indispensable commodities of any New England small town.

But about a decade before I moved to Nemaseck, it had fallen on hard times again. The tourists dried up and businesses boarded up. That was perfect for me, though. I was looking for someplace small, nondescript and out-of-the-way, but still within driving distance of an airport, and the town's backslide had made real estate prices appealing.

Enjoying the aroma of my vintage tobacco, I walked south past shops that were either closed permanently or not yet open for the day. The side streets ran perpendicular, to the left coming to a dead-end as they approached the river, to the right up the steep slope out of the valley.

I turned right down one of these side streets and stopped in front of an old Victorian house, well tended, with a lovely garden in front of the wraparound porch. The flowers were mostly gone now, and the few that were left were faded beauties from another season. They just didn't know their time was up yet.

Over the porch was a sign that read "Nemaseck Historical Society." I opened the door and stepped in.

SATURDAY – CHAPTER 5

Charlie was sitting at his desk, leaning over an aged yellow newspaper.

"Put that damn thing out, Asa. You know there's no smoking in here."

He went back to his paper. I stepped back out and knocked the dottle out of my pipe on the heel of my shoe and it fell into the garden below. I went back in.

"Good morning to you, too, Charlie."

He looked up at me, a sour look on his face.

"You always do that. You always walk in smoking your pipe and you know there's no smoking in here. You just don't give a damn about the rules, do you?"

"I give a damn about the important ones," I said. Charlie gets a little crabby sometimes, especially when he thinks somebody is bending "the rules." I looked at him, staring at his paper again. "What's into you this morning?"

"Ah, this," he said, waving at the paper. Every morning, Charlie pulled an old paper from that same date years ago and read through it. Sometimes it was from a decade earlier, sometimes fifty years back. Keeps history alive, he said. "Happened twenty years ago today. That's when they found her. What a horror."

He turned the paper so that I could read it.

"Missing Girl Found Dead," the headline read. Below it was a picture of a girl.

Not a girl. The girl.

The girl I had seen in my vision the night before. She was smiling for a photographer taking her high school yearbook picture. She had wavy blonde hair, parted in the middle and falling to either side. Her face was a little chubby with cheeks that rounded to her smile. She looked...well, happy. She wasn't dead.

"Jesus," I said, not taking my eyes off the picture. "What happened to her?"

"Helluva story, Asa," Charlie said. He grabbed the wheels of his chair and pushed himself back from his desk. Charlie had close-cropped hair touched with gray, and even sitting in a wheelchair he had the straight-backed bearing of former military. He had done a couple of tours somewhere— someplace with rocks and mountains and scrub, someplace cold and hard. He had, according to his own account, come back pretty cold and hard himself and had made a name as one of the region's best rock climbers. He'd climbed solo plenty of routes which others had looked at and said "no" to, and he'd established new ones on cliffs that everyone else thought had been all done.

Then he fell. He fell a long way, and the only reason he survived the fall at all was because he was cold and hard. He lost use of the lower half of his body, and his shattered pelvis would never let him be out of pain again, but he dealt with it without falling into drugs or alcohol as so many of his peers did. He had rules. And his rules kept him alive and sane.

"She goes out one night to get together with some friends, and doesn't come back. Mom gets a little worried but doesn't really check up on her. The girl was a little wayward, I guess, and Mom wasn't the most attentive parent. She figured the girl had spent the night with one of her friends. The following night, Mom still hasn't heard from girl. She calls the police. They don't think much about it, either. Search for her doesn't get into full gear until a couple days later. They find her a week after she disappeared. By this time, whole town's up in arms.

Charlie tapped the yellow newspaper page in front of me with a thick index finger.

"That's not the worst part," he said. "They find her dead. Drowned. Hands and feet tied. She had a tattoo. It was cut off her body. Just peeled right off."

"Jesus," I said.

"Even that's not the worst part," Charlie said. "She'd been sodomized. Not while she was alive. After."

"Jesus. Who did it?"

Charlie took a deep breath, as if he were coming up for air.

"They never found him. They had some suspects—some of the local lowlifes—but nothing they could pin on anyone. Killed this town. Used to be real busy here, with tourists. But that stopped pretty fast when the story got on the news. Made us look like a town of creeps."

He leaned forward and reached toward me.

"Fold that paper for me, would you?" he said. "I'll take it back to the stacks."

I took one last look at the girl in the picture. It was her face I'd seen, no mistake about it.

But this picture was before the screams, before the pain, before the drowning. She'd been alive and vibrant, and so what if a little wayward. Weren't we all at that time of life? Looking at her face made me sad. And old. It had been a long time since I had been filled with that vibrant energy of youth.

I folded up the paper and gave it to Charlie, who wheeled into the back room with it on his lap.

He came back a minute later, this time with a package. It was a long, thin box, wrapped in newspaper, Hindi from the looks of it.

"This is what you came here for, right?"

"Kautilya?" I asked.

"Yup," he said, handing it over.

I took it. Inside the box was a manuscript, nearly one of a kind, *Arthashastra*, written by one of ancient India's greatest kingmakers. Kautilya was the man behind the Mauryan Empire, and only one of the original Sanskrit manuscripts was thought to have survived. In my hands I held, presumably, a second.

"You're sure of the provenance?"

Charlie nodded. "Dead sure. Pakistani source. Never steered me wrong back in the day. Not stolen. Well, at least during the past century. Before that, I can't say." Charlie reached under the desk and pulled out a plastic grocery bag. "Here,. You may need this too." He took the box back from me and wrapped it in the bag.

"I'll send you your payment," I said. "Bitcoin, as usual?"

"Yep."

"And our usual game of Go on Tuesday?"

"Unless you have to swim. Rain's s'posed to be pretty bad. Already started."

"And they say this is just the beginning. It's just going to get worse from here."

"What worse?" Charlie said.

"Climate change. It's ramping up."

Charlie waved his hand in the air.

"Meh," he said. "The world's been going to hell since there have been old codgers like you to complain about it." He held out the bag.

I took it and headed to the front door. I began to open the door, then stopped and turned around.

"Charlie," I said, "what was the girl's name?"

He looked at me. "Oh, her," he said after a second. "Elle. Elle Anderson"

I went out on the porch. Charlie was right. Raindrops had begun to fall, big heavy drops, like the tears of a child. I tucked the bag under my arm and began walking back to the shop.

Neveah's coffee was going to have to wait.

SATURDAY – CHAPTER 6

Nev took the loss of her morning coffee in stride, but I still felt bad about it so lunchtime found me at Not Debbie's Donuts. Not Debbie's was in the old post office, left vacant after the postal service put up a new building south of the center of town, and a couple miles closer to the highway. The move, according to the postmaster, would save the USPS a million dollars each year is its new location. The donut shop moved in a few years later.

When it had opened up, it wasn't "Not Debbie's Donuts," it was "Debbie's Donuts," named after one-half of the couple that owned it, Debbie and Paul Lambe. Paul was a Bermudan immigrant. His father was a banker who had worked his way up through the Byzantine ranks of one of one of Bermuda's famous offshore banks and eventually won a slot in the bank's New York operations. His mother was a Haitian whom Paul said was the best cook on the island—which every son says about his mother—but in Paul's case it might have been true because Paul himself had become a singular chef, educated at the Culinary Institute of America, and later a pastry chef at one of the city's best-known restaurants.

After marrying Debbie, Paul decided to leave the city, part of the Latino migration from cities to suburbs to the rural Northeast. Many of them, like Nev, had found their way to Nemaseck.

It hasn't been an entirely popular demographic shift. The average rural Yankee is not exactly a cheerleader of multi-ethnic culture. On the other hand, the only thing rural Yankees like less than cultural change is people sticking their heads in other people's business, so the average Nemaseck residents balanced themselves on those two core values and mostly kept their mouths shut as the town began to change.

It also began to grow. Only the most hard-headed refused to see what was happening. With the decrease in tourism, the influx of Latinos was bringing new money and new business to the region, and once again Yankee practicality won over old racial divides. As one small dairy farmer, who sold the non-homogenized milk from his cows directly from his farm told me, "the milk's white, the guy buying it is brown, but the money's always green, so who gives a shit?" On the basis of tried-and-true Yankee values, the residents of Nemaseck grudgingly accepted the newcomers.

Within a couple of years of opening, Debbie's Donuts prospered. The problem was that the couple had brought a drug problem with them from the city. Restaurant kitchens are not exactly the place to go for clean and sober living, and Debbie—a line cook herself—as well as Paul had picked up a bad habit or two along the way. As the profitability of their donut shop grew, so did their habit, until one day Paul had an epiphany and realized if he didn't quit, he would lose his business. In a town the size of Nemaseck, he understood it would only take a few outraged Yankee customers to start the ball rolling downhill, particularly if your skin isn't the right color.

So Paul quit. Detoxed. Started going to NA meetings, even found a little higher power in his life. Debbie, unfortunately, did not, and the not-unexpected result came to pass, with Paul filing the papers. He later told me she was so deep into it that he had to physically hold her upright the day they went to court to finalize their divorce. It was all very clean and simple, split fifty/fifty. Debbie got the house and some money and Paul kept his business.

The very next day, Paul came to his shop with a ladder and a can of red paint, climbed up to the sign and painted a red circle with a diagonal stripe across it over Debbie's name.

That was how Debbie's Donut shop became Not Debbie's Donut shop. But the donuts were still the best around.

SATURDAY – CHAPTER 7

Paul had the coffee house ambiance down to a T. Brick walls, hardwood floor, hardwood table and benches, and background sound that could be anything from Dave Brubeck to Tash Sultana, depending on the time of day and who was working.

At the moment it was a screamingly fast banjo, backed by mandolin and fiddle. A long glass case held the day's selection of donuts and pastries, and a cappuccino machine about the size of a Mini Cooper sat on the counter in back. A door to the kitchen was off to the right.

Tom and Myra Miller were sitting at a corner table, drinking coffee and arguing quietly. I waved to them anyway, and they interrupted their argument to wave back. Everybody knew they argued about everything.

Behind the display case was a petite redhead with bobbed hair wearing overalls and an apron. Chloe looked to be in her mid-twenties, and she'd been working there about six months, which was about one month less than she'd been dating Paul, I figured. Her head was bouncing to the music. She smiled.

"Who's the picker?" I asked, nodding toward one of the speakers.

"Richie Ricks," she said. "Old-time player, from down around Tennessee. He hasn't recorded in years," she said. "Want the usual? Double-shot and a coconut donut?"

Out of the kitchen, a voice roared. "Make sure that guy pays cash up front, Chloe! He's got a reputation around here!"

The bellow was followed by a man as large as the voice, brown as a pair of old work boots, with a black beard that would command respect even absent the size of the man it was on. Paul was about forty-five, six foot four, and had only a bit of extra padding on him. Any more than that and he'd be going through doors sideways.

"I love you too, Paul," I said. "You ready for the storm?"

"Heck, yes," Paul said. "My mother said there's always a storm brewing somewhere, so you'd best be ready when it comes to your backyard. So I'm always ready."

"Actually," he continued in what passed for his inside voice, "the only thing we have to do for the storm is what we do every closing. Sweep up, put the chairs on the table, turn everything off and lock the door."

Paul claimed that he got his extra-large voice from years of yelling at idiots in the kitchen, but I'm pretty sure it was original equipment. Just like his natural friendliness, and a knack for putting anyone in his presence at ease and feeling welcomed.

"You got a couple of minutes to talk, Asa?" he said, and without waiting for my answer added, "Chloe, can you fly solo for a few minutes?"

Chloe nodded, with a smile on her face that said she would pick up the building and move it five feet to the left if Paul asked her to.

"I'll bring your coffee out back to you," she said.

Paul flipped up the counter top and waved me back. I followed him through the kitchen and out the back door, where a couple of stools were waiting, protected from the rain by the roof's overhang.

SATURDAY – CHAPTER 8

Paul settled himself on one of the stools. It accepted the burden without visible complaint. He pulled a pipe out of his pocket.

"Before you go any farther, you'll be wanting this," I said and pulled a pouch of pipe tobacco out of my pocket and sat down. He opened it up and sniffed.

"Mmm, Virginia and, let me guess, a little Perique, and something sweet," Paul said. "Smells like raisins and plums." He filled his pipe and handed it back to me.

"It'd be hard to fool you at this point, Paul," I said. "There's like twelve different Virginias in there. I got it from a guy who does a little blending on the side, only sells to a few friends because, you know, ATF and all. I tried a batch and bought a couple of pounds. He said he may not be able to get all those Virginias again, so this is a one-batch blend. You like it, I'd be willing to trade out for coffee and donuts."

Paul lit and took a few puffs while I filled my own pipe. He smiled.

"Deal," he said.

Paul and I had become friends when he was trying to quit smoking cigarettes some time after he'd gotten clean. I was sitting at one of the outside tables, drinking my cappuccino and having a bowl when he'd come up to me and asked me if I thought switching to a pipe would be a good way to quit the cigarettes.

We must have spent an hour that afternoon talking about pipes and tobacco. I told him that pipe smoking as a hobby was a lot like being a wine connoisseur. There are thousands of blends, being made by companies large and small, and, like my home blender guy, people who made their own blends on the side, just for the pure joy of it. Some were sweet, some were savory, some smelled like leather and a campfire, some smelled like apples or other fruit, in the same way that a fine wine carried those tastes. A pipe was smoked not by taking long drags on it and filling your lungs, but by sipping it, not inhaling it, and basking in the aroma.

And though there was caffeine in the tobacco, it wasn't addictive, at least not in the same way as cigarettes. The addiction to pipe smoking comes from hitting the pause button on the world for thirty or forty minutes to think and ponder and watch the smoke curling through the air.

The other thing about pipe tobacco was the way smells trigger memories, although for me it was not so much distinct memories as much as sensations and feelings from previous times.

It would be the perfect pursuit for Paul, I had told him, because his chef's trained nose would enjoy teasing out the different tastes without having to have a drink. The argument had made sense to him. The next day I brought him one of my pipes and a couple of samples of tobacco, and we had enjoyed many bowls together since.

"Mmm," Paul said. "This is wonderful. I think it will make an excellent marriage blend."

"Excuse me?" I said.

"Me and Chloe," Paul said. "We're tying the knot."

"Really?" I said. "Well, congratulations, but I thought you had kind of soured on the whole marriage thing. Also, isn't she a little young?"

"I did, but then I met Chloe," Paul said. "She's something special."

"No doubt, but, umm, what about the whole 'clean and sober' business?"

Paul looked at me. "We met in the rooms," he said. "She's got as much time there as I do. Not gonna be a problem, and will probably help us stay with the program."

I smiled. "Well, congratulations, then," I said. "Have you set a date yet?"

"Yeah," Paul said. "Tomorrow."

I laughed. "Jesus, Paul," I said, "Don't wait *too* long."

"We'll never have a chance to go away, not for months, the way business has been growing. And we'll be shutting down the donut shop for at least a few days while the storm passes through. So this is the best chance we'll have for a bit of a honeymoon," Paul said.

"And, speaking of Jesus, that brings me to another point," he said. "We need someone to do it. My mother practiced Vodoun back on the island, and my father's only god is Mammon. Chloe believes in water fairies and tree spirits and other stuff like that. So, Father Peter or Rabbi Thomas aren't exactly our choices for presiding. And neither would be willing to do it on such short notice, either. So, Chloe and I were wondering if you would be willing to do the honors."

SATURDAY – CHAPTER 9

"You're a JP," Paul said. "We looked it up."

I smiled and shook my head.

"Yeah, I am. JP's can notarize signatures, and I need Nev's signature notarized from time to time. I looked into it, and becoming a JP was easier than becoming a notary public, so that's what I did. But I've never officiated a wedding before."

"Well, we can be your first, then!" Paul said.

As if on cue—and I couldn't be certain that she hadn't been inside the door listening to us—Chloe walked out with my coffee.

"There you go, Asa," she said. She looked at me hopefully. "Will you do it?"

I looked at her genuine smile, and Paul's big grin, and I knew that the fix was in.

Ok, ok. I'll do it. How big will this be?"

"Just us," Paul said.

"I'll need two witnesses," I said. "Also, everybody has to be sober."

Both of them laughed at that.

"No problem, Asa!" Paul said.

"And a license?"

"Done and done," Paul said.

"Thank you sooo much, Asa," Chloe said. She leaned over and kissed me on the cheek. "You're the best!"

She turned and walked back inside. I looked at Paul.

"That was a setup," I said.

Paul laughed, a big, booming laugh.

"Of course it was, Asa! I know you all too well."

"Alright, well, there are a couple of other things that we need to discuss. Like, what kind of ceremony do you want? I don't know much about Vodoun, and I know you have a higher power, but can you maybe spell things out a little bit for me?"

"Like I said, Asa, I know you. I trust you. You do you."

"Dear lord. Are you sure this is what you want?"

"What do you mean?"

"Well, I just mean, are you really ready? And is she old enough? I mean I know, legally, but in terms of the two of you?

"This from the man who's joined at the hip with Ms. Half-Your-Age Yoga Teacher?" Paul said.

"Oh, crikey, Paul, no. It's not like that with Tanya and I. It never has been. We're just friends."

Paul laughed again. "Suure you are," he said mockingly. "Everybody who knows either one of you in this town has been waiting for one of you to move in with the other. Heck, I think somebody has even put together a betting pool on it. Frankly, you should move in with her. I've seen that salt box you live in."

"And I'd never get to smoke inside for the rest of my life," I said.

Paul raised his eyebrows. "Well, that's a tell," he said. "You don't object to the woman, just to the lifestyle adjustment."

Thank the gods, my pipe had gone out and I had to re-light it. "It's hard to explain it, Paul," I said when I got it stoked up again. "It's complicated."

"Isn't it always?" he said.

"No. Now...really. I just...it's just..." I fell silent.

"I'm waiting," Paul said after a suitable interval.

"Ok, I admit it," I said. "We're deeply connected on some level, I know that. But there's something there that just holds both of us back. I'm not sure what, but something in my gut tells me that it would be the wrong thing to do, to fall in love with her. Or for her to fall in love with me. I'm a confirmed, happy, satisfied bachelor, and too damn old to make the kind of changes that a relationship like that would require. And I don't know but what she feels the same way about her own life."

"Have you asked?"

"Asked what?"

"Have you asked her, knucklehead? Have you guys, like, even talked about this?"

"We don't need to. I know how she feels."

Paul looked at me like he was peering over a pair of half-rims.

"Dude," he said, "I don't think you have a clue."

SATURDAY – CHAPTER 10

I spent the remainder of the day working with Nev, printing manifests and address labels and packing boxes. There weren't that many orders, but some items, like the orrery, required fairly detailed preparations. The rain continued steadily, not a downpour yet, but not sprinkling either. I wanted to get as much as possible out in case the hurricane started messing with the airplane flights more than it already had.

The busywork of taping, printing and dealing with errant packing peanuts wasn't enough to keep my mind off Elle Anderson and the vision I'd had of her and the scream that still echoed in the back of my mind. At first I'd thought that the vision was only a manifestation of some dark part of my unconscious, some urgent message being delivered to me while the barrier between conscious and unconscious was open, like a waking nightmare.

But the discovery of her existence made it more than just an eruption of psychic bile. She was real – or had been – and that fact tethered my vision to a horrific reality. I didn't like that. I didn't like the deep sadness I'd felt when I saw her picture in the paper, or the revulsion I'd felt when Charlie told me her story.

And I really didn't like the feeling that she was asking me for help.

The UPS guy was late for his pickup, as usual, so I made up for my earlier coffee failures – I'd been too distracted to remember to bring back one from Paul's for Nev—by getting us some takeout Chinese from down the block. I let Nev wait up front for the driver, and I went back into my office to spend some time on the phone making arrangements for the delivery of the

Arthashastra manuscript. Some things just can't be shipped by normal methods.

My office is much like the rest of the store but a little neater. The shelves are lined with books, some, collector's items, but most of a practical nature, books on archaeology, architecture and history. At one end is my desk, the size of a square piano—because it was made from a square piano—and an old safe the size of an icebox, but I'd replaced its lock with more modern technology. It was as immovable as the mountains up north. Lining the top of my desk was two dozen briar pipes and a dozen canning jars in which I kept different blends of tobacco.

I was looking at a note that I had scribbled to myself a week earlier, trying to decipher what it said, when Neveah poked her head through the door.

"Somebody here for you, boss. Says he knows you, but, shit, he looks like a drug dealer. Want me to shoot him for you?"

"Jesus. No. Just bring him back. I'll see what he wants."

She laughed and went out. She came back in a few minutes later with a short, thin man, soaking wet from head to toe, black stringy hair clinging to his face, a courier bag on his shoulder. She moved in through the door after him and sat on a wood chair that had been liberated from Harvard's Skull & Bones club.

The man pulled his hair away from his face.

"*Saluton, Lao Shen,*" I said. "*Mi ne havas vidas vin por longotempe. Kio alportas vin ĉi tien?*"

He made a short bow. "*Mi havas pakon por vin, io vi serĉis.*"

I raised my eyebrow. "*Mi ne mendis io ajn de vin.*"

Neveah cleared her throat. "Umm, boss . . . "

"Sorry, Nev," I said. "Lao, let us continue in English. My partner does not speak *la lingvo internacia.*"

He glanced at her.

"She's your partner?"

"Yes. Get over it. What's this package you say you have for me? I haven't spoken to you in a year."

"I was sent here by one of my clients, specifically to deliver this to you. It is not for you to keep, but they need help with the translation. My clients suspect you may be the only one who can do it."

"I'm not a linguist, Lao. You know that."

"Yes, but you have some . . . certain knowledge that may allow you to do the translation."

"What are we talking about here, Lao?"

"I'll get to the point," he said. "My bus leaves soon anyway." He unlatched the cover of his bag, flipped it open and pulled out a flat, square box wrapped in plastic. "Take a look," he said. "It's the *Lingvo Universala.*"

I stared at him. "Bull," I said. "That manuscript was burned by Zamenhof's father."

"As it turns out," Lao said in his precise manner, "that was not the case. He *said* he burned it to avoid trouble with the Tsarist police. But he'd hidden it. And it has been found."

I opened the box. Inside were several pages, yellowed with age, handwritten. Each page was encased in a plastic sleeve. I tried to read it. It was deceptively familiar, but the words looked strange, not like the language I'd expected it to be. It didn't quite make sense. The words were like I was trying to read Middle English. Which, in a way, I was. I turned each page slowly, examining them, then looked back at Lao.

"This is nothing but the prototype," I said. "Anyone with a decent understanding of the final language could figure out what this says quite easily."

"One would think that," Lao said, "but the best scholars have been unable to translate it. There's something different about it. You will see. You've heard of Watson, have you not?" he said.

"Of course. It's the IBM supercomputer that first beat the best chess master in the world and is now on its way to beating the best Go master."

"Yes," he said, "and the Chinese have their own Watson. Actually, they call it Laotze. And it already has beaten the best Go master in the world. My clients, having access to this computer, fed the *Lingvo Universala* into it, and it said it could not translate this manuscript. It told us something entirely different."

"What'd it say?" I asked.

Lao brushed his hair back from his eyes.

"It said to ask you."

I looked at the manuscript again. The first page was numbered 4 in the same handwriting as the lettering. Then it jumped to pages 13, 7, 5, 8, 18 and 22.

"Wait," I said, "Some of the pages are missing."

"Laotze says not. You have everything you need," Lao said. He stood up. "I'll be back in a month to retrieve the manuscript and its translation from you. You've dealt with me before. You know you may be paid handsomely for your work."

"And if I fail?"

Lao shrugged. "You know how it goes. Some things should not be seen by the wrong eyes."

He smiled, cold and empty. He looked at me, and then Neveah. She stared back at him, her expression equally hard.

"Well, I must catch my bus. It leaves soon." He bowed to me again and left the room.

I followed him out to make sure he didn't miss finding the front door, and then walked back into my office. Nev was standing there with a pistol in her left hand.

"Told you he was shit, boss," she said.

"Where the hell did the gun come from?"

"I always have one. Like you don't know."

"The hell," I said. "You're wearing yoga pants. Where the hell do you—" I stopped myself. "Never mind. I don't even want to know."

I walked over to my desk and looked at the manuscript.

"Shit," I said.

SATURDAY – CHAPTER 11

They say don't shoot the messenger, but at that moment I felt like I should have let Nev follow her instincts.

Lao and I had first crossed paths many years ago, when I was looking for a specific jade carving. Lao had gotten in touch with me and said he could get it, clean, not stolen. His price was good.

I met him in New York, outside of Grand Central. It was a sunny summer day, and he suggested we go somewhere to finalize the transaction. We walked down 42nd Street until we found a busy deli with a table open. Lao had an odd formality about him. I was never sure if it was his natural way of communicating with people or just an act. I thought that once we had a few dealings together, he might get a bit more casual, but he never did.

"*Ĉu vi kredis kiel delikateso esas bona?*" I said, asking him if he approved of the deli I picked.

Lao was from Hong Kong, and although I knew he spoke English, we always spoke in Esperanto for the reason that everyone who speaks Esperanto uses the language. It put us on common ground. I think it was one of the reasons, over the years, that he liked to work with me.

"*Jes, ĝi esta bela,*" he said. It was fine.

Once we had sat down and ordered a couple of iced teas, he reached into his courier pouch and pulled out a silk bag.

"*Regardu,*" he said. Look.

Inside the bag was the jade piece I was looking for. Was it the real one? That was the big question. Fake jade pieces can be made from a variety of substances, but a visual examination in good light can separate the good from the bad. Jade's translucence lets you see slightly below the surface, creating a visual effect quite unlike its imitators. Older jades that were polished using soft abrasives will also often reveal a slight "orange peel" effect on the surface. And real jade, though it comes in a variety of colors, has a hue all of its own. This piece had all three.

I pulled a penknife out of my pocket and looked for Lao's reaction. He didn't blink. Real jade is harder than steel, and my quick attempt to scratch the bottom of the piece left no mark.

Finally, there was the age of the piece. Fake jade abounds, and there is no sure way—such as carbon-14 dating—to tell the age of a carving. The best you can do is a stylistic analysis by knowing the details of the carving style of the time period the particular piece is supposed to have come from.

I spent several minutes looking closely at the sculpture, turning it around in my hands, while Lao sipped on his tea. Finally, I put it in the bag, set it down and looked at Lao.

"Sorry, *mia amiko,*" I said, "but this is a fake. I can't buy it."

Lao put down his tea and smiled. "Perhaps this will suit you better," he said and pulled out another silk bag. He swapped it with the first one.

This one proved to be real.

As we concluded our transaction, with me using my phone to transfer funds to the bitcoin wallet number he gave me, I said, "Was that a test, or what?"

Lao gave me another one of his slow smiles. "Perhaps," he said. "I like to know the quality of the people I'm dealing with."

"Also," he added, "what's the point of selling something once when you can sell it twice?"

His statement was so unexpectedly honest that I had to laugh. We both worked in a world where truth and fiction, history and reality, were constantly being played with for mercenary reasons.

We made small talk for a few minutes while Lao waited for the confirmation to come through on his phone. Once it did, he gave me a little smile.

"*Mi ĝuis fari negocon kun vi,*" he said. I've enjoyed doing business with you.

We stood, shook hands, and I watched him leave as I stowed away my new purchase. He moved with precision, without haste, but without wasting time, as he turned left out of the deli.

All of my subsequent dealings with Lao went more or less the same way although his subterfuges got more subtle over time. I asked him once why he did it, and he said—in his straightforward way—that it kept us both on our toes. It was obvious that he enjoyed our games. To be honest, so did I.

What was the subterfuge here, I wondered, with the *Lingvo Universala*? Was there something I had missed?

There was a lot that had been different about this latest meeting. It was clear that Lao was in haste and under some kind of pressure, but the one thing that stood out to me, the one thing that rang false in that whole encounter, was that Lao had mentioned payment, but never a specific amount. For Lao, that was a substantial omission. For all of his games, Lao was always, in the end, about the money. How much I would get, how much he would receive. He never, ever left without some sign of firm confirmation, either in terms of payment or a letter of intent, or—in one odd deal that was a three-way transaction where multiple parties were involved—some form of hostage.

This time, there had been none of that. Here, Asa, figure this out, I'll be back in a month or so and yeah, you'll get some money, and don't fuck up. That wasn't Lao. At all.

Perhaps the subterfuge this time was a message, a message he knew that only I would understand. There would be no payment.

Lao was telling me that, whatever happened, I was a dead man.

SUNDAY – CHAPTER 12

Sunday morning I got up early and drove to the shop to start looking at the *Lingvo Universala* manuscript. I was going to have to assume that this was actually what I had been given. Though anyone can be fooled, Lao's clients were probably not idiots.

The rain was coming down harder and the wind was beginning to pick up. The weather pages on the internet were already yelling Category 4 or 5 within a few days. Maybe we'd get lucky here and miss the worst of it.

I fooled around with the oddly numbered pages for about two hours before getting frustrated. It was a bit like trying to understand a Chinese ideogram with no clue as to content, and damn few clues as to context.

L.L. Zamenhof, a Jew in 19th century Poland, was the author of the manuscript I held in my hands and the inventor of Esperanto, the most successful created language in history. It was designed to be a universal second language, easy for almost anyone who was a speaker of most any Western tongue to become fluent in. Zamenhof's idea, conceived in the revolutionary and nationalistic tumult that consumed Europe in the late 19th century, was that if people could speak to each other—without one having to adopt the "dominant tongue" of another—then wars would become less likely. Diplomacy could be carried out free of the cultural baggage embodied by first languages and free from the dominance implied by using the other person's language rather than your own. It also eliminated the imprecision of interpreters. The average person could speak to his peers across borders of politics and language.

In Zamenhof's new language, the verb "esper," meant "to hope." Esperanto, thus, meant "one who hopes." It was, indeed, the language of hope.

It was also, for me, the language of commerce. I didn't speak Japanese, Mandarin, French, or any of the other languages I was likely to come into contact with in the course of my business. But today Esperanto is spoken by anywhere between two and eight million people worldwide. English makes claim to be the universal language of business, mostly on the strength of the US dollar and English-speaking countries' ferocious periods of colonization. Before that, it was French, and before that, Latin.

Any of those languages has based its claim of universality on the projection of wealth and power.

And now that's changing. Cryptocurrency is taking commerce out of the hands of banks and governments, and America, hobbled by its own demons, is demonstrably less fearsome to the rest of the world than it once was. Esperanto is flowing into this gap, slowly filling it with a language that, like the cryptocurrencies, is governed by no one. I didn't mind. It made more room for people like me who made their lives by fishing at the edge of the current.

Hell, I made my first inroads into trading through the language. Esperanto has been adopted as the preferred language by both the Ba'hai faith and the followers of Oomoto, a modern Japanese religion derived from ancient Shintoism. That has led to volumes of sacred texts, always moneymakers in the right circles. Over time, the language has developed its own corpus of literature, leading to a small but ferocious demand for first editions and signed copies. There are books in Esperanto ranging from sex how-to manuals to detective mysteries to everything else in between. In fact, my first big sale had been a manual on Taoist sexual practices in Esperanto, of which maybe two copies in the world existed. People with means rarely flinch at the cost of satisfying their desires.

Esperanto was Zamenhof's actually second attempt at creating a language. He had abandoned his first attempt, it was said, because he found it incomplete and flawed. He gave the manuscript of this proto-Esperanto to his father when he had gone off to school to become an ophthalmologist, and his father had, as I had mentioned to Lao, thrown his son's work into the fire.

If that had been all to the story, Lao's visit to me last night and the importance his clients assigned to this manuscript of proto-Esperanto would be a bit of a puzzle. On the basis of this history alone, it would be of interest only to a few linguists and of slightly less interest to those who actually used the language.

But there was another version of proto-Esperanto's origins, one largely of the told-around-a-campfire variety. This version held that proto-Esperanto was actually a language of magic and could be used to cast spells and summon demons and the like. Perhaps Lao had tapped into a group of well-to-do occultists who sought their own version of the Holy Grail.

I tried to read the manuscript forward, backward, upside down and via a mirror. I got nowhere. The words *seemed* like Esperanto vocabulary, but were not. The script itself was not quite Roman, either. Squinting, or looking at it from a distance, the writing almost seemed like Hebrew. Up close, the characters might have spelled words in an Indo-European language. It was, if nothing else, unique in my experience, and I'm long past the age when I use the phrase "for the first time" very often.

Thinking of Zamenhof's life, and the odd way in which the letters were formed, gave me an idea. I had, almost in my back yard, one of the country's foremost Jewish scholars, a fallen Yale professor who had published a number of controversial Hebrew and Aramaic sacred text translations and interpretations. He'd eventually gotten tired of academic backbiting and had dropped out and had come to the synagogue in Nemaseck many years ago to lead its small congregation as its rabbi.

I had little doubt that Rabbi Thomas, himself a convert from Catholicism, would be anywhere besides the synagogue today. It was not only the High Holy Days, the week between the Jewish New Year and Yom Kippur, but a hurricane was coming and the synagogue was on a flood plain. He would be there. I made a copy of one of the manuscript pages and drove south to where the river valley flattened out and the river flowed calmly along a winding channel.

SUNDAY – CHAPTER 13

"Asa, how delightful you have come to help us build Ezra's walls!" The Rabbi's baritone boomed over the noise of a dozen people talking and shoveling, and two pickup trucks maneuvering around the synagogue. "He had fifty-two days. We have only a few!"

He dropped the shovel he had been using to fill a burlap bag with gravel, wiped his hands on his pants, and came over to greet me.

"How it is that such a goy ended up with such a Jewish name, I'll never know," he said.

"Says Rabbi Thomas . . . "

"I know, I know. How can I help you, my friend? I'm sure you didn't come to fill burlap."

"Let's go to your office where we can talk, Rabbi. I have some questions."

As we walked to the office, I noticed the river on the other side of an adjacent field. We were only slightly higher than the surrounding land. If the river rose significantly above its banks, the synagogue would be in trouble, no doubt about it.

We sat, he on the far side of an ancient oak desk. He clipped the end of a cigar while I stuffed my pipe with some Dunhill.

"I must thank you again for these cigars," he said. "They're like nothing else I've ever had."

"Pre-war Syrian tobacco," I said. "It is literally not grown anymore, not like this. When they're gone, they're gone."

"But somehow, I suspect, you'll stumble on some more, won't you?" the Rabbi said.

I smiled. "And you'll know as soon as I do," I said.

Both of us lit up. With clouds of smoke about our heads, I handed the copied page from the manuscript to the Rabbi. He looked at it and then looked at me, questioningly.

"Believe it or not, I've never seen this language before," the Rabbi said. "What is this?"

"I'm not surprised," I said. "It's the manuscript of a language that the inventor of Esperanto, L.L. Zamenhof, created before he created Esperanto. He abandoned his original attempt, thinking it incomplete and inchoate, and gave this manuscript to his father for safekeeping while he was away at school and developing Esperanto. It was thought that the manuscript was destroyed, burned by the old man so the Tsar wouldn't catch his kid and send him to the dungeons, or worse. But it seems that wasn't the case. The manuscript was handed off to me last night with the assignment of deciphering it. Not a whole lot of luck so far. So I figured I'd come see you. Zamenhof was Jewish, and some of the lettering resembles Hebrew . . . or Sanskrit . . . or something. And you know more languages than an African tour guide. So there it is. Ideas?"

Rabbi Thomas looked at the page. Then, as I had done, he turned it upside down. He held it up to the light facing away from him to read it backwards.

He set the manuscript down again, staring at it, and thought. His cigar had long gone out from inattention and I was reaching the bottom of my bowl before he shook his head and looked up.

"You know, Asa, in Genesis, it speaks of God seeing man's aspirations to the heavens—and beginning to achieve them—and being somewhat unappreciative of the effort. 'Let us go down and confound their speech there, so that they shall not understand one another's speech,' is what Adonai said. That mankind could create a universal language, a divine language, spoke to God about our hubris. We needed to be taken down a notch. So he made it hard for us to talk to one another. So here, many millennia later, we have man, a man, trying to reverse God's work by creating a single language—a single language that we could all use. For peace. For progress. For the reunification of a divided species. It's a beautiful idea. A marvelous one. And one that absolutely subverts God's will. If Zamenhof were any sort of a Jew at all, he realized that was what he was doing."

The Rabbi looked down at the page again before continuing.

"He didn't discard this first attempt because it was a failure. He did it because he was entirely too successful." He handed me the paper. "Languages have power, you know. Languages don't necessarily grow and become successful because the people who speak them are the ones who build empires. It is the other way around. Societies become successful because the languages they use are powerful enough to create the world they want. What Zamenhof realized was that he had created a language all too powerful. You can see it in the script, in the letters, in the words, even without understanding what they say. This language is dangerously powerful, and Zamenhof buried it before it could become a reality. Here," the Rabbi said, handing me the paper. "Take this. I don't want it. We Jews, we have enough problems."

"Thanks, Rabbi," I said. "I'll repay you with a little shovel work outside."

He waved me off.

"There's no need for payment, though I won't turn down the assistance. We'll call it a mitzvah, and I'll pay you when the next batch of cigars comes in."

SUNDAY – CHAPTER 14

Outside, the synagogue's members were still shoveling away. I could see the river on the other side of the mowed field where every fall the synagogue built its sukkah, a framed-in shelter, covered with branches and leaves. During the festival of Sukkot, the congregation held services and ate meals there to celebrate the harvest.

A few thin trees lined the bank of the river, but they would be no impediment to a current swollen with heavy rains. Should the hurricane stick around long enough, the sandbags would likely make no difference either. But what are you going to do? It's nature's way to flood the plains, its mankind's way to struggle with the inevitable. Me, I preferred the mountains, from which water and soil flowed to meet their fate far below.

I stuffed my pipe in my jacket pocket and adjusted my hat so the water would drip in front rather than down my back when I bent over. I grabbed one of the burlap sacks and walked over to one shoveller, a doughty woman all of five feet, and of not inconsiderable waistline, wrapped in a yellow slicker.

"Got enough in you to fill another bag?" I asked.

"If you've got enough in you to carry it when I'm done, old man, I can surely fill it," she said.

I laughed and held out my hand.

"Touché," I said. "This old man's name is Asa. Asa Cire."

"Anne Goldsmith here," she said. "Everyone calls me Annie." She squinted at me. "Asa, yes, you're the fellow that runs the antique shop in the center of town, aren't you?"

Close enough. "That would be me," I said. I held out the empty bag. "Looks like you'll be needing as many of these as can be filled."

"Doubt it'll be enough," she said, "but we're moving what we can out of the synagogue, too. Rabbi Thomas will be taking our Torah home with him this evening, and the rest of us will be taking anything else that can be easily moved." She nodded at the river. "It's already angry. I haven't seen anything like this in a long time."

She grabbed her shovel, stuck it into a pile of sand, lifted it and spilled it into the bag.

"Lived here long?" I asked.

"My whole life," she said. "My family was some of the first Jews around. Came from a shtetl in a place in Poland which doesn't exist anymore. In between Russian pogroms. New York was a bit too crowded for a farming family, so my great-great grandfather got in with his brother selling coal. As soon as he had enough money, he upped his family and bought some farmland here." She dropped another shovel full into the bag. "Been here raising cattle and growing corn ever since."

With the third shovelful, the bag was full. I tied it shut, carried it over to a pickup truck that in turn would ferry the sandbags to the other end of the building, where more people grabbed them to build the rising wall. I grabbed another empty bag and went back to Annie.

"So you must have been around here back when Elle Anderson was killed."

Her mouth drew back a bit. "Yup," she said, "That was a bit of a dark time," she said. "'Specially for us Jews."

"Really? Why?"

"Ah, people and their prejudices. Her murder, it was so, so grisly," she said. "And the stuff that happened to her. Satanic is what people called it. And when something gets called satanic, you can bet it's the Jews they'll be giving the evil eye to."

"They thought one of you did it?"

"Yup, or that's what a lot of people thought. The police, though, the police had a couple other people in mind."

The bag was filled, and I quickly tied it off, hustled it over to the truck, grabbed another empty and hoofed it back to Annie. I didn't want any of the other baggers jumping in my line.

"You hustle pretty good for an old guy," Annie said. "You ever get tired of selling overpriced junk to tourists, stop by my place. I got a barn that could use your help."

"I'm only this good on every third Sunday," I said. "The rest of the time, I'm a bit of a wastrel, I'm afraid."

She eyeballed me. "Yup, I believe that," she said, "...as much as I believe in leprechauns."

"You know leprechauns are what's left of the original Celtic gods—oh, never mind," I said. "So, who were the police after for Elle?"

"A couple of guys, both druggies, but one especially. Name was Donald Perkins, but everyone called him Budgie."

"Budgie? Really?"

"Really. I guess he'd been fooling around with her. If nothing else he shoulda been put up for rape as he was twenty-three at the time, and she was what...fifteen, sixteen? Something like that. Anyway, she'd been hanging out with him so the cops got interested in him. Nothing came of it, of course. But his name was certainly ruined in this town."

"So I guess he did the smart thing and left."

Annie laughed. "Smart wasn't in that boy's deck of cards. In fact, he wasn't even playing with a full deck. Stayed around here, he did, worked for his brother-in-law's landscaping business for a while. Don't know what happened to him after that, but I'm pretty sure he still lives in town. Think it might be in the old Wilson place over on Prescott Street. Yes, it is, 'cause Frannie – that's her over there by the pickup truck—told me he's got a dog from Hades chained in his yard."

I tied up another bag and trotted off to the truck. When I came back, Annie had stuck the shovel in the mound of sand.

"Well, that's it for me," she said. "Gonna move inside and grab some books."

I felt my phone buzzing in my pocket.

I nodded to Annie. "Nice to meet you, Annie. Maybe I will stop by your place sometime."

"Come at dinner," she said. "Best steak around."

With that, she walked off, and I ducked my head to answer the phone without it getting soaked.

SUNDAY – CHAPTER 15

It was Neveah. "Got a message for you, boss," she said.

"Sure, go ahead."

"Mr. Policeman stopped by the store this morning," she said. "Wants to talk to you."

"Did he mention why?"

"Nope. 'Cept I'm pretty sure he was working his way up to asking me out to dinner again."

"You ever gonna say yes?"

"Like hell," Nev said. "Cops aren't really my thing. Especially white cops."

"Well, it wouldn't be a bad connection to make, a girl with your history."

"Are you fucking kidding me, boss? I don't need that shit. Just no."

"Pfft," I said. "Picky. So what did he want?"

"I dunno. I just told you. Give him a call and talk to him yourself."

The phone beeped as she hung up. I probably shouldn't have brought that "girl with your history" up, I thought.

I looked up the number for the police barracks and called. Nemaseck was too small to have its own police force so we bought a state trooper who was assigned to the town for various periods of time. Officer Peterson had been around longer than most, about seven years. For some reason he liked the Nemaseck beat.

The duty officer told me Peterson was over at the bridge, directing traffic while the DOT did its storm prep thing. I walked back down the driveway to the jeep. Before I hopped in, I took one last look at the river.

Annie was right. She was angry.

SUNDAY – CHAPTER 16

Nemaseck has two bridges. The northern bridge crosses the river at the Cauldron and is always lined by cars in the summer as tourists stop for the obligatory pictures from the middle of it. The southern bridge is below the center of town and is the easiest route to the nearest divided highway, about ten miles away. That's where Peterson was.

I hadn't intended to piss off Nev, but she was a bit feral and I could never quite tell when she was going to bite, even after working cheek to jowl with her for several years. I had gotten to know her about as well as anyone, but she kept her personal history close to her chest. I knew that she had grown up in the projects, and I had gotten the impression she had been mixed up in some business, probably drugs, though she never said.

What I did discover, though, was that her history had given her an immediately practical outlook on life. She never had much, and never held on to much. But she turned out to be more than an e-commerce manager for me. Her instincts immediately sorted out the good from the bad, and I had learned to listen to her advice.

Especially after the time I had come back from a trip overseas. I had come across a rumor about an old timepiece, dating back to 1505, the first "watch" ever made. Its shape was a sphere, reminiscent of an oriental pomander, and built by a German watchmaker. At last sighting, it still ran. It had been sold at auction in 1987 and then disappeared into a private collection. A few people had hinted that they had heard it had become available again with the death of the owner, and I had gone to Europe to track it down.

Nev had warned me that something was hinky with the whole story, but I had brushed off her warning. Two weeks later I had returned with the watch and, when I got back, had walked right into an ambush outside the train station that would take me back to my car. I always used mass transit when I could, especially when carrying valuables,

I was negotiating, rather unsuccessfully, with the man who wanted to relieve me of my burden and have me spend the last few hours of my life in the trunk of a car when Nev showed up out of nowhere. Neither my assailant nor I knew she was there until a split second before she pistol whipped him on the side of the head. He went down, and Nev ushered me to her car.

Once inside, I looked over at her.

"What the hell was that?" I asked Nev.

"Told you not to go, boss," Nev said, not taking her eyes off the road. "Told you it was shit."

"But how . . . ?" I waved my hand. "How did you know here? And where'd the gun come from?"

"Saw that someone had gotten past the security and was pokin' around our system two days ago," she said. "IP address said they were from Ukraine. All they did was find the emails with your itinerary and tickets, and left. I figured you were in some shit, so I figured you might need a hand," she said in the same tone of voice she used to tell me she had picked up the mail.

"The gun? Where'd that come from?"

This time she did look at me, like I was an idiot.

"You gotta be kidding me, boss," she said.

And that was all I got out of her, although she got a hefty bonus out of me when the timepiece was sold.

So, all in all, I couldn't blame Nev for being a little skittish about going out to dinner with a cop.

SUNDAY – CHAPTER 17

By the time I pulled up at the bridge, I was halfway through a bowl of a nice Virginia/Perique mixture. I didn't want to put it down, so I just clenched it and got out. The DOT crew was working to secure the aging guardrails against the wind and rain, but I doubted that that would make any difference should the hurricane get cranky.

Peterson was standing in the rain, slicker on, state trooper hat covered with the regulation rain cover. He was directing traffic on the bridge and he didn't look entirely happy.

"Man, this is what supernumeraries are for," he said as I walked up. "I graduated from this shit years ago."

"Cop life," I said. "Can't all be donuts and babes."

He shook his head, rain scattering off the brim of his hat.

"What's wrong with that woman?" he said. "She's colder than ice."

I shrugged. "You know about as much as I do," I said. "She's not one for a lot of interpersonal sharing."

"You can say that again." He stepped into the road and waved oncoming traffic through, then walked back.

"So what's the story?" I asked.

"C'mon. Let's get out of this rain," he said.

We walked back to his cruiser and got in. It was running, and dry. He feathered through some papers in a big clip on the console, found a picture and yanked it out. He held it up.

"Know this guy?"

It was a picture of Lao. Looked like a passport photo, his long hair brushed back and tied in a pony tail, a white shirt and tie.

I looked at it for long enough to seem interested.

"Nope. Not a friend. Should I?"

Peterson threw the picture on the dash of the cruiser.

"He came through customs a few days ago and he pinged someone's radar. Chinese have him on a list."

"Chinese got a lot of people on a list, I've heard," I said. "What's special about this guy?"

"They say he was sneaking some stolen documents," Peterson said. "After he got through customs, he bought a bus ticket. Bus passed through here on the way to Montreal."

"Well, that's nice, but he picked a bad year for leaf-peeping. By the time we hit peak, the hurricane will have knocked all the leaves off the trees."

"And probably knock some trees down, too," he said. "Couple people saw him get off the bus. You deal with a lot of that crap. He mighta stopped to see you."

I picked up the picture and pretended to study it for a minute.

"Oh, that's right," I said. "He called me. We met for tea and crumpets at Not Debbie's, and he tried to sell me an original copy of the Constitution."

"Fuck off," Peterson said. "So you're saying you don't know this guy?"

"Haven't a clue. What's the guy's name, anyway?"

"Wang Xiu Ying," Peterson said.

I raised my eyebrows. "Nice inflection," I said. "Work on that a long time, did you?"

"Fuck off, Asa," Peterson said. "They had the pronunciation in the bulletin. I'm just checking things out." He pulled the picture out of my hand and clipped it back on the console.

"Hey, you want an in with Nev, you gotta be nice," I said.

"That girl ain't got no in," Peterson said.

"Maybe it's not her. Maybe it's you," I said.

"Yeah, maybe. Well, you see this guy, you wanna give me a call?"

"Sure," I said. "But how about a favor for a favor?"

He glared at me. "What?"

"You know anything about Elle Anderson?"

"Before my time," he said, "But there ain't anyone who's been in this town for more than fifteen minutes who hasn't heard of her, except maybe you. What do you need to know, secret cop stuff? And why do you care?"

"Writing a book," I said. "Maybe. All I know is she was found, drowned, victim of necrophilia, and a tattoo cut off of her body. You guys had a couple of suspects, but nothing panned out."

"You're late. That book's been done about eight times already. And I don't know shit. Like I said, before my time."

Headlights appeared on the road ahead. "Fuck," he said. "More fucking traffic. You trip across Wangy boy, you give me a call," he said. "Right?"

"Sure. No problem."

We both got out of the car. He headed off to steer the traffic away from the DOT workers, and I went back to the Jeep. My pipe had long gone out and I stoked it back to life.

So Lao Shen was traveling under a forged passport, I thought. Not unusual, given what he did. I wasn't pleased to know that the Zamenhof manuscript was stolen, but I should have assumed that anyway. Lao's business was often the funny kind. I wondered who he was working for.

I looked at the clock on the dash. I had just enough time to get a donut and then get changed and over to Tanya's studio for our weekly date.

Then, sometime soon, I guessed, I might as well go find Budgie. Who the hell gets a nickname like "Budgie," anyway?

I pulled into the road. Peterson looked at me like he had indigestion and waved me on through.

SUNDAY – CHAPTER 18

I lay on my back on the mat, eyes closed, feeling my body, warmed and stretched, breathing slowly and deeply, arms relaxed at my side. Tanya had ended our yoga class today, as she often did, with the corpse pose. Tanya frequently claimed that I snored while doing the corpse pose, but I thought she was lying because I'd never heard it.

After a space of time, I felt, rather than heard, Tanya get up. I opened my eyes and sat up as well. She looked lithe and trim and strong, and after years of practicing Zen Buddhism and teaching yoga, she emanated a presence that was at once calm and unignorable.

"Thank you, Tanya," I said. "I needed that."

"You're welcome," she said, nodding slightly. Strands of her long black hair fell in front of her shoulder, and she brushed them back. "Next week, it's your turn."

For the past several years, virtually since we had met, Tanya and I had taken turns teaching each other our individual disciplines, or at least parts of them. A full-time yoga teacher with her own studio, Tanya welcomed the chance to expand her own skills by working with me before bringing new routines live into her classes. I reciprocated by teaching her the martial art I knew. There's a limit to what you can practice by yourself. Good training requires a good partner, and Tanya had gotten very good over the years. Though I outweighed her by a good fifty pounds, Tanya now threw me across the mat as easily as I could chuck a piece of firewood.

She eyed my stained and torn-at-the-knee gi pants and black t-shirt with "Vintage" written across it. "Wait here, while I put the water on. I'll be back in a couple of minutes."

After she left, I moved over past the mats to the side of the studio where the rain ran down the windows. There were two cushions there, separated by a low table. I sat cross-legged on one of the cushions and looked out the window. Her studio was the top floor of an old Victorian house on a steep side street leading out of the center of town. Gazing out of the window, I looked past the buildings on West Street to the river below. The water was black in this deep stretch, and the only way I could tell how hard it was running was by the speed with which the occasional branch or piece of debris crossed my sight line.

She returned a few minutes later, a long shirt over her tank top and yoga pants. She was carrying a tray with a stoneware teapot and small cups, and a vase with a single flower in it. After moving it all onto the table, she sat down across from me. She closed her eyes, took a few deep breaths, opened her dark eyes again, and poured with studied precision.

"Someday, you'll have to invite me to a full tea ceremony," I said.

She smiled. "I will. It takes so much concentration, though. There will have to be a big occasion to warrant it."

"A *bris* perhaps?"

She looked at me, startled, and then laughed. She didn't belly laugh. She laughed like a stream in springtime.

"Why, Asa, is there something you would like to share with me? Are you converting, or has someone's ninth month arrived?"

"No, no, nothing like that," I said. "I was out at the Beth Shalom Synagogue helping them fill sandbags and stack them in case the river floods."

"Of course you were, dear Asa. You just got up this morning and said to yourself, 'My, I really need to help the synagogue today. I don't see how they'll get anything done without me.' "

"Well, sort of. I—"

"Sort of." She snorted.

Then it was my turn to laugh. A Japanese woman snorting is a sight and sound to behold. It breaks our stereotyped notions about how a person who looks like that ought to behave. And at the same time lets you know that you are among her innermost circle, because she knows she's breaking stereotype. It was lovely, at any rate.

"No, really," I said. "It went like this..." and I told her the whole story about a bedraggled Lao Shen showing up at the shop, and the manuscript, and the history of the manuscript, and what the rabbi said. I didn't tell her about my conclusions from Lao's odd behavior.

Tanya poured me another cup. "So what did the Rabbi mean, the language is too powerful? And why can't you decipher it, or one of the other six thousand Esperanto experts who are probably more knowledgeable than you? Or that giant computer?"

"Good questions, all. Here's the thing. A language is the sum total of not only a culture's knowledge base, but that culture's view of the world. It's both a filter on how we see reality, and a doorway into reality. It's how we manipulate reality to make it suit our needs. And if you look at history, certain languages are very, very good at certain things. Take, for example, Latin. Latin is the language of law, not simply because Western scholars and rulers learned that language in the Catholic Church, but because Latin is very, very good at delineating things. This, not that. Then, not now. His, not yours. Lawyers first learned Latin because it is a good language for making law."

I sipped my second cup of tea and nodded once to show my approval of it.

"Compare that to English," I said. "English is the language of technology. Hell, it requires hardly any adaptation to be used to code computers. Even if you don't 'speak' a computer language—especially the early ones like Basic or Cobol—if you know a little bit about how a computer works, you can sort out the basics of what a few lines of code may be doing. That's not because the first computer designers and programmers spoke English. It's because English enabled them to see the world in a way that allowed a computer to be built."

I watched her dark eyes to make sure she was following me. She was.

"Now," I continued, "look at an Asian language, like Japanese or Chinese. The words themselves are ideographs, pictures, and while they represent things by themselves, their meaning is incomplete without the ideographs around them. And how do you tell that an action occurred in the past or in the present, or only might have occurred in the past, but will happen tomorrow instead? You can't change tense simply by conjugating the verb. You have to change the context around it, making the meaning of the word completely different, not by changing the word itself, but by changing its environment.

Tanya nodded, slowly.

"Now think about how that changes your view of the world," I said. "If your native language is Chinese or Japanese, *of course* time is relative. *Of course* this is related to that in seventeen different ways. And when you see the world like that, you see correlations among things that aren't seen in the West. And then you have the development of philosophic systems like Taoism, or the *I Ching,* or you have concepts such as *qi* or *shen,* you know, "life force" and "spirit.""

A smile tickled at the corner of Tanya's mouth. "You're smarter than you look, sometimes," she said. "But that still doesn't explain your proto-Esperanto or whatever it is."

"The Rabbi was right," I said. "This isn't proto-anything. This manuscript has a language to itself, full and developed, and Zamenhof threw it away."

"Well, if every language is good for something, what is this language good for?" Tanya asked.

"If I knew that," I said, "the manuscript would translate itself."

SUNDAY – CHAPTER 19

I collected the cups and the teapot and put them on the tray.

"I'll take care of these," I said. Tanya nodded, and I carried them out of her studio and downstairs to her apartment.

As I washed and rinsed the dishes, I looked around the kitchen. In one corner sat her "go bag," the accessory of every first responder, ready to grab when she went out on a call in her side hustle as an EMT. Hanging from hooks in the ceiling were herbs of various sorts, drying until they were used in one of her herbal preparations, and not all of them for cooking. Tanya was a healer at heart, and though ambulance-running was more lucrative, her true love was the old way, and there were many people in the area who sought her advice over seeing a mainstream doctor.

The herbs, hanging loosely in front of the rain-soaked windows, gave the room a curious smell, a mixture of fresh hay and lavender and something that smelled strong and slightly unpleasant. It took me a minute to recognize it as valerian, a strong sedative if prepared correctly. Tanya had learned traditional healing from her mother before her mother had up and left and disappeared out of Tanya's life, returning to Japan to a prefecture that a quarter century before still had one foot in Japan's deeply-rooted traditions. Tanya had never seen her again, but had grown up the rest of the way with only her father, the pharmacist here in Nemaseck. After her father had died, she had changed her name to her mother's surname. Tanya had once told me that was because she feared losing that heritage that had left with her mother. Tanya was now thirty-five and could pass for being either Western or Eastern, depending on her mood or dress.

Thirty-five, I thought. So young. I thought of Paul's comment. I did the math.

Drying my hands, I climbed the stairs to the studio and saw Tanya had passed the time in the same manner as I had, watching raindrops roll down the window. I watched her reflection. Her face was quiet, giving nothing away of her inner thoughts.

I sat down on the cushion again. "Tanya, did you know Elle Anderson?"

Her face turned toward me and for a split second I got a glimpse of deep sadness.

"Yes, I did. She was in the class ahead of me in school," she said. "Why do you ask?"

I told her. I told her about the vision I had while meditating, and then seeing Elle's picture in the newspaper the next day. I told her about what Charlie had said, and what Annie had told me.

She shook her head at me. "This doesn't really make a lot of sense, Asa. Why are you going around asking people about her?"

"Just trying to understand," I said. "That girl looked so terrified. I want to know why she's in my head."

"You think she wants you to find her murderer?"

"I was thinking that. But who am I? I own a shop, I sell oddities to people who are willing to pay a high price for them, I know an odd language. Why not get in Peterson's head? He's a cop."

"Maybe it's because of who you are, Asa," she said. "There's something different about you. You don't shrug stuff off, but at the same time..." Tanya looked down. Her finger was tapping idly on the table. "I've known you how long, Asa? Seven years?"

"More or less," I said. "After real estate agents and bankers, you were one of the first people I met here."

"I remember," she said. "It was midsummer down by the river, there in town where the bank is all grassy and mowed. I was doing some yoga. I saw you walking along the side of the river, smoking your pipe."

"Yeah," I said, "I was trying to figure out if I'd made the biggest mistake of my life by moving here."

Tanya looked back up at me. "I was struck by your, your *singularity.* You were by yourself, but you didn't seem alone. You looked deep in thought, but

I could tell the slightest movement in the water, in the sky, caught your eye. I knew I wanted to meet you."

"And you did, and we became friends," I said.

"And, oh, did my boyfriend at the time get jealous when we would get together," she said. "Brian was a bit of an ass. He used to ask me why I spent so much time hanging around with an old fart."

"You date a lovely woman, you got to keep your eyes peeled," I said. "Even for old farts. You remember what I told you?"

"How could I forget? It was that first time, down at the riverbank. You said, 'you know, if I were twenty years younger, we'd burn this town down." She laughed. "The unimaginable—I don't know—presumption of that statement. You'd known me all of ten minutes! Do you remember what I said back, Asa?"

"Of course," I said. "You looked at me, serious as a heart attack, tapped me right here on the chest"—I tapped myself on the sternum—"and said 'I may come to love you, Asa Cire, but not like that.'"

"Yeah. Not like that."

She nodded. "And in all these years that I've loved you not like that, I've never asked you."

"Asked me what?"

"Was there ever...was there ever someone you *did* burn the town down with?"

I looked out the window and thought. The raindrops were rolling down the window in well-defined streams, speeding along the path of least resistance only to pool up and wait on the sill for their next drop down.

"No, not really, Tanya. Least not that I can remember."

'So you're telling me you *may* have known the love of your life, but you don't remember?"

"I'm old, Tanya. Lotta years between there and here. Some things fade, get lost. Some things you keep."

"And the love of your life—or if there was one—wasn't something you kept?" She shook her head. "Sorry. I just find that hard to believe. You know a little about everything, forget nothing anyone has said to you, can look at a piece of jade and know its age, where it was carved, by whom, and what the artist's second child was named. And you don't remember 'her'?"

Our eyes met. I held her gaze, softly, like it was a cloud.

"It's true, Tanya. There's really nothing to remember."

Tanya brushed some imaginary crumbs from the table. "Well, enough of this cheerful walk down memory lane," she said. "I have things to do, and you're going to help."

"With what?"

"There's a bunch of foxglove growing not too far from the river. I want to collect some now, before the river floods."

I squinted at her with one eye. "Foxglove? Really? Going from healer to assassin, or what?" Foxglove, I knew, was the source of digitalis, a heart medicine or a deadly poison, depending on the dosage.

"I'm going to try to make a homeopathic preparation of it. *Aconitum napellus* is a very useful remedy, and when prepared homeopathically, is absolutely harmless."

"As long as you know what you're doing," I said.

"I do." She stood up and held out her hand for me to grab. "Let's go. I'll help you up, old man."

She had just watched me do ninety minutes of yoga. But she held out her hand, and I took it.

SUNDAY – CHAPTER 20

Going home to change into something more suitable for a walk in wet woods, I thought of one time a year or so after Tanya and I had met.

Tanya liked nothing so much as to walk in the woods, often going alone into the rocky hills and valleys upstream from the Cauldron. Sometimes she was in search of an obscure herb, but more frequently she was just, as she put it, "tree hugging."

Sometimes she would invite me along. I'm not sure why. Tanya seemed just as content in the company of herself as with anyone else, and she certainly did not need me to help her enjoy rambling.

This trip with me, in particular, Tanya had been in an oddly joyful mood. She and Brian had broken up recently. I suspected our friendship was a part of the cause, but as I remembered them, there had seemed to be a fundamental disconnect between the two of them as well. She had found something, she said, deep in the woods, and she wanted to show it to me.

It was a sunny day when we drove to the parking lot off the bridge crossing the river across the Cauldron. From the lot a steep short trail led to a landing above where the river folded itself into the Cauldron's narrow rock channel and began its boiling run down nature's sluice, splashing over rock outcroppings and finally exploding into a pool far below. When the river was running high, the mist from the pool would rise to the top of the chasm like steam, thus giving the place its name.

The landing was posted with "No Swimming" signs, but of course every few years somebody did. And, of course, they got sucked into the Cauldron and were spewed out broken and dead at the other end. There, the undertow would turn them around and around underneath the falling water, unreachable until the current finally let them go drifting into the pool.

A by-then waiting crew of divers would retrieve the body, family was notified, the newspaper posted the obituary the following week, and the episode would be forgotten until it all happened over again. It would be easy to castigate the dead as fools, or idiots, or drunks, and such accusations were usually on target, but that never struck me as being just cause for their death. After all, the world was full of fools and idiots and drunks, many of whom lived uneventful lives, and a fair share of whom would reach heights of success or fame denied those considered more worthy.

The river chose its victims by its own criteria, and the crashing of the waves against its rocks did not speak of such things.

From the landing Tanya led us along a trail that climbed diagonally up to a ridge, where it turned south again to loop back to its start. Halfway up we passed an old shack slowly returning to nature. I imagined the floor was mostly beer bottles and cannabis ash at this point. We passed it without stopping.

She continued north and along the top of the ridge. Rocks stuck out of the ground, and between the poor soil and the deep shade of the fir and pine overhead, there was little undergrowth. After a period of time, according to some signpost visible only to her, Tanya headed southeast, dropping off the trail and the ridge, and descended diagonally down a steep slope.

We reached the bottom of the narrow valley and followed along a small stream. The undergrowth was thicker here, encouraged by the water and the gradual slopes on either side which allowed the sun's presence for at least a few hours each day. We came to a marsh and Tanya skirted along the east side of it. Sometimes we had to balance toe-to-heel as we walked across fallen logs with muck on either side. The marsh smelled of decay, as marshes do, and water birds flew in and out somewhere to the left of us, indicating that there was some open water deep in there.

We spoke little as we traveled. Tanya was concentrating on the land and the signs directing her where to go, and I was content to be led and to breathe in the woods and the rocks and the birds. At one point I stopped to light my pipe, but Tanya kept going, and as soon as I had a nice plume of smoke, I hustled up to rejoin her.

Two more ridges and three hours later, we reached a broad, grassy expanse. We hadn't stopped the whole way. No marsh here. The ground was firm underfoot. Ahead of us was a steep, rocky outcrop, a cliff extending straight up from the ground. For the first ten feet, there was the occasional small shelf with scattered hemlock clinging on it for dear life, their roots reaching into cracks in the rock to hold them in place. Above that was sheer rock with a crack or two shooting up to the top of the cliff fifty feet above us.

My stomach was growling with hunger. Ahead of Tanya I could barely make out a faint break in the grass where somebody had taken passage through, a path so faint I would have missed it had I not been expecting to see it. Tanya looked back at me.

"Try to keep up, old man," she said with a smile, and then broke out into a trot.

We reached the base of the outcropping, the ground covered with fallen needles, and Tanya pulled up in front of a fallen log. She turned, and with as big a grin as I'd ever seen on her face said, "We're here." She pushed her hair behind her ears and sat down.

SUNDAY – CHAPTER 21

She reached down and started fishing through her shoulder bag. To this day
I've never been sure what's in it. It's huge, and there's a flap over the top, but
I'd seen her pull everything from a size three Phillips head screwdriver to a
pint of Jack Daniels out of it, so I suspected it might be one of those "larger
on the inside" things.

This time she pulled out two water bottles and tossed one to me. Then
she fished around some more and delivered a couple of sandwiches wrapped
in brown paper. I took a sandwich, sat down on the ground with my back
against the rock and peeked suspiciously between the slices of bread.

"Watercress, cucumber, onion and radish, and a little butter," she said,
and laughed. "And because I know you, Asa, this as well." She tossed me
something wrapped in waxed cotton. "Baked chicken, with basil and
rosemary." She laughed again after seeing my smile of relief.

I was finished with the sandwich, halfway done with the chicken, and
two-thirds of the way through the bottle of water before I felt on firm
enough ground to speak.

"This all very lovely and whatnot, but y'know, we could have just sat on
the landing and had a delightful meal without all of the crashing about
through the woods, Tanya."

"But you wouldn't have appreciated it nearly so much that way," she said.
"Plus, you wouldn't have had the chance to go caving afterwards."

"Caving?"

"Yes, caving. You've been caving before, haven't you?"

"Well, not really," I said. Actually, I was pretty sure that I had, but the details escaped me at the moment.

"To your left, about fifteen feet away, there's a crack in the rock," she said. "There's just enough room to slip in. And then . . . well, you'll see." She smiled again, excitedly, pulled her hair back and tied it into a ponytail. She reached in her bag one more time, pulled out a couple of headlights and tossed one to me.

"Let's go," she said, "and leave your pipe here."

I got up. I could swear I felt my joints creak as I stood.

SUNDAY – CHAPTER 22

Tanya's slender body fit through the crack easily. I had a little more difficulty, even turned sideways, and had to exhale fully before the rock would let me pass.

Once I was inside, though, the cave opened up into a larger passage. A thin shaft of light from the entry hung in the air. I turned on my headlight and looked around. It was a small room, four feet by six feet and seven feet high. I imagined the slab of rock we had passed through cracking off the face of the cliff and sliding down with thunder to form the room ages before there was man or animals or likely anything but single-celled amoeba swimming around the green seas of early earth.

Tanya was beside me and in the stillness I felt, as much as heard, her breath, slow and even despite her excitement. She took my hand.

"Follow me," she said in a whisper, as if to speak louder would unsettle the sanctity of the world we were entering. Trailing her hand behind her as I held it, she walked across the room. I scanned the floor with my light, looking for scat or other signs of animal life. There was none.

The wall, it turned out, was two facing pieces of rock, at different depths, and she slipped behind one of them and pulled me with her. The rocks met overhead and the passage formed by them gradually became shorter. Finally she had to let go of my hand and begin crawling.

The tunnel had come to a sudden end, I thought, until Tanya lay on her side and bent to the left, jackknifing herself through another crack. I followed suit, grabbing the edge of the rock ahead of me, and dragging myself through the opening.

On the other side Tanya was standing again. I felt a cool draft of air and stood up. Except for our headlights stabbing through the dark, it was pitch-black. Again, I swept my light across the ground looking for signs.

Tanya kept her head pointed away from me so as not to blind me with her headlamp and whispered again.

"Look up, Asa. It's beautiful." Her soft voice resonated through the room.

I looked up to where her light was shining. On the wall were drawings. Pictures. One was clearly a bird. Another, a tree. A third, a series of long wavy lines. That had me stumped for a minute, and then I realized it was water. A river.

Next to the river was a mound and then hills, and then three deer. I stared, unmoving for a minute, then walked closer. The drawings were at head height for me, a man of today. These would have been above the head of most prehistoric people, I thought. Or were the people who drew these unusually tall for their time?

"Art," Tanya said. "Ancient artists lived here." Though spoken softly, her voice echoed throughout the room.

"Not only artists," I said. "Authors. They're telling a story." I turned my head to look at another wall and saw more paintings. "Or several stories."

The next wall showed a mountain and what looked like a dog, or a wolf, and a giant bird flying overhead. Two vertical stripes, going down almost to the ground, ended that sequence. I walked over to a third wall and two large drawings, a life-sized figure of a man little more than a stick figure, one hand held overhead, his other angled down to the ground. Next to him stood a similarly-drawn figure of a woman, the near-universal representation of a fertility goddess with exaggerated breasts and a bulging stomach. On the other side of the man was a bowl, or a gourd, with wavy lines drifting out of it.

I couldn't see Tanya, but I could feel her standing close to me in the dark. I could smell her, the mixture of sweat and dirt, and, faintly, a floral smell. Jasmine?

"This wasn't a home, Tanya. This was a shrine. A place of worship. Songs were sung here. Let's turn our lights off. Listen."

I took a deep breath and let my jaw loosen, my lips parted slightly and I exhaled and let out a long, low, tone, the sound of someone meditating or a monk chanting. Though I wasn't loud, the sound began filling the room, then reverberating, and by the time my exhalation had reached its peak, my voice resonated as if a hundred men were chanting with me. My breath reached its end and faded. The hundred dropped away, one by one, until once again there was only one voice left.

Tanya's hand found mine and clasped it, not hard, not soft, just holding to me.

"My god, Asa," she whispered. "I could feel them. All of them."

"Your turn," I said. I felt, more than saw her shake her head. "Go ahead," I said.

Her tone was higher than mine, not loud, but equally as strong. As it built, it filled the room with brilliance, with sun sparkling off a stream and trees and leaves growing overhead and the cave's draft grew into a breeze of fresh air. Then it too faded into a sunset of gold, and then darkness.

"What did you see?" she whispered.

"A forest. Full of life, and a stream running through it, and trees taller than the cliff," I said.

"Yes," Tanya said. "What *is* this place?"

"I'm not sure," I said, "but I have an idea."

"What?" she said.

"Let's do it together," I said.

"What?"

"Both of us. At the same time."

Silence. "Ok," Tanya said.

I heard her draw her breath in, as I did mine. Then I let out my low chant and she her higher-pitched *ah.*

It took us a second to harmonize. Then our voices gelled, and a world began to grow around us. We were standing on the shore of a vast, gray sea. The sun was barely over the horizon, and in another quarter, a full moon shone, its milky whiteness a counterpoint to the sun's growing brilliance. The vault of the sky was purple and a few stars were still visible. Off to one side there was a field of deep grass where a man stood, a dark, vaguely threatening silhouette visible only in the distance.

To the other side was a high cliff with two figures on it, a man and a woman, also staring out into the sea.

The waves lapped at our feet, gurgling, but as our voices faded, so did the image, until we were engulfed in darkness again. I don't know how long we stood in the dark and the silence, but finally Tanya spoke.

"Did you see what I saw?"

"I don't know," I said. "A man?"

"And a woman."

"And the sun," I said.

"And the moon," Tanya said.

"We were standing on the edge of a sea," I said. "Did you see a man standing way off to one side?"

"No. Just the people and the sea and the sky."

We stood, holding hands, for a few more minutes.

"We should go, Asa. It must be getting late, and I don't know if I can find our way out of the woods in the dark." She let go of my hand.

As we turned toward the crawlspace out, I took one last scan around the floor, looking for...I don't know what. Pottery? A painting stick?

What I saw was the last thing I expected.

It was a knife. In a sheath. I knelt down and picked it up. Covered in dust, it was almost indistinguishable from the ground, even in the light of my headlamp. I pulled the knife out. It was military issue, a standard K-Bar. It felt cold, even colder than the ground it had lain on, and it was corroded from hilt to tip. It had been there a long time. I put it back in its sheath, grinding against the leather, and shoved it in my back pocket.

"What are you doing?" Tanya asked, looking over my shoulder.

"Not too surprising, Tanya, but we aren't the first ones to find this cave. But this doesn't belong here," I said. "It needs to leave."

I don't think we ever spoke again about that experience. It was something, we both knew, that could never be put into words.

In any language.

SUNDAY – CHAPTER 23

After I had gone home and changed out of my torn gi pants and "Vintage" t-shirt into wet woods gear, I drove back and picked up Tanya in my jeep.

Upstream from the center of town—before the bridge across the Cauldron—there was a dirt road that ran along the river bank for several miles. Several pull-offs along the way made it mildly two-way, and there were trails that wandered up from the banks into the woods above the river. The trails weren't maintained by anyone. They were just commonly accepted pathways, and they didn't get enough foot traffic to need maintenance.

The jeep bounced its way down the road, splashing through puddles. The ground was still firm underneath and the soil was rocky, so there wasn't much in the way of mud. The little trickles of water that usually came down from the hillside had become rivulets, eroding small gullies into the road as their little currents swept toward the river.

"There." Tanya pointed to a pull-off next to a dark grove of hemlock climbing up a steep slope.

I pulled over and we got out. The raindrops were big and fat and plopped against my hat and jacket. That combination kept me near-enough dry, but everything has its limits, and soon my outerwear was reaching its. I had really been looking forward to a bowl of Three Nuns tobacco, but the rain was coming down way too hard to get my pipe successfully filled and lit.

I looked at the grove, dark under the closely packed trees.

"Shade aconite, eh? The most potent kind. I guess when you want a heart to stop beating, you mean it."

Tanya looked across the hood at me and shook her head.

"How did you know that? I mean, really, Asa, is there anything you *don't* know, or at least pretend to know?"

"Yeah, there is," I said. "Like right now, I don't know why I'm standing in the pouring rain with a beautiful woman chatting about deadly plants."

"Probably because you're too old to do anything else," she said. She reached into her shoulder bag, still on the seat of the jeep, and pulled out two small, muslin drawstring bags and handed one to me.

"Here," she said. "You can help me pick. Since you know every damn thing, I'll assume you know what it looks like. You probably also already know that I only want the flowers and leaves."

"No problem," I said.

Tanya led us into the grove of trees to where she'd seen the foxglove.

We were both bent over, water dripping off us onto the plants we were collecting, when I remembered the previous conversation I had gotten sidetracked from.

"So, Elle Anderson. You knew her. And probably Budgie, too." Tanya and I had never talked much beyond the basics of our pasts. Her Buddhist training kept her focused on the present moment, and I was never one to delve into those sorts of thing on my own account. What had been had been, and was long gone.

"Didn't know Budgie. He was like five years older than me. I knew him by reputation back then, though. Used to sell weed and coke to the kids in high school. And if you were hard up for money, and you were a girl, he'd always be willing to 'trade'. What an ass. And to be honest, I only kind of knew Elle. Everybody always wants to claim how close friends they were with the deceased, but I knew her better in elementary school. Regional school was bigger. We didn't really hang out with the same people."

Tanya stood and paused to wipe the rain drops from her nose.

"She came from a lousy family," she said. "No dad that anyone knew of, mom only paid attention about half the time. So of course she took any attention she could get as good, and drugs to make that kind of attention easier to swallow. She got a rep, hung out with people mostly older than her, and wasn't really a part of things. So we were both outcasts. I guess we had that in common."

"You were an outcast?"

"Oh, yeah, but for the opposite reasons. You're looking at the High School Ice Queen here."

"Really, Tanya? I'm surprised. You're so warm hearted and—"

"Look at me, Asa. What do you see?"

I looked. "A very wet woman," I said.

Tanya didn't smile. "There's no mistaking my heritage," she said. "Worse, I'm hapa."

"Hapa? What's that?"

"It's a Hawaiian term for someone who is half Asian, half white, and doesn't really belong anywhere," she said bitterly. "For me that meant half the boys in high school had bamboo fever, half the girls didn't get past 'half-Asian slut.' The only way to shut that down was to distance myself from it. In a way, though, that was good. That's when I started hiking, and finding out about the healing plants around here. Until then, all I knew was what my mother taught me before she ran."

"I'm sorry, Tanya."

"It's ok, Asa. Like you always tell me, it was a long time ago."

We picked some more in silence until our bags were full, and then walked back to the jeep. Once inside I reached across Tanya into the glove compartment and grabbed my pipe and tobacco pouch.

"Really?" Tanya said. "In here?"

I sighed and shoved them back in.

"You know, that's one of the six hundred and fifty-seven reasons I never-" she stopped herself.

"Never what?" I said.

"Never mind. That's what," Tanya said and looked out her window.

SUNDAY – CHAPTER 24

Instead of turning around, I headed the jeep upstream toward the bridge below the gorge. The road dead-ended at the pool below the gorge where the river pounded through the narrows then suddenly dropping to the pool. I thought that the sight of the gorge with all this extra water blasting through might nudge Tanya out of her suddenly sour mood, but I kind of wanted to see it too.

I had to trudge along in second gear to navigate my way through the gullies and washouts, and it was a good thing I did. Otherwise I would have missed it.

I was nudging our way out of one gully when I caught a glimpse of something hanging over a branch on the passenger side. I got the jeep up and out and stopped.

"Wait here," I said to Tanya. I jumped out without grabbing my hat.

Just a few steps off the muddy road I could see the body much more clearly. It was a man, hanging over a branch, not moving. I ran over to him.

I pulled him off the branch and he fell to the ground. I rolled him over. His eyes were empty, and his face cold. Tanya ran up beside me.

"Oh, my god," she said.

I looked at the face. Shit.

"It's Lao," I said to Tanya. "You know, the guy who brought me the manuscript."

"Let me get my phone," Tanya said. "I'll call the police."

"No." I said. "Wait. I have to think this through."

I flipped his coat open, rifled his pockets. I pulled out a thick wad of bills and a passport with a picture of him, but not his real name. Or at least the name I knew him by, or the one Peterson had given me.

Guy like Lao had several names. We all do, when it comes down to it.

I stuffed the goods back in his pocket. There was no blood, no sign of a gunshot or knife wound. I unbuttoned his shirt and saw the big bruise on his chest. I pushed. Ribs were broken.

"Shit," I said. "He was murdered. Killed by a blow to the chest. A hard enough percussion can stop a heart, and that's what happened. He died in seconds." I looked him over for signs of cuts or broken bones. "It happened fast, so they didn't have a chance to, umm, interview him—or they didn't need to. Then they dropped him like a hot potato and ran."

"Get back in the car, Tanya. Get in the driver's seat. If something looks wrong, get the hell out of here."

"No," Tanya said. "I want to know what is going on, Asa."

She was right.

I sat back on my heels, squatting. I was soaked through and through.

"Somebody wants to kill me." I said.

"You...what? What do you mean?" she said.

"Somebody wants the manuscript, and they also want me," I said. "Whether they want to kidnap me and hold me until I've deciphered the manuscript, or whether they just want to kill me and take the paper, I'm not sure. One way or another, though, I've got a target on my back."

I stayed crouched in the rain, thinking some more. Tanya was silent.

"Ok," I said. "Here's what we're gonna do."

"The Zamenhof manuscript was stolen. I suspected that when Lao came here with it in the dead of night, and I knew it after talking to Peterson. Somebody has come looking for it, and they found Lao.

"If we call the police, then they'll know he's dead, which means they'll tell the Chinese. Peterson told me Lao had gotten flagged on the Chinese hot list when he came into the country. Somebody connected to the Chinese government wants that manuscript back. Whoever that was—when this gets back to the Chinese—will ask them if there were any documents on him, and they'll say no. But it will point the finger directly at me. Next thing you know, I'll be dead and the manuscript will be on the first plane back to China. Or I'll be in the cargo hold with it. I can't let that happen, Tanya."

She looked horrified. "If the Chinese government wants it that bad, let them have it! It's not worth it, Asa. Can't you give it back to the people who hired Lao?"

"I don't know who they are, Tanya. I don't know any of the players here, and with Lao dead I have no way of finding out. Even if I did know, it doesn't matter. Lao was giving me a message that they'll want me dead, too. I'm caught between a rock and a hard place. The only thing I can do right now is try to buy myself some time to translate that language, whatever it is."

"You can't, Tanya said. Her normally serene face was creased with fear. "Whoever killed them were probably on the phone as soon as they were finished."

"Which means one side knows and the other doesn't," I said. "Maybe. It's slim pickings, but I have to hope that Lao's people were willing to give me some time. If they know that Lao was compromised, everything's going to start moving fast. Too fast, and I'm gone, one direction or the other."

Tanya's hand was over her mouth and her tears were mixing with the rain. In all our years I'd never seen her so upset.

"So I'm going to buy myself some time. And Tanya, if you really do love me, you'll let me do what I need to do to protect myself."

"Ok, Asa." It was barely more than a whisper.

I took off my coat and handed it to her. It didn't matter, we were both already soaked to the skin.

"Take this to the car. I'll be right there."

I crouched down and tried to lift Lao's body. It was wet and stiff and too heavy. I couldn't pick it up. I stood up and looked at the river, thirty yards away, through brush and across the dirt road. I looked back down at Lao's lifeless form. Everything that had made Lao who he was, was gone. What made him move and laugh and think and seek and love—all of that was gone, leaving only this behind. Nothing more than some tissue, already seeking, no doubt, to dissolve into the dirt beneath it. Just a husk, just the shell. I crouched down again, put my arms under the body and lifted it up easily.

Lao, I couldn't carry. This shell, I could.

I carried it to the river's edge and without pausing, walked into the river. I carried it as far from the bank as I could and with half my body under water and the current threatening to pull me the rest of the way, I shoved the body away from me after turning it face down.

I watched it glide downstream, joining in the main current with the other debris that was beginning to collect in the swollen waters. I felt my feet begin to slip under the force of the river and I started working my way back to the edge. Tanya stood there, looking at me, her eyes hollow. I reached shore twenty feet downstream from where I'd gone in.

There's never fighting the current to go upstream, I thought. There's only finding the smoothest passage down.

SUNDAY – CHAPTER 25

I dropped a wet, sad and angry Tanya off at her house and then drove down to *Tempo Gardas.* Neveah was there, as I knew she would be. She often uses Sunday afternoons to handle nonessential and catch up work. Today she was perusing Nike club dresses.

"Hey, Nev, you got someplace where you can go?" I asked.

"Like, for dinner?"

"No, like, for a couple of days. Things are going to get kind of weird around here for a bit."

"Fuck, boss, what'd you do?

I weighed telling her a sanitized version, but scrapped that. She couldn't do any more damage by knowing so I spilled it.

"And that's why you have to get out of town for a few days," I said.

"Naw," she said. "I'm good."

"No," I said. "You aren't. Scram. Vamoose."

She cocked her head. "Vamoose? Really, boss?"

"Well, ok, maybe not. Just stay away from the store for a while. I'll call you when the coast is clear."

"Still gettin' paid, right?"

"Right."

" 'K, boss. Lemme just find this dress I wanted, then I'll 'vamoose' " She giggled and turned back to the screen.

I went to my office in back, spun a couple of knobs and opened my safe. The manuscript was still in there. I pulled it out and dropped the pages on my desk. I thought about everything I knew about manuscript preservation. Controlled environment, proper humidity, filtered air . . .

Screw it. I reached for my pipe and scrabbled around the piles on my desk for a tin of Three Nuns. The day had pretty much gone to shit, but at least I would have a nice smoke, I thought. Some days just went like that.

Pipe lit, tamped down and lit again for smoking, I sat down and looked at the manuscript. The letters didn't suddenly jump out at me and tell me their names.

So instead I thought about the man who had written them. Zamenhof's goal in creating a new language, he had said, was to make a universal second language, a language that could be learned by anyone, easily. It was to be a language as free as possible from cultural baggage, with simple grammar and spelling, yet robust enough to express complex ideas. With Esperanto, he had certainly succeeded.

Take, for example, the common Esperanto greeting. "*Saluton!*" you would say, as an English speaker would say "hello," or a Swede would say "*hej!*" "*Saluton*" is a simple translation for an English or French speaker, who might also say "*salut!*" Association to similar words quickly make "salute" or "salutations" come to mind. In other words, a greeting.

Or take this simple sentence. "*Cxu vi parolas Esperanton?*" translates to "do you speak Esperanto?" Again, easily translated, at least in part by a speaker of any one of several languages with Indo-European roots. With a dictionary and some rudimentary grammar, any one of these speakers could make themselves understood in Esperanto in a matter of hours.

But this manuscript? This wasn't that.

I drew on the pipe and puffed out the smoke. The cloud rose in the air. If the language on these pages was an attempt to make a universal second language, it was, by any account, a dismal failure. It was impossible to decipher, apparently even by an artificial intelligence presumably skilled in the world's languages. Zamenhof must have known it was a flop. He was anything but a dunce. So why give it to Dad for safekeeping? Why not just chuck it in the fire himself and go on and design the language that became Esperanto?

He must have seen some worth to it. What value would it have been to this man? A Polish Jew, he spoke many languages, from Yiddish to Polish to Belarusian. He'd studied Latin, Greek, Hebrew and Aramaic in school. He later developed a proficiency in German and Lithuanian, and he knew a smattering of English. Having grown up in the midst of violent conflicts among people, his underlying goal was to make one language that could create peace. A language of diplomacy.

He was a doctor, a man of medicine, an ophthalmologist—a specialist in eyes. A man of science, of reason, who had dedicated his life to giving birth to Esperanto and giving it to the world. What he'd created was logical, consistent and clear. Its meaning was visible on the surface, and that was one of the reasons it had been adopted so readily by those who shared his vision.

This manuscript was the opposite. Unclear, obtuse. Perhaps it was the opposite in other ways. Irrational. Illogical. A language, not of peace, but of discord. This was the yang to Esperanto's yin. There can not be one without the other. In the words of Lao Tzu, "All things carry Yin yet embrace Yang. They blend their life breaths in order to produce harmony."

Maybe this was crazy thinking, but before Zamenhof could create Esperanto, what if he created its opposite? Maybe what sat silently in front of me was not proto-Esperanto, but anti-Esperanto? And if so, what did that even mean?

My pipe gurgled and offered me its last puff. I cleaned it, put it back in its stand, opened the safe and locked the manuscript inside.

It was time to go marry Paul and Chloe. Then I needed to have a talk with Budgie.

SUNDAY – CHAPTER 26

For the second time that day, I went home, showered and put on some clean clothes. Given all that had happened, I hadn't given more than a glancing thought to what I was going to say as a wedding officiant. But that's one of the advantages of being old. As Nev would put it, I've seen some shit. When you're older, you can sometimes talk your way through situations that would have left you stammering and staring at your shoes as a younger man.

Which was all well and good, but then again, this was Paul. He and Charlie were my two best friends in Nemaseck, aside from Tanya. I needed to do a little planning, but in order to do so, I needed more information from the two of them. I hurried up my preparations to get to Not Debbie's on time. I briefly wondered if Paul planned on changing the name.

I made a quick stop at *Tempo Gardas*, which was now empty of Nev, and then proceeded to the donut shop. I wasn't expecting what I walked into. Four or five people were already there rearranging tables and setting up chairs. A couple of long tables had been set up on one side, and a plates of food were already sitting on one of them, and wrapped boxes on the other.

I walked over to one woman while the others were setting up some chairs.

"Expecting a crowd?" I asked.

She nodded. "About twenty of us," she said.

"Where's Paul and Chloe?"

"In the kitchen. We told them to stay the hell out of here."

I flipped the countertop open. One of Paul's other employees was already behind the counter pulling levers on Paul's mammoth coffee machine. Paul and Chloe were in the kitchen, sitting on stools next to the kitchen's work counter. Chloe's lightweight cotton dress fell to her ankles and moved gently in the breeze from the open back door. Paul wore black slacks and a white collared shirt. Both looked happy, and a little bit scared.

I had to wonder that Paul wasn't on the edge of taking a runner, given his last experience with marriage, but despite the edge of concern on his face, he looked present and grounded.

I couldn't help but smile. After what I had just done, this felt like a renewal of sorts. A cleansing of the river's water that I couldn't wash away in the shower.

Paul stood and we clenched in a strong hug. Then Chloe, more gentle. Now they were smiling, too.

"You, umm, got a few witnesses for the wedding, I guess?"

Paul laughed. "News to us, too," he said. "Word gets around fast in the rooms. We mentioned it in a meeting last night, and the next thing you know we walked into all this. It's not what we planned for, but," he shrugged, "they're here. It's all good."

"Good," I said. "You guys deserve a sendoff. But I'd be willing to bet you didn't have time to get any rings, did you?"

"No," Chloe said, speaking quietly as if to balance Paul's cannon of a voice. "Paul and I don't want them. Too traditional. It's not us. And when you're working in a kitchen, a ring is just a bother."

"Wonderful," I said. "Because I brought you something that might work better."

I reached into my pocket and pulled out the items I had grabbed at my shop, two pendants on thin gold rope necklaces. Each had an intricate design of criss-crossing gold filaments within a platinum circle. One held a small onyx stone, black as midnight, and the other an iridescent opal. I held them out in my hand.

"I thought you might want to give these to each other instead."

"My god, Asa. they're beautiful!" Chloe said. Paul looked at them, and then at me. His silence spoke his approval.

"They're more than just jewelry," I said and set them down on the counter. "They're talismans, with magical properties, if you believe the legends. Onyx, that is the stone of personal power. It gives the wearer the ability to make oneself heard, the ability to persist in one's desires, the power to stay strong during tough times. Opal contains the fire of the human spirit. It helps the wearers keep their passions burning, keeps their spark of life bright and shining, even during the darkest of hours. And there's one other thing, too," I said. "Let me show you."

I reached over to the counter and placed one of the pendants on top of the other. I twisted the top one until the bails of the two lined up. I took my hand away. The intricate weaving in each, when viewed together, gave way to a circle filled with gold on one side and nearly empty on the other. A curving line crossed the center, and on the upper left side of the clear circle was the onyx. The lower right held the opal. Together, they formed a *taijitu,* or as it is more commonly known in the West, the yin-yang symbol.

Chloe fell silent. I waited for a minute, letting each of them ingest the pattern just formed.

"You each need to decide which one you want to wear. Whichever it is, reach out and take it."

This could have been the only hiccup in my gift, but my instincts proved correct. Without hesitation, Paul reached out for the opal. Chloe took the onyx.

They looked at the pendants in their hands, then at each other, and finally at me.

"Now trade," I said. "During the ceremony, where the rings are usually put on each other's fingers, you will clasp these pendants around each other's necks. Paul, you put Chloe's in your pocket, and Chloe, you can . . . "

I looked at her in her flowing dress with, of course, nothing to put the pendant in.

"I'll hold it in my hand," Chloe said, tears in her eyes. "And I'm never letting go."

SUNDAY – CHAPTER 27

I looked at both of them, their eyes glistening. There was no longer any fear, any worry, in either of them. Only joy.

As I watched Paul and Chloe, the haunting sight of Lao's body floating face down in the river finally began to fade from my mind. This was a time for beginnings, not endings.

"Where did these come from?" Paul asked. "I've never seen anything like them."

"You're not likely to, either," I said. "They came from Down Under, and I got them in kind of a strange way—but not a bad strange way. Several years ago, I took a trip through Tasmania. It was, in part, a business trip—there was an auction there with some items I was interested in—but I decided to make it a bit of a pleasure trip as well. The auction was in Hobart, near the southern tip of the island, but I decided to take the ferry from Melbourne and hike from the north to the south. Have either of you been to Tasmania?" I asked.

They shook their heads.

"Maybe you should take a second honeymoon there, sometime," I said. "It's beautiful. Most of the time I hiked on public lands through the bush, but there were times I had to cross private land, and not always with permission. One day in particular I remember. I had hiked across a long expanse of savanna. There were only a few gum trees in the distance, and a rock outcropping or two. This was as I was on the southern half of my trip, and I had been walking a little over a week, seeing nobody. It was so remote, almost at the bottom of the globe, and the land felt like it hadn't been touched since prehistoric times. And though I wasn't on a mountain, somehow the sky seemed very close to the earth. It was like I was walking at the ends of the earth, in the beginning of time. As I came over one outcrop, I saw the sea, the Tasman Sea. It was deep, deep green, and the shore was a pure white beach. I scrambled down to the beach and sat down on a rock, sitting there and feeling the land and the sea around me. It was one of the most beautiful places I had ever been."

Paul waved away with his right hand one of the guests who had tried to come through the kitchen doorway.

"It was so beautiful," I continued, "that I sat there too long and suddenly noticed my long shadow stretching out in front of me. I'd long overstayed my welcome and really had no idea where I was. As I looked behind, I saw storm clouds, a front coming in behind me, and felt the wind picking up. I knew this beach would be no place to be in a Tasmanian storm. I grabbed my pack and took off. Still, it was nothing but grass and the occasional gum tree around me, nothing I to use for shelter or to stop the wind from battering my tent to pieces. The sun had set and I was walking in the last of dusk when I spotted a house. It was a shack, really, but there was a light on inside."

"Now, encounters like this—coming up to someone's home in the evening in the middle of nowhere—can go two ways. One way ends up with a shotgun pointed at you as you run in the direction you're told. The other is a warm dinner, and if you're doubly lucky, a place to sleep. I walked up to the house. There was no activity outside, and no barns or equipment that told me this was a farm, so I was a little bit on edge. I knocked on the door."

"A woman, older than me, if you can believe it, answered."

"'I'm a traveler,' I said, 'a bit lost, really. I was wondering if you could point me to a safe place to stay the night, during the storm?'"

"She looked me up and down for a minute, and then said, 'Well, you look right old, and probably not one to give me trouble. Come on in.'"

"It was a one-room shack and sparsely finished. Just a bed, a chair, and a table and a stove, and what looked to be an ice cooler in the corner. 'I'm just about to cook dinner. I'm glad to have the company.'"

"I dropped my pack on the floor, weary from its weight, and sat down on it. The old woman opened the cooler and pulled out a fish, filleted it on the table and threw it into a pan on the stove. No spices, no rice, just a fish. We talked about what I was doing and where I was headed."

"'One oldster to another, what are you doing way out here?' I asked. Her filmy eyes looked into a distance that I couldn't see, and she began to tell me her tale."

"It was really her son's shack, she said, one of several built to stay with his flock of sheep as they grazed their way through the area during the summer. 'If you look close in the morning,' she said, 'you'll see the track where his four-wheeler used to run. You can follow that out in the morning, and that will get you pretty far south, and back onto Crown land.'"

"As we ate, she told me about his son, and how proud she'd been of him. He'd married a wonderful girl, she said, and together they'd built up a good-sized herd, and had been doing well. Then the drought hit, and the horrible summer when the temperatures had soared for weeks over one hundred degrees. 'Climate change,' the old woman said. 'Don't tell me it don't exist, 'cuz it killed my son. They found him, right over yonder, with half his flock, all dead of heat exhaustion.'"

"We finished dinner and talked until it was late at night while outside the storm howled and blew. Eventually we grew quiet, two strangers running out of things to say."

"'So what are you doing out here?' I finally asked."

"She peered at me through her bad eyes. 'Come to die, I have. Got the cancer, and pretty near the end. Just a few more days, I figure.' She stared at me for a minute, a searching look on her face. Then she said, 'You aren't who you say you are, are you?'"

"I looked at her, trying to muster all my honesty into my face. 'No,' I said, 'I'm exactly who I said I am.'"

"She chuckled, and said, 'Don't try and fool the dying, sonny. We know better.' She kept staring at me, and then said, 'You don't even know, do you?' I didn't know what she meant, so I said nothing. She nodded to herself, and then said, almost to herself, 'So that's why I'm here.'"

"She got up, walked over to a shoulder bag in the corner and began rooting through it. 'There it is,' she finally said, and pulled out a small, drawstring bag."

"She handed it to me. Inside were the two pendants that I gave to you guys. 'Here,' she said. 'I made these myself, back when I could see, not long after my son got married. 'Tasmanian rocks, they are, from Mother Earth herself, before she got angry at us. Meant to give 'em to my son and daughter-in-law on their seventh anniversary, but he didn't last that long. Daughter-in-law's long gone, dead of the grief, and I've been holding on to them since. I was gonna take them with me, but you know, you can't do those things.'"

"'They were made with love,' she said, 'They were made for love that lasts. You take 'em. You're gonna need 'em one day.'"

"I thanked her and tried to refuse, but she wouldn't hear of it. Eventually my eyes wouldn't stay open any more and I fell asleep, right there on the floor, my head on my pack.

"The next morning, when I woke up, she was gone, and so was the storm. I went outside to look for her. The sun was rising and the air had that fresh, new feeling to it, that clarity it always has after a hard storm. I never did see her again, but I did find the old track that she said would lead me south. I eventually picked up my pack and left, with the pendants stashed in one of the pockets."

"As it turned out, the old woman was wrong. I never did need them, and I'm too old to use them. But I think you will. They're made for love that lasts. They're strong."

Paul and Chloe nodded their heads silently. I mean, what can you say to a story like that?

SUNDAY – CHAPTER 28

It was all a lie, I thought to myself, as I stood against the far wall of the shop, opposite the curtain.

The woman I'd talked to when I'd arrived was unfolding the legs of a table from which I could officiate, putting a white tablecloth over it and setting three candles on it. Paul and Chloe were sequestered in the kitchen, where I had told them to keep waiting while we got things set up.

Well, some of it was a lie, anyway. I actually had taken a walk across Tasmania on my way to an auction in Hobart, and that was about where the truth ended. The afternoon on the remote beach on the shore of the Tasman Sea, that was true, too, but there had been no storm. I had actually spent the night on the beach in my sleeping bag, without a tent, looking at the strange display of the heavens above. None of the constellations or stars that I knew were visible in the southern hemisphere, and I felt adrift and a bit lost in that strange land. But that had been ok. That had been what I wanted. I took great measure of comfort in the wild and unfamiliar beauty around me.

There had been no shack, no wise woman offering me gifts on the evening of her self-designated final day on earth. From the beach, I had walked on south without incident. I had, unfortunately, been disappointed at the auction, where the items I wanted failed to materialize, but I had been struck by the wares being offered by an Asian street vendor on the way back to my hotel.

Australia is almost entirely European Caucasian and, unlike here, there were no African-Americans or Hispanics or other ethnicities common in the States. The only other ethnicity of note were people from southeast Asia, and they were a rapidly growing population there, I gathered. In fact, when people asked me what Australian cuisine was like, I said that the Thai food there was great and authentic.

The street vendor had such beautiful jewelry, and it was from him that I had bought the pendants, as well as some other items at unusually low prices compared to their quality. I had asked him where the pendants had come from, but he was a bit nonspecific, pleading unfamiliarity with English and looking sideways at me when I tried to converse in Esperanto. Probably stolen, I had thought, or "fallen off the back of the truck," in the fiction used by gray market vendors everywhere.

So I had sold Paul and Chloe a story, one that only barely held together when examined rationally. But the rational part of their minds was not the part I was speaking to. That's not what stories are for. I was talking to their unconscious, their hearts, their emotions. I told them a fable of enduring love, and in so doing linked it to the pendants that they were to give one another.

For those with a religious leaning, the wedding ring is already empowered by the myth of their sacred tradition, whatever it might be. These myths, these stories we tell ourselves, are possessed of immense power. Some change sinners to saints. Others fill us with courage or enable us to realize that we are never really alone, in joy or in suffering.

SUNDAY – CHAPTER 29

The table was in front of me and the eyes of the guests were on me. I gestured to the two in back who had been delegated to bring the bride and groom forward, and they disappeared into the kitchen and returned a minute later with the couple.

Paul and Chloe were escorted down the aisle, and stood in front of me. I looked at them, Paul, serious and thoughtful, Chloe, nervous and happy.

"Welcome, good friends," I began. "We are here to celebrate the union of Chloe and Paul, Paul and Chloe, as husband and wife. They are to be joined together, not only by law and custom, but in the presence of, and with the blessing of, Heaven and Earth. I will now invite these most important guests to our ceremony."

I picked up a lighter placed on the table for me and lit the candle on the far left.

"With this flame we recognize the power of heaven above us. The power of light and of heat, the energy through which our days are made and the work of our lives conducted."

I lit the candle on the far right.

"As we light this candle, we recognize the wax from which it is made, the material essence of all things, the power of the cool, dark earth below us by which all is given life, nurtured, and through which the sustenance of all things comes."

I moved the third candle slightly back so that the three candles now formed a triangle. "And here are we. Humankind, through which Heaven and Earth are manifested."

"All three of these powers are necessary for the creation of a reality, the creation of our reality. Unending light and heat can only scorch and burn, rather than create. Neverending depth and darkness is only a cold and lifeless rock spinning through empty space. But when we, as people, recognize our proper place in the cosmos, light and dark, hot and cold, action and stillness come together in us to make the rock spinning in darkness a home. So as this is true in the universe, so is it true in a marriage. We each bring our light and our darkness, our passion and our peace, our joy, and our sadness. And none of it can come to be..." I looked out at the congregation and nodded "...without the community around us, those who co-create the reality in which we live."

I looked back at Chloe and Paul, both now calm and attentive to my words.

"Chloe," I said, "before we go forward, do you have any words to say to Paul?"

She looked at me, startled. I hadn't warned either of them about this, preferring a spontaneous response.

She turned her gaze to Paul.

"Paul," she said, "I met you—you came to me—when I was in darkness, scared of the world, who I had become—scared of everything. And you stood beside me, an unmovable rock. I held onto you for dear life. And, if you will have it, I will hold onto you for the rest of my life."

Paul, usually never one to be without a word, stood for a minute in silence, and I could see his eyes glisten.

"Chloe," he then said, "you have given me new hope. Inside me, I *was* a rock. I was tired, and suspicious and, and almost ready to turn around and go back to what I had been. But you gave me hope. You showed me it was ok to love again. You gave me back my trust and I have been repaid a hundred million times since. And I will never let go of that again, or of you."

They weren't the only ones with tears in their eyes, I could see as I looked out toward the guests. I took a breath. Time to make the magic happen.

"It is time," I said. "Paul and Chloe, I believe you have something to exchange with one another. Would you please do so now?"

Paul reached into his pocket and pulled out one pendant and tenderly fastened it around Chloe's neck. Chloe opened her hand, unclasped the other necklace and reached up to Paul, but his height exceeded her reach.

Instead of bending forward, Paul reached out to Chloe, encircling her waist with his hands, and lifted her to his level. She fastened the pendant on his neck. He held her a second more—both immersed in one another—and then lowered her down.

In a slightly louder voice, as if speaking to those outside as well, I said, *"Ni naskiĝas, ni restadas, kaj tiam ni moviĝi. Kaj ni pasigas tiun tempo serĉas por amon; Amo por la lando ni estas on, Amo por la belo firmamento. Ni perdas nia vojo kaj ni trovas ĝin. Kaj, kune, ni kreias eternecon el momento. Permesu ĉi tiu momenton estas tian eternecon!*

Then I repeated it, in English:

"We are born, we linger here, and then we move on. And we spend that time in search of love, love for the land we are on, love for the beauty of the sky. We lose our way, and we find it. And, together, we create eternity from an instant. Let this moment be your infinity!"

I paused.

"I now pronounce you husband and wife."

SUNDAY – CHAPTER 30

Paul and Chloe had been enchanted with the ceremony, although Chloe had later confessed to a small heart attack when I'd asked her to say her vows.

Before the reception started in earnest, Paul pulled me aside into the kitchen.

"Thank you so much, Asa," he said. "That was beautiful."

"You're welcome," I said, and then, "I've been meaning to ask you. Are you going to rename the donut shop now, or what?"

"Ah. Well, about that," Paul said, looking around the kitchen. "We're going to sell it, I think. Chloe wants to get a little closer to the earth, and I want to begin creating food straight from the ground. So we're going to find some land, a farm, and maybe I'll start a farm-to-table restaurant right on the premises. "Thing is," he added, "it probably won't be around here. Land's too tough, seasons are too hard, winter's too long. We're going to look further south." He looked at me sadly. "I'm sorry, Asa. I will miss you. You've been a good friend."

I nodded, slowly. "You have as well, Paul. But I won't say goodbye quite yet. Tonight is a time for hellos, not goodbyes."

"Yes. Yes it is," Paul said, but he was still thoughtful. "One thing, though, Asa, while I have the chance..."

"What?" I said.

"Don't be afraid to be yourself," Paul said. "As long as I've known you, I've always felt that you're holding something back, that there's more—or more to you—than you let on. Our wedding ceremony, for example. That was Asa, unleashed. That was magic." His eyes looked into mine.

I wasn't sure what to say. "You're welcome, Paul. I'll think about it. But now I have to go, and you should get with Chloe and your guests."

He said goodbye and I slipped out the kitchen door. The wind was beginning to pick up as I got in the red Jeep, and things were already starting to get damp around the edges inside. The soft top had a few points of entry that shouldn't have been there. They had been there when I got it, and I had always intended to patch the roof, but had never got around to it. I tried telling Tanya once that they were bullet holes, but she laughed at me.

"I know exactly where these holes are from, and they aren't bullets," she said.

"Oh, yeah?" I said.

"Yeah. This was Curtis McCandel's car, and it was parked underneath that old elm on the town green in the middle of some storm," she said. "The tree came down. It missed most of Curtis' car, but some of the small branches went right through this top. He tried to get the town to pay for it, but got nowhere, of course," she said. "Also, the holes are on top. Where were they shooting at you from, a helicopter?"

That wasn't totally inconceivable, but I let it go. Looking at the holes now, I wondered why I hadn't bothered to even duct tape them, and then let it go. What Paul had said before I left still rattled around in my head. He said that except during the wedding, I'd been holding back, but I had no idea what he was talking about. Holding back what?

The ceremony had been an exercise in showmanship, and had certainly been successful from the tears of joy on everyone's faces.

But he had a point. I have always been cautious. It's in my nature not to say too much, not to do much that will attract attention to me. I do exist on the margins of things, coming and going, never staying too long. That's where I'm comfortable. And that's why I'm good at what I do.

I wondered how much of that story I'd told Chloe and Paul was also a story I needed to tell myself.

My stomach growled and I realized that I hadn't eaten anything since breakfast. I figured it might be a good idea to have something now, as I didn't know how long this show was going to take, but I was pretty sure that Budgie wasn't going to offer me dinner.

I swung into the town's one fast-food place, rolled around to the drive-up line, picked up my order and backed into a parking space to eat. I hated actually eating inside those places, all bright colors and grease and sixteen-year-old girls with stitched-on smiles and braces and about a year away from getting knocked up.

Probably a lot like Elle, I thought, to be honest. At her funeral, I was sure a lot had been said about the bright future she had ahead of her, what a good and steady friend she had been, and loving everyone and being kind to animals. Only some of it true. I had no idea what she was like, really, Probably no one did, least of all, her. She was still being molded by the world when she had been killed.

Which is about when I realized that the girl at the drive-up window had forgotten my coffee. I put down my half-eaten burger, got out and went inside. The same girl was standing at the counter. She was fighting off some acne, a losing war in this work environment, and her blondish hair was braided on either side of her head and pulled back. Tattered hair ends stuck out of the braids like pieces of straw. And, yes, she had braces.

Showing no trace of recognizing me, she put on her trained service smile.

"Are you ready to order?" she asked.

"I just went through the drive-thru," I said, "but I didn't get the cup of coffee that I ordered."

Her smile never left her face as she said, "Certainly, sir. I'm sorry. I'll get that for you right away." She turned and left the counter for the coffee station.

I followed her with my eyes. I wondered if the life path I had made up for her were true. I was willing to bet the guy sitting by himself in the lifted pickup truck in the parking lot, tapping his thumbs on the steering wheel to unheard music, was her boyfriend, killing time until there were no customers there and he could go in and flirt with her. If she hadn't already lost her virginity in the front seat of that thing, she soon would. It was a story as old as humanity.

She came back with my coffee and I was suddenly sad. Sad for opportunities wasted, sad for truncated lives, sad for lives crippled by bad decisions. And all of these lives—all of them—so very, very short.

I guess I had lost track of things because she was standing there looking quizzically at me. I smiled at her wanly.

"I'm sorry. What did you say?" I asked her.

"I said 'would you like anything else?'" she repeated in a slightly louder voice for the old geezer.

I picked up my coffee and touched the brim of my hat.

"No thank you, miss," I said. "I'm sorry. I hope you don't being called 'miss.' Old man talk, I'm afraid."

"Oh, no problem," she said, "I don't mind at all. But actually it's missus," she said. "See?" She held out her left hand so I could see her ring. Her smile was genuine now.

"That your husband out in the lot?" I asked. "In the sky-high pickup truck?"

She laughed. "That's Josh," she said. "He waits for my shift to end every night, and then we go to my mom's and pick up the baby." Her smile never faltered. It was real. She wasn't playing me just to get rid of a creepy old guy.

"Well, bless you both. Or the three of you, I guess."

I nodded and walked out of the store. Can't drive, can work second shift, got kid, I thought. I'm getting old. I pulled the old old cup out of the console holder, threw it on the floor, and put the new one in. I reached into the glove compartment and pulled out a pipe. It was a roughed-up Canadian, all long shank, and one of my favorites. I stuffed the bowl with enough Night Owl tobacco to last the ride and lit up. I still had enough time to get to Budgie's house before the sun set.

SUNDAY – CHAPTER 31

I drove down Prescott Street, pulled up in front of Budgie's house and turned off the jeep. The front yard was about the size of a postage stamp and intermittently studded with grass. A child's Big Wheel, faded from sunlight, lay on its side and an aluminum softball bat lay half in the mud.

Also half in the mud was the dog. A big one from the looks of it. There was a stake in the ground and a chain hooked to its collar and an overturned bowl which had been stepped on and bent. The dog's chain was long enough for it to reach Budgie's front door.

The screen door itself stood slightly ajar. If I'd had to guess, it had problems closing. The house needed a paint job and dirty curtains hung from the upstairs windows. The downstairs windows were equipped with Venetian blinds. In the fading light I could make out the dance of blue light coming from a television behind the window furthest to my right.

My eyes focused back on the dog, just lying there. Alert. Probably angry. I know I would be if I were chained in a mud puddle. He wasn't a short hair, I could tell he had a coat like a husky's, but he didn't have the eyes or build of a husky. He was longer. Taller. Meaner. He'd be one hundred pounds if he were well fed. He looked at me. His eyes gleamed eerily in the fading light and I saw his right brow was thick with scars.

Well, nothing for it, I thought, and got out of the jeep, keeping my eyes on the dog. As soon as he heard the squeak of my door hinge, he jumped to his feet and stared intently. He couldn't see me until I began walking around the front toward the yard, and then his eyes jumped toward me. His ribs stuck out, as he stood, soaking wet. He was hungry. He leaned toward me against the chain and growled, low. I could be dinner.

The last thing you do in front of any assailant, animal or human, is show fear. I stood still for a minute, letting my fear drop into the earth, become absorbed by the mud, and then slowly but steadily I began walking toward the house, keeping one eye—but only one—on the dog.

I was halfway there when the dog lunged. Only a growl betrayed his attack. Before he took the two steps to reach me, I turned and with my arms wide and my hands open, I stood and looked into the dog's eyes.

In my own mind, I made myself as large as possible, looming over him with a fearless determination to match his attack.

He stopped. We looked at each other.

Years ago—how many, I can't remember—I was walking through the woods...in Canada, I think. I was in a bit of a hurry—why doesn't really matter now—but I had two hundred miles of wilderness to cross. I was carrying little, only a rucksack, and I'd been out for eight days. Eight days since I had seen anyone, eight days of checking maps and climbing ridges and skirting many small lakes. There was a certain lake that I was headed for.

It was mid-morning. I was walking through a virgin pine forest, trees one hundred years old or more rising up endlessly into the gloomy distance. Inches of needles lay on the soil making my walk smooth, comfortable and silent.

I stopped for a minute to take a rest and dropped my pack to the ground. After a couple of minutes I saw something moving through the trees. It was a bear, slowly making its way on all fours, foraging its way toward me.

I watched it, silently.

Black bears have miserable eyesight, and what slight breeze there was put me upwind. He walked closer and closer until he was only twenty feet from me. I was holding my breath, being so still that no movement would betray me.

He was huge. On his hind legs he would dwarf me, and if he weighed less than six hundred pounds, I was a mutton chop. Which I might be anyway, I thought.

Ever so slowly I twisted around to keep him in my sight. A twig snapped.

As poorly as bears see, their hearing makes up for it, and his huge skull swung toward me. I looked at him. He looked at me. Our eyes locked, and all I could see in his eyes was wildness. No fear, no anger, no sadness, no thought. Just pure, primitive, feral being.

Then it happened. Suddenly I was looking, not at him, but at myself, from his eyes.

Everything else was distorted, like there was an aura around each rock, bush and tree, except for one keyhole of clarity through which I appeared, in crystal-clear focus.

At the same time, I was overwhelmed by smells, the moist aroma of the needles and the earth, the pungent fox scat yards away, and then this strange, strong smell from what was standing in front of me.

I heard a chipmunk run up a tree behind me and listened to the rustle of needles underneath the feet of a mouse a few feet away. And I knew, I felt, I breathed deep into and from that woods and then...

It was over. I snapped back into myself and was again facing the bear, now staring at me and seeming neither fierce nor wild.

Should I run, I thought? Climb a tree? Yell at him?

I realized what I must do. I opened my mouth and with a voice that hadn't seen use for a week, I spoke.

"Well, good morning, Mr. Bear!"

At the sound of my voice, the bear turned and ran as fast as a bear can run—it can peak at thirty mph in a sprint—and he was swallowed by the forest.

And here I was, now, staring at an angry, hungry dog, certainly no worse than a six hundred pound bear.

Neither of us moved, and then he tilted his head and looked at me with one eye, his ears cocked ears, the way dogs do when they are trying to figure out where a sound is coming from.

I had an idea. I backed away from him, but did not take my eyes off him. I was careful not to slip in the mud and when I reached the jeep, I opened the door without turning around and grabbed my half-eaten burger. I walked back toward the dog.

He was still looking at me as if he couldn't quite figure out what was going on.

"Here, pup," I said.

I squatted to his level, which to be honest, wasn't that far down, and held out the burger to him. He took it, gingerly, then settled back on his haunches and gulped it down. Probably the first food he'd had all day.

"Stay right there," I said. "Got fries in the car."

I turned my back toward him with a confidence I didn't feel and walked toward the broken screen door. I felt him looking at me from behind. I wondered if he'd ever had French fries.

SUNDAY – CHAPTER 32

There was no point knocking on the half-open door. I peered into the empty kitchen and stepped in.

A angry voice came from the living room to my right. "Who's that?"

"It's Asa," I said, in a tone of voice that indicated that he should know who I was.

I walked into the living room, where a forty year old man with long hair pulled back in a ponytail was sitting on a Rent-A-Center couch. His right hand was between the couch cushions. I looked at it.

"No need to freak out, son," I said. "I just want to talk to you."

He pulled the gun out from the couch and put it on his lap, his hand still on the grip.

"Old man like you can't do much more than talk, can you, anyway?" he said and laughed at his own joke. His eyes flicked back to a sixty-five inch flat screen, drawn by the flash and dazzle of a professional wrestling show.

"Don't need to do much more," I said. "I got a question."

"Sorry. I quit answering questions after five. Call tomorrow and leave a message with my people." He chuckled again. "My people."

"You're Budgie, right? I got a question about Elle Anderson."

He blew his lips at me. "I don't answer questions about Elle Anderson," he said. "I told the last asshole writer that."

"I'm not a writer," I said. "I'm her dad."

He looked at me for a second, all still.

"Bullshit," he said. "Elle didn't have a dad, at least not one that gave a shit."

"I didn't know," I said, "at least not until a few months ago. Trying to find out what happened. You're a father too, right? I saw your kids' toys out front."

I looked past the TV to the rain on the window and tried to look troubled.

"Naw," Budgie said. "Those are my sister's brats. I came home and found the little assholes tearing up the front yard with their shit so I ran 'em off and told 'em they could have their toys back when I was ready."

"Yeah, I get it," I said. "Other people's kids. I never knew I had a kid, y'know? Her mom was just one of those things."

Budgie laughed. "Yeah, she was one of those things with a lot of guys."

"Was Elle?"

"Yeah," Budgie said with a locker-room smile. "She was."

"Oh," I said.

"Hey, don't feel bad, Dad," Budgie said. "She had a thing for guys in uniform. She woulda ended up a nice, happy dependapotamous. Coulda been worse. She coulda ended up with a loser like me."

"You got a big-ass TV, though," I said. "And a dog."

"Yeah," Budgie said. He looked suspicious. "How'd you get past him?"

"I got a way with dogs," I said.

"And women that look like dogs, if you're Elle's father." He chuckled again. Budgie did like his own jokes.

"What kind of dog is he?"

Budgie had to think for a minute.

"Keto...or something like that. I'm not real sure. I got him from . . . this guy. A friend. Owed me some money, I said I'll take the dog. Wanted to keep the place safe. Bastard eats like a pig, though."

"He's kind of a big dog," I said.

"Still eats like a pig." He looked at the TV and the match that had begun. "Yeah, I knew Elle. Yeah, she was a good fuck...if you like pudgy. No, I didn't kill her. That's about it, Dad. I got a show to watch. Anything else?"

His hand fidgeted with the gun.

"I guess not. Thanks for your time, Budgie." I got up and put my hat on.

Budgie wasn't even looking at me as I walked into the kitchen. Out the window I saw the dog looking toward the house expectantly.

As I slipped past the screen door, the dog didn't move. He sat on his haunches, ears forward, looking at me.

I reached out my hand, slowly. He sniffed it, and then looked at me again. I reached around his neck and unbuckled his collar. I wasn't altogether sure what was going to happen next. I didn't think he'd jump me, being the Bearer of Burgers and all, but I did figure he'd bolt. If he was as smart as I thought he was anyway, he would.

Instead he sat there for a moment, still looking at me. Then he trotted over to my jeep and sat down next to the door, waiting for me to open it.

I could swear I heard a voice in the back of my head say "*what took you so long?*"

I opened the door. He hopped in, sniffed toward the back and then sat down in the passenger's seat.

I looked back at the house, and I saw Budgie's face peering out the window.

"Oh, shit," I said to the dog.

I ran around and jumped in and had the jeep running before my door was shut. I peeled out—if that's something you can actually do in an old jeep—and I looked in the rear view mirror. I watched Budgie running up to the edge of the road. His gun hand was at his side, though.

I looked at the dog. He looked at me.

"Lemme get down the road, and I'll give you the fries," I said. "I think we'll be safe. Budgie doesn't strike me as the kind of guy who goes running to the cops with his troubles."

SUNDAY – CHAPTER 33

A mile away from Budgie's, I looked over at the dog. He was a muddy mess and was getting dirt all over my seat. I reached around, grabbed the fries from the back seat and handed him the bag. He took them, bag and all, right out of my hand and munched down the fries before letting the bag drop to the floor.

He looked at me.

"You don't talk much, do you?" I said, and without thinking about it, reached over to scratch him behind the ears. His ears pointed forward, not in an "I'm paying attention" way, but more in an "I'm going to kill you and eat your entrails warm" kind of way. I held my hand motionless, keeping one eye on the road and one on the dog. A low growl came from his throat. I moved my hand away and dropped it back on the wheel.

"Heh. Guess you can when you want to, though, eh?"

I kept both hands on the wheel for the rest of the ride home. The wind was picking up and the rain was starting to come down pretty hard. The jeep got pushed into the middle of the road with one gust and the dog leaned into it without shifting position. He kept his eyes on the road as if he were driving.

"I don't think we got a whole lot out of my visit," I said. "though the dad ploy wasn't a bad idea. And we did find out that she liked army boys, I wonder if there used to be a base around here somewhere."

The dog didn't reply. He was probably still pretty hungry.

I guessed I was sharing that night's salmon and rice.

SUNDAY – CHAPTER 34

I opened the door to my house and the dog followed me in. He immediately started sniffing the floor, the chairs and around the dining room table and then he followed me into the kitchen. I shrugged my jacket off and hung it out in the mud room to dry.

"Like salmon, boy?" I asked as I pulled the fish out of the refrigerator.

He immediately sat, and gave me the gravest attention as I unwrapped the fish and turned on the oven to pre-heat. I poured water and a small amount of oil into a pot and set it on the flame to boil. I went to the cabinet and poured out a half cup of white rice. I looked at the dog and his ribs and added another quarter cup.

I cut off a third of the salmon steak and put the rest aside. I squeezed a slice of fresh lemon on it and then sprinkled it with a little salt and pepper. Not too much, though. I never liked the taste of the condiments overriding a good centerpiece. Finally I cut up some broccoli to steam and put another pot on the stove.

The dog didn't budge the whole time.

Once everything was cooked, I put it all on a plate and put it on the table. The dog hadn't taken his eye off the remaining two-thirds of the salmon steak. I went back to the kitchen, grabbed a serving platter, put some rice in a bowl and the raw salmon on top and brought it back to the dining room with me.

He followed.

I wondered just how well he was trained.

"Sit," I said.

He sat.

"Stay" I said.

I walked a couple feet away from the table and put the bowl down. The dog remained where he was. I went back to the table, sat and then said "Ok."

The dog leaped forward. I think he was done with the fish before I'd cut my first piece.

I got up once during my meal to fill a bowl with water for the dog, but we mostly sat in a companionable peace. After his dinner he stretched out near his bowl and rested his head on his front paws, his good eye never leaving me...or rather, the food I was eating.

For my part, I just ate. Good food, even simple food like this, is a magical thing. Too often we rush through our meals, not appreciating the gifts of the earth and the sea.

I'd done enough thinking for one day. It was time to not think.

Finished, I pushed my chair away from the table. I'd decided to push my luck and see if I could get the drying muck off him before he decided to rub it all off on the Persian rug. I went to the bathroom and ran a tub of lukewarm water. The dog followed me. When it was half full, I turned off the water. I looked at the dog, pointed to the water, and said "In."

He tilted his head at me.

"In," I repeated. I reached my hand in and splashed some of the water around. He sat there, looking.

I sighed. Well, what's good for the goose is good for the gander, I thought. I dropped my sodden clothes on the floor and climbed in the tub. It was a little chilly.

"C'mere, boy," I said.

The dog hopped into the water, his bulk sloshing the water over the sides, and I spent the next fifteen minutes rubbing his coat and getting out layer after layer of dirt.

He had scars across his body, from what I didn't know. He sat quietly as I moved carefully about his head and found the network of scars around one eye. He'd been pretty torn up there. With cupped hands I poured water on his head and his snout and gently rubbed the dirt off his head. I wondered where he had been, what his life had been like until now.

Fighting dog, was my guess, though he was nowhere near aggressive as far as I could tell. Bait? I couldn't imagine that, either. No fear, no timidity.

On the other hand, he was too well trained for a pit fighter. He'd been a hunter. I wondered what his owner had owed Budgie to end up giving a dog like that to him.

When we were done, the bathtub had turned into a mud puddle. I got out and grabbed a towel, but before I could throw it on the dog, he jumped out and shook himself. Dirty water splattered all over the floor, the walls, even the ceiling.

I couldn't help myself. I started laughing.

The dog flipped himself over and rubbed himself dry on the bath mat. He was scarred and bony. He was no show winner, that was for sure. I caught my reflection in the mirror. Neither was I.

My body had long ago left behind the taught strength of youth. Its muscles had sagged with age and my hair, my beard, even the hair on my chest had turned white. One knee was bigger than the other—from some accident or another—and a once angry looking scar ran down my right thigh. All old injuries from something, I thought, but I didn't remember what.

My hands were hurting again from all the rubbing and hand-combing I'd done on the dog, and my back hurt from being crouched in the tub for so long.

I wrapped the towel around me and walked into the living room. There was a touch of coolness in the air, a hint of what the weather actually should be at this time of year, and I was chilly from the half-cold bath. I lit a small fire in the wood stove, lit my pipe, and sat down on the floor in front of the stove. Leaning back against the couch, I looked at the flames licking up around the logs. I was exhausted.

The dog—finished abusing the bathmat—came into the room. He sat down next to me, his body touching mine.

Then he got up and moved a few steps away and lay down, but still facing the fire. I heard that voice again, the same voice I'd heard when the dog stood beside my jeep earlier in the evening, a small voice in the back of my head filling a vacancy I'd never noticed was there. It would have been easy to miss if my mind had not been still.

"*Home,*" was all it said.

MONDAY - CHAPTER 35

The dog slept next to my bed that night.

The next morning I got up and scrambled five eggs and two pieces of ham. Four of the eggs were for the dog. I split the ham with him. There were limits to my empathy.

The rain was hard and the wind blowing, but the temperature was again unseasonably warm as the storm got stronger. I put on my gi pants and Vintage t-shirt and went to the back yard to train. I took my jo, a five foot wooden staff with me. The jo was a laminate, one piece of lighter blood wood sandwiched between two harder, darker pieces of ipe. It gave the jo some heft and a fair degree of hardness without being brittle.

As a weapon a jo was hard to beat. It has two ends and can not only be swung at your target, but thrust directly into it. Once you know how to use it, a jo is marvelously difficult for any opponent to take away because his own grip can be used against him.

The dog and I were soaked within the first minute of being outside, but he didn't seem to mind. He picked up the broken maul handle where I had left it, found a semi-protected corner of the woodshed and curled up, happily gnawing on the wood.

I began practicing my kata, a fixed series of moves alternating between attacks and parries against an imaginary opponent. They are initially learned, and practiced, alone, but the intent of the kata is to teach the correct sequence of moves against a similarly trained opponent. Much like the standard opening moves in chess or go, a kata progresses through a predictable sequence in which both parties respond to one another in ways that best advance their position without creating dangerous openings.

I began slowly and gradually picked up speed until, after half an hour, the jo was flinging water droplets off as it hummed through the air, fending off imaginary strikes from invisible attackers and downing them in turn. After forty minutes and the completion of one of the most complex katas, I decided to call it quits. I was doing the final moves when I saw the dog sit up and stare at something behind me.

I turned. It was Budgie, standing at the fence gate, a gun hanging from his hand.

"I want my dog back," Budgie said. He opened the gate and walked into the yard.

I glanced back at the dog. He was sitting very still, his eyes and ears on Budgie.

"That was fast," I said. 'How'd you find me?"

"Old prick like you, ain't hard," Budgie said. "Everybody knows that piece of shit jeep you drive, and the ones that don't, know the old asshole selling used shit over at his pawn shop."

Pawn shop. That kind of stung.

"It's not a pawn shop," I said. "I deal in difficult to find objects that—"

"Shut up," Budgie said, raising his gun up. "I'm taking the dog and if you so much as move, I'll shoot you."

"Really, Budgie?" I said. "Really? You're going to kill me over a fucking dog?"

"Fuck no," he said. "I'll fucking kneecap you. You can sell from a wheelchair. Now, how about that?"

Frankly, I doubted that Budgie could even remotely hit one of my knees, even the swollen one. My bigger problem was what else he would hit instead. I took a step toward him. He raised his gun and pointed it somewhere in the vicinity of my head.

"Right fucking there, asshole," he said. "Not letting you near me with that stick in your hand." He looked to my left behind me, where the dog was sitting. "C'mere, Keto! C'mon, boy!"

I felt, rather than heard, the dog's movement, and then I saw the fear in Budgie's eyes. His gun hand flicked to to the left as I caught the dog out of the corner of my eye, running full tilt at Budgie. A growl cut loose from him, leaving little doubt of his intention.

I heaved the jo at Budgie's head. It flew end over end and with his free hand he fended it off. That diverted his attention for just enough time, and in the next moment the dog leapt onto Budgie's chest and knocked him backwards. I followed in behind the dog, grabbed Budgie's gun hand and gave it a sharp counterclockwise twist. The dog was biting at Budgie's throat and I heard the loud "snap!" of a wrist torn from its ligaments.

He dropped the gun. I kicked it away.

"Stop!" I yelled to the dog.

Whoever had trained him had done a hell of a job, because the dog pulled his head back, but kept his front paws and his weight on Budgie's chest. Budgie tried to roll over and pull his hand toward himself, but my bare foot was resting on it, holding it down. I ground down on it, and Budgie yelped in pain.

"Off," I told the dog, and he stepped back and sat on his haunches, but he never took his eyes off Budgie.

I lifted my foot and Budgie curled up and brought his hand to his chest and held it. A little bit of blood mixed with rainwater running from the tooth marks on his neck. The dog hadn't gone too deep.

In less than ten seconds Budgie had gone from gun-wielding, small-town bad guy to a soaking, sorry mess.

I crouched down in front of him and shoved my hair back.

"I don't think the dog wants to go with you, Budgie. It might be smarter of you to leave him here."

Budgie groaned.

"So here's what we're gonna do. I feel bad about stealing him from you—I really do—so let me make it up to you. I'm gonna keep the gun and the dog, but I'm not going to call the police. You're going to leave me and the dog alone, and if you come here again, I'm going to shoot you with your own gun. Got it?"

Budgie groaned again.

"Got it?" I repeated. I reached down and pressed on his wrist with my hand.

"Got it, got it!" he yelled.

"Good," I said. I felt inside the drawstring of my gi pants and found the pouch on the side. I pulled out a five dollar bill and stuffed it into his good hand. "Take this and go to the deli while we both forget this ever happened."

The dog and I watched as Budgie gathered himself up and stumbled toward the gate. After he'd left, I looked down at the dog.

"Damn," I said. "You got game."

MONDAY – CHAPTER 36

As I let the dog and I in through the back door of Tanya's kitchen, I could hear the shuffling of feet from upstairs. Morning yoga class would be over soon.

I put water on the stove to heat and pulled tea and two cups from the cupboards. The shelves were overflowing with the herbs she had collected over the summer and were drying before packaging, mixing or extracting. I remembered the objective of our last outing and double-checked the jar of loose leaf tea before putting it into the pot. Wouldn't do to get the wrong brew right now, I figured.

The teapot was filled and steeping, and I put it and the cups on the kitchen table. The dog sat down next to me, alert but not unfriendly. His nose quivered as he sorted out all of the unusual scents from the herbs.

I had timed it perfectly. I heard the many pairs of footsteps coming down the stairs and heading out the front door, and then I heard Tanya's bare feet coming quietly down the hall.

She reached the kitchen door and her eyes flicked from me, to the dog, and back to me. The dog, for his part, leaned forward, ears pointing forward, not aggressively, but eagerly, maybe.

"Hello, Asa," she said. "Who's your friend?"

"He's apparently my new dog," I said. "He's friendly, if he likes you."

"Well, let's see about me," Tanya said. She leaned forward a bit, put both her hands on her thighs and said, "Come here, boy."

The dog jumped up and in three quick steps was standing in front of her. He put his muzzle in her hands and gratefully accepted her rubbing his face and head. Tanya grinned and looked up at me.

"I'm pretty sure we're good," she said. "Where'd you get him?"

She sat down and I told her about my two encounters with Budgie and how he ended with a five-spot and a recommendation for a gyro. The dog sat beside her and she absent-mindedly stroked his neck as I gave her more details about my dealings with Budgie.

She had regained the calm serenity that had left her yesterday, and her face betrayed little of what she might now be feeling. Tanya would sometimes get like she'd been yesterday, and I understood, after hearing yesterday's story, how she must have morphed her ice-queen adolescence into what I saw now.

Years of Buddhist training had allowed her natural inner warmth to emerge, and she had converted what had once been a defense into an integrated character trait. She was both engaged and caring, yet detached at the same time. The first fresh version of that was what I had first seen all those years ago at the riverbank and what had made me impetuously make the comment that I had. We had never really talked about each other's histories before yesterday. There had never seemed to be any need.

I finished my story and fell silent. She said nothing, sipped her tea and petted the dog.

"So what's his name?" she asked.

"Who, Budgie?" I asked. "It's Budgie. Well, he has another name, but you know that."

She shook her head with a wisp of a smile.

"No, Asa," she said. "The dog."

"Oh," I said. "Budgie called him 'Keto,' but that's just a mispronunciation of his breed. He's an akita. They were originally a Japanese hunting dog. They were used to hunt boar and—"

Tanya interrupted me. "I know all about akitas," she said. "Part of my mother's heritage." She looked out the window as a gust of wind blew rain onto it and rocked the old sash. "She used to tell me a story about one, but not Hachiko, that dog that was so loyal to his master that, even after his death, he used to sit at the train station every day, waiting for his master to return, cared for by everyone until the day he died. This story is older, far more ancient. This akita, too, was loyal to his master, but in an entirely different way. A hunter in the Odate region in northern Japan was with his dog when they accidentally strayed onto a local lord's territory. The hunter was captured by the lord's soldiers, but not before he told the dog to run back to his house and get his hunting license. The dog ran for miles, during a blizzard and through deep snow, and got his master's license. He turned around and ran back to the lord's castle as fast as he could make it, but his journey took days. By the time he had returned, it was too late. His master had been executed. The dog was heartbroken. For days he sat out in the snow, howling at the castle. His howls were so fierce that nobody dared go out of the castle. Eventually he grew weaker, and his howling stopped. When the soldiers eventually gained the courage to go out, they found his frozen body standing in the snow, as fierce in death as he had been in life.

Tanya took a sip of her tea.

"For the next two years, the lord's province was rocked by natural disasters. Floods and earthquakes destroyed crops, homes and houses. The people, starving, sick and faced with imminent collapse, made a shrine for the dog and made offerings to his spirit until the curse was removed. To this day that shrine still stands, and people still leave him offerings so his spirit doesn't get angry again."

She fell silent and we both looked at the dog.

"Don't you think," she asked me, "a dog like that—a dog like this— deserves a name?"

I nodded. I thought of that mythical dog's courage and his unwavering loyalty. I caught this dog's eyes, and he and I looked at one another. I, too, was a hunter in my own way, and now I was likely to come under attack by forces much larger and stronger than myself. His tail wagged once, twice, then stopped.

"Kuraĝa," I said. "It means 'courageous' in Esperanto."

MONDAY – CHAPTER 37

Tanya nodded her head in agreement.

"We need to talk," she said to me.

"I know. That's why I came this morning. I wanted to see how you were doing."

"I'm doing fine," she said. "Really. I'm ok. But what happened yesterday got me to thinking. I'm leaving Nemaseck, Asa. After this storm is over. I'm putting the house up for sale and leaving."

I paused for a second, not sure of what to say, or what I even wanted to say.

"Where are you going?" I finally asked.

"I'm going to become a monk," she said. She paused too, watching how I took the news. "You know that Buddhist monastery in upstate New York where I go a couple of times a year for a retreat?"

I nodded.

"I've been talking to the abbot up there for the past couple of months. She said they would be very happy for me to take the vows there."

"But what about your life here, your school . . . your herbal practice . . . your . . . "

"My friends, you mean? I don't have many left here."

I was still trying to get in touch with the feeling I had in my gut, but I wasn't sure what it was.

"I noticed you haven't had any boyfriends for a while," I said, "but you haven't seemed unhappy."

"That's just the thing, Asa. I'm not unhappy. But as my spirituality – let's call it—has grown, my need for others has diminished. And let's face it, the pickings for relationships are pretty slim around here, especially at my age. I really don't have the desire to go cougar cruising on Tinder. I have little that I need, and less that I want. I am close . . . close to something new. I want to be somewhere where I can nurture that, let it grow." Her look grew sad and she stared at me a minute. "What I need is a new pot, where my roots can grow out and my leaves get green again."

"But . . . " I began.

"But what about *us*? Is that what you're thinking?

"Well . . . yes," I said.

She reached out and took my hand. "There is no *us*, Asa. There never was. Our times got screwed up. I was too young, and you are..." she looked out the window for a few seconds and then back at me, "...I don't know what you are, Asa. Particularly after yesterday."

"You mean I'm too old to mean that much to you," I said. "I get it. It was always that way."

"No, not that," she said, shaking her head. "Not that at all. I just don't know who you are. Yes, you're funny, and adventurous, and the most brilliant man I've ever known, but I've never known *you*."

"I am exactly who is sitting across the table from you, Tanya," I said. "Just as I always have."

"That's right," she said. "That's exactly it. Over the time that I've known you, I've grown older. My waist is thicker, my thighs are thicker. I've aged. But you haven't. You're the same old man I first saw walking along the riverbank."

"At my age, Tanya, things change more slowly," I said. "Time goes faster when you're old, but an older person walks through time at a slower pace."

Her gaze at me hardened. For an instant I had an image of her, alone, on a hilltop in a storm, wrapping her shawl around herself. Then she spoke.

"Yes, Asa. And...exactly how old are you?"

"Oh, I go way back, Tanya. I—"

"Cut the crap, Asa." Her voice was angry. "Tell me. When were you born?"

"A long time ago," I said. "The exact—"

"Stop it, Asa! Stop it right now!"

Silence.

"Did you go to school? Where? What was your childhood like? Who were your parents?"

"I...I." I closed my mouth. Inside, my gut was churning. I thought for a minute. It was so long ago, so terribly long ago. I closed my eyes, trying to pull something back to tell her.

I found nothing. It was empty.

I tried for a minute to push back on that emptiness, to find the earliest memory I had. And then I found it. I was on a bus, riding into Nemaseck for the first time.

And then, something else. It was hazy. There was someone, and then they weren't. A mountain, not here, far away. And then something - someone - a woman - holding me, whispering into my ear.

Then I thought to myself, what the hell does all this matter? It doesn't, really. Who would care about twenty, thirty years ago? That's insane.

"Do you have amnesia, Asa?" Tanya's voice pulled me back to the present. "Were you injured, sick? Did something bad happen to you?"

"This is ridiculous, Tanya," I said, not angrily—I wasn't angry—just firmly. "Ten years, twenty years, who cares? It's ancient history. It. Doesn't. Matter. Or at least it doesn't to me, in which case it shouldn't to you."

"Why not? You're someone I care about...cared about. You asked me all about my high school years yesterday, Asa. Personal history certainly mattered then. Why don't the rules apply to you?"

The question sat between us.

"Because the rules don't apply to me," was what I wanted to say, but I kept my mouth shut. I looked at the table, at the empty teacups. Tanya and I had shared so much over those two cups, so much laughter, so much of what we felt and what we knew and what we saw. In my mind's eye, our shared history rolled out before me.

Kurağa whined. Why, I wondered.

"You are not exactly who I see in front of me Asa, not at all. Yesterday, I saw a man I never met. A man who was willing to throw a corpse in a river, who calculated the odds of living and dying without a single emotion, a man who looked into the future at his own possible death and sacrificed the sanctity of another man's death without batting an eye."

"Yes," I said. "For my own survival. And yours."

"Survival against what? Against who? Who are you, Asa, really? Who are you?"

I was silent. I had nothing to say.

She stood up and looked at me, her expression a mixture of anger and affection and fear, like I was a wounded dog she had found on the street, similar to the way I had first looked at Kuraĝa.

"Until you know that, I can't love you, Asa. Not like that and not in any other way. I'm sorry."

I rose from my chair and searched for words that refused to come to mind in any language.

"I'm sorry, too," I said.

It was the best I had. For a moment, we stood, facing each other. Woman and man. Yin and yang. Young and old. Completion in two words, two faces, two minds. There was nothing more to say.

I turned away and opened the door. Kuraĝa stood up and followed me as I left. I stepped out into the rain and the wind.

As I walked to the jeep, I finally identified what I'd felt inside me. It was grief. How long had it been since I had felt that, I wondered. I didn't know. All I did know was that those weren't only raindrops running down my face, and they didn't stop for a long time.

MONDAY – CHAPTER 38

Driving aimlessly through the storm, I finally pushed out of my mind my conversation with Tanya—and the confusion that had come with it. I didn't have room for that right now.

I parked, somewhere, and called Charlie.

"What?" he said in his curt, no-nonsense voice.

"Charlie," I said, "Was there ever military base around Nemaseck?"

"Define 'ever.' There was a small garrison here during the Revolutionary War. Is that what you want?"

"No, I mean twenty, twenty-five years ago."

"What for?" he asked. It was strictly quid pro quo with Charlie.

"I talked to Budgie Meyers last night," I said. "He said that Elle Anderson liked military guys. I wondered if some might have been around back then."

There was silence for a few seconds.

"What the hell are you doing, Asa?" Charlie said.

"I'm just asking around. That girl's death's got me bugged."

"It got a lot of people bugged," he said. "Why you?"

"Long story," I said. "But I think I can find out who killed her."

"Get in line, champ," Charlie said. "Lotta people thought that. Some of them were actually policemen and stuff and knew what they were doing. Not manuscript peddlers in their dotage."

"Yeah, well, it's all a matter of the right stone in the right place at the right time. You know that."

"Pfft. I've been working on my end game. You're going to suffer, come tomorrow."

"Right, yeah. Just set the board up. I'll be there."

"Ok," he said. "See ya."

"Wait. So was there a base here or not?"

"No. And you're fucking crazy."

"Established already. I'll see you tomorrow." Well, so much for that idea, I thought.

The line went dead.

What the hell? Was this National Hang Up week or what?

A gust caught the jeep and tried to push it sideways. I gripped the steering wheel tighter even though I was still parked. I had been going to ask Charlie if he wanted me to bring anything, but the hell with it. Charlie didn't take anything that smelled faintly of assistance to him, but sometimes you could sneak it up on him if he wasn't paying attention.

I started up the engine and jerked the jeep back onto the road. Kuraĝa bounced off the door.

"Sorry, boy. Tough day for all of us."

He glared at me.

I stopped at the post office to pick up the mail. It might be the last to come in for a couple of days.

MONDAY – CHAPTER 39

The post office didn't have much for me, only a plain brown envelope with no return address. Standards must be slipping for that to get through, I thought.

I chucked it in the back seat and drove back to the shop. As I pulled up, my business neighbor, Liz, wrapped in a bright yellow slicker, was standing in front of her store, a high-end kitchen boutique. She was a petite woman and I thought the wind was going to take her down the street any second.

"Asa, you going to board up your windows?" Liz asked, as a man in soaked overalls tried to wrestle a piece of plywood into place while his partner nailed it in front of her window.

"Hadn't really thought about it, Liz," I said.

"Well, you should. They're predicting really high winds for the next couple of days. Haven't you been watching the weather?"

Sometimes I felt sorry for Liz, her nice bright shop all decked out with holiday-appropriate themes in the windows, right next to my dingy, messy place. On the other hand, I probably made her place look better in comparison.

"Been kind of busy," I said." Trying to get stuff in the mail before the worst hits us."

"This is the worst one there's ever been, they say. And maybe not the last. I don't know what's going on, Asa, I don't." She pulled the raincoat closer around her as if to keep out the fear.

"It's climate change, Liz," I said. "And they're right. It's not going to let up, not until something changes. Maybe not until there's a lot fewer of us."

Liz looked at me and shook her head back and forth. "We have to do something," she said. "It can't be too late."

"I don't know, Liz. I'm not a climate scientist. But I've been around a long time…" How long? a piece of my mind blurted out—"and I know that this hasn't happened before. And sometimes you go down a road that you can't come back on."

She nodded. It was then that I noticed the car parked down the street, a shiny black BMW. I wouldn't have given it a second thought any other day— just another tourist in town—but only idiot tourists would be here at this point in time. I nodded in its direction.

"Know who that is?" I asked her.

She looked. "Not a clue. Not anyone from around here, that's for sure."

I took a second glance at the car and then looked at her boarded up windows. "Well, maybe I'll at least pull stuff out of the window display," I said.

She laughed. "Always on top of things, aren't you Asa?"

"Yup. You closing up now?"

"Yeah," she said. "No point in being open. There's nobody around."

"Okay, then. I guess I'll see you on the other side," I said and then unlocked the shop and stepped in. I stood there until I was certain the store was empty.

Kuraǧa wandered around and sniffed, but didn't sound any alarms. Nothing looked like it had been moved. Nev had turned off the computer and unplugged it before she left. Somehow the silence and emptiness annoyed me.

I threw the envelope on her desk, walked in the back to my office. Nothing out of place here either. I spun open the safe and found the manuscript where I had left it. I closed and locked it, and then leaned on my desk.

"Shit," I said to the dog. "They didn't toss the place. Looks like it's me as well as the manuscript that they want. I wonder when they'll be here."

He sniffed, shook off the extra water and curled up on an oriental prayer rug in the corner. If they had simply wanted the manuscript, they would have searched the store and busted the safe open. I pulled an earthenware bowl off the shelf. It was modern stoneware, had been used by a Druid grove in Ohio as a bowl for offerings to the gods, and had drawings symbolizing the gods and goddesses, ancestors, and land spirits embossed along the rim. Perfect for Kuraĝa, I thought, and went to the bathroom, filled it up and placed it next to the dog.

I didn't keep a gun there, but I wasn't entirely defenseless. There was Kuraĝa, for one, though he was still a bit of a wild card in my mind. I also had a nice, hard jo propped up in the corner. I pulled it out and leaned it up on my desk. Then I sat and looked around at the room, gauging distances and angles and footing.

Now, where had I learned to think like that? For that matter, where did I learn how to wield a jo or throw a man across a room? I sat down. How right Tanya was. What is a man without his past?

For that matter, what did it matter if they did capture me? I would be missed by no one, except briefly by Tanya, but so what? It would be painful, yes, and uncomfortable, but I had weathered similar situations. That much I knew.

And when would that have been? I shook my head. I shouldn't think about this shit, I realized. I needed a clear head. I also kind of felt like I needed a gun, but that was Neveah's shtick, not mine. I wished I hadn't sent her away. She was good in a fight.

I got back up and grabbed the envelope from Nev's desk. Might as well make myself busy while I was waiting for the grab-n-snatch.

MONDAY – CHAPTER 40

I sat down at my desk, grabbed my knife and slit open the envelope. I pushed on the edges, gently, and dumped the contents out.

It was another manuscript, each page encased in a plastic sleeve, just like the one Lao had given me. I turned them over, one by one. Same yellowed paper. Same page numbering. Same letters, ideographs, hieroglyphics, whatever they were.

The same manuscript as the one Lao had given me?

I looked back at the envelope. It had been addressed to me in a formal, Victorian script that looked like it had been written with a fountain pen. No return address. No postmark.

I looked inside the envelope again and saw a piece of manila about the size of an index card stuck on the bottom. I pulled it out.

"Not all is what it seems," the card read, "neither outside nor inside. And what we seek most will always be found within ourselves."

It wasn't signed. It had been written in the same floral script as the address on the envelope. The handwriting was exquisite. Whoever wrote it was an expert in calligraphy.

"Shit," I said to the dog. "This whole thing is getting out of control."

And then I laughed. Because it had been out of control from the beginning, from the night I had the vision of Elle. There was absolutely nothing that was remotely in control. I had no idea what was going on, what I had, who wanted it, why the goddamn manuscript was important to anybody in the first place, who killed Elle, why I was even trying to find out...and why the hell was Tanya going to a monastery, anyway?

My laughter stopped at that thought. Which was a good thing, because I was beginning to sound a little hysterical, even to me.

I took a deep, slow breath. And then another. And a third, drawing into my lungs the ephemeral essence of the universe, bringing it to my center, my core, and holding it there for a moment until I exhaled. With each breath I released everything I was worried about, everything I wanted, everything I was afraid of, until all I felt inside me was a bright warmth.

I sat there with that for a minute as I reconnected myself with the chair and the room around me. Whatever was going to happen was going to happen, and the choice I had was how I would respond to it.

I pushed aside the card, squared up the manuscript pages and set put them down in front of me.

What do I know? I asked myself, staring at the small stack.

I knew it was probably a woman who had sent me this. The handwriting was decidedly feminine. On a hunch, I picked up the card. Perhaps the woman had worn a perfume, a scent that might have attached itself to the card.

Nothing. No perfume, no cologne, no faint smell of oil or cigarettes or cognac. But I did smell something else, faintly. I sniffed again and put the card down, wondering what it was.

Then I caught it. I was smelling the ink. Unlike ballpoint pens, fountain pens leave a trace behind that you could smell if the item had been written recently. That was what I was smelling. I knew that from having dealt, although rarely, with forgeries. The aroma of ink was the quickest and most certain way to spot a forgery done on the cheap.

Slowly I put the card down next to the manuscript. I picked up one of the plastic sleeves and—against every rule of dealing with aged paper—I reached in the slot at the top with my bare fingers and pulled the page partly out. It certainly had the feel of century-old paper, dry and brittle. I put it up to my nose and inhaled.

The paper might have been old, or have been made to look old, but the writing certainly was not. The page held that same smell as the note card. This was, most decidedly, a forgery.

I slid the paper back into the plastic, spun on my chair, opened the safe and pulled out the document that Lao had given me. I placed them side by side. Visually, they were indistinguishable.

Or were they?

I pulled a pipe out of the desk drawer, a Canadian lumberman style with a huge bowl. I reached for a tin of the darkest Latakia blend I had and stuffed the pipe and lit it. Latakia blends are nothing like the aromatics that most people these days associate with Grandpa's pipe. Latakia tobacco comes from Syria or Cypress, and is cured by smoking the leaf over fires of various aromatic woods. As it dries, a dark, strong smelling tobacco is created and then usually blended with other tobaccos to create a mixture that often smells like a cross between a campfire and a grassy field.

Pipe lit, I focused on the manuscript on the desk. I had quite the chore in front of me.

Ninety minutes later, I finished my bowl and my examination at about the same time. The documents were not identical.

At a couple points on each page, the letters—or whatever they were—were transposed, or removed or extra ones inserted. One page had had the number altered by one digit, not that it mattered anyway. The forgery was intentionally doctored, but not in a readily apparent way. I put my pipe away, shuffled the pages of each stack back into their original order and sat back.

I heard the front door open.

MONDAY – CHAPTER 41

I didn't know how I'd left it unlocked, but there it was. I grabbed my jo and walked out of my office. Kuraĝa walked beside me toward the front of the store.

Neveah was dropping a duffel bag on the floor. It sounded like it had bricks in it.

"I thought I told you to skedaddle," I said.

"I did, boss," she said. "And now I'm back."

She looked at the dog. "The fuck is that?"

"It's my new dog," I said. "His name's Kuraĝa."

"Looks like a damn wolf."

"Wolves don't have coats like that, Nev," I said.

"Well, that one does. Keep it away from me."

"Why?"

"I don't like wolves," she said, "and I don't like the way he's looking at me."

I looked a Kuraĝa. He sat there with his usual acute attention when somebody new had appeared in his range of vision. He didn't look pissed off.

"I'm pretty sure you're ok," I said.

"Oh, yeah?" she said. "*Pretty* sure? I'm not down with that."

"You'll be ok. You shouldn't have come back," I said. "It's not safe."

"Never is," she said. "Gimme a hand with this, 'k?"

"What's in it?"

"You'll see," she said. "Grab one end and we'll carry it back to your office. I don't want all this shit on the floor out here."

I picked up my end and we carried it back, Kuraĝa leading the way. It felt like a bag of hammers.

"Bag o' hammers?" I said

"Fuck no," she said and zipped it open. First out of the bag was an AR-15. She put that on the Skull & Bones chair. That was followed by a sawed-off shotgun, two 9mm Glocks, a Smith & Wesson Shield and a decidedly well-used .45 ACP M1911, both of the latter with twelve-round magazines. There were several boxes of ammo for each of them.

"Jesus." I said. "Where the hell did this come from?"

"You don't wanna know, boss," she said.

"Seriously, Nev. What the hell?"

She picked up the AR, clicked a magazine on and jacked a round into the chamber.

"Know some people in New York. Had to go on the run when they fucked over some Mexicans. They left this shit behind. I, kinda, knew where they stashed it, y'know?"

She reached into the bag again and pulled out a couple of flash-bang grenades.

"Here. You should have one." She tossed it to me.

I hefted it in my hand for a few seconds, then tossed it back.

"You keep it, Nev," I said. "Not my thing."

"Be your thing if it saves your life," she said and stuffed it into her jacket pocket. "Guess I'll stick around in case you need it."

"I might," I said. "You see the BMW parked down the street?"

"Yup," Neveah said. "Tourists stuck in the rain, I guess."

"I don't think so," I said. "I think somebody is going to be paying me a visit."

"You mean 'us,'" Neveah said.

"Well, it's me they're after. And the manuscript. You remember what Lao said about me being the only one who can translate it, right?"

"Yup," she nodded.

"Well, they're going to come for both. Sooner rather than later, and my guess is that they saw you come in, with that duffel, and you just jacked up their degree of difficulty in making a quiet extraction. So it's gonna get nasty."

Nev laughed. "They ain't Mexicans. Mexicans are nasty."

"Well, these guys are too, in their own way. So, we need to be ready."

"Got it, boss," Nev said. She picked up four of the guns. "Gonna make this, you know, strategic."

She walked out of the office. I had no idea what she was planning on doing, but I had my own plans. I took care to safeguard the manuscripts and put a stool next to my chair at the desk for Nev. This was going to be ninety percent theater and ten percent reality. I hoped it was going to work.

I sat down at my desk and waited.

MONDAY – CHAPTER 42

The knock on the door came about the same time I was contemplating how I was going to manage dinner for all of us and wondering if Kuraǧa would prefer General Tso's or Kung Pao Chicken.

"Got it, boss," I heard Nev call from the front. I didn't know what she had been up to and didn't really want to.

I heard the front door open and close with a bang. A minute later, Nev ushered in two men, one Caucasian and one Asian. Neither was what I would consider of diminutive size, but neither of them gave off the air of being leg-breakers, either. They were both dressed casually. I couldn't tell if either was armed, but I felt it was safer to bet on it.

Kuraǧa stood up from his rug and moved to sit beside me. Nev perched herself on the stool on the other side of me, and I waved my hand at two chairs across from it.

"Have a seat," I said. "Can I help you?"

They opened their raincoats and sat.

"Asa Cire, I presume?" the Caucasian said. I nodded.

"My name is Lamont, and my associate here is Peter. It's late, the weather is bad and getting worse, so we'll cut to the chase, if you don't mind."

"Not a problem," I said. "*Tempo estas mono.*"

"Money is not the issue here," he said, "but we need to get our work completed and leave before the weather makes that impossible. We came to retrieve the Zamenhof manuscript, and to offer you...and your associate," he nodded at Nev, "...a job."

"I don't have it," I said.

Lamont looked at his partner, then back at me.

"Of course you do, Mr. Cire. We know that Lao Shen delivered it to you on Saturday."

"He did not," I said.

"Of course he did," Lamont said. "He came here on the bus and left it with you before he was killed."

Damn. They were already starting two steps ahead of where I wanted to end things.

"He's dead?" I asked.

"Yes. He was, ah, eliminated by agents of the Chinese government."

"Which, of course, wouldn't be you," I said.

"Of course not," Lamont said. "We are part of the consortium that sent him here. Why would we kill him?"

I leaned back and reached for my pipe and stuffed it with some of the Latakia blend I'd been smoking earlier. I tamped it down and lit it, while I considered what he had said. One of the beauties of pipe smoking. It gives the wise man time for thought and the foolish man's mouth something to occupy it.

I felt a little of both.

"Let's assume, for a minute, that I believe you," I said. "How do you know that he was killed?"

Lamont nodded. "Dead man switch," he said. "Lao has missed his last two check-ins. We are, of course, presuming the worst."

"Or the best," I said, thinking of the various means humans have devised of coercing unwilling people to speak. I took a puff on the pipe and let the smoke drift up between us.

"We know from our last communications that he delivered the manuscript to you, with our instructions. I assume the payment he offered was satisfactory to you?"

Guys who worked for money often assumed that was everyone else's motivation, too, Frankly, they weren't often wrong.

"We discussed that," I said, "and I thought it was a little low at the time, given the nature of the work."

"Well, we're prepared to double the amount," Lamont said.

"To five hundred thousand?" I asked.

At that, Lamont sat up a little straighter and permitted himself a smile. Peter smirked.

"Ah," Lamont said. "It appears that Lao had been prepared to give himself an unauthorized cut."

Peter—who had been sitting there as still as a mountain—perked up.

"I told you," he said, directing his comment at Lamont. "That's classic Lao. I knew we should have put more controls on him, I told you guys that."

Lamont glanced at Peter and then looked back at me.

"In that event," he said, "my news is even better. We will be quadrupling your reimbursement. One million is what we will give you."

So they were who they said they were.

"I appreciate the largess," I said, "but I assume it doesn't come unencumbered."

"No," Lamont said. "You are correct, but it is actually a favor as well. The Chinese picked up on Lao's movements when he entered the country, and they are likely not to be too far behind us. Trust me when I say that their offer will be...well, let's just say it will be unpleasant in comparison to ours. So we want you and your associate—and, of course, the manuscript—to come with us to a safer location. There you can complete your work on it in safety...and collect your fee when you are done."

"Or, being safely out of touch from everybody else, just eliminated ourselves," I said.

"No," Lamont shook his head. "That's not our style. We are a community of scholars, of people seeking knowledge. We don't wantonly destroy."

"Of course," I said. "Naturally you'd say that, but I'm not sure I believe you at face value. Before I confer with Nev about your offer, though, perhaps you could answer a question for me. Why's everybody so damned interested in this manuscript? At best, it's an offshoot work by a man who invented a language that's barely spoken in the world. I know most everyone who is interested in Zamenhof and Esperanto at a certain level. Why have I never heard of you?"

"We'll explain that when we get moving," Lamont said. "Right now, it's imperative that we get you, and the manuscript, to a safe place. We really have very little time."

Beside me, Nev shifted on her stool. I didn't look at her.

"Give me a piece," I said. "Just a piece, so I know who is where. I would hate to end up on the wrong side of history."

MONDAY – CHAPTER 43

Lamont looked at Peter, who nodded faintly.

"Each tick of the clock brings you closer to having no choices at all, Mr. Cire," Lamont said. "But here's the elevator version. As you've probably already guessed, that manuscript is not what it seems to be. The truth – or part of it – is that it contains the essence of all languages, every language that has been spoken by mankind throughout history, and before. Somehow Zamenhof, in his pursuit of a universal language, uncovered or recreated it. We don't know which. What we do know is that this language is to the human nature and psyche what mathematics is to physics. Just as physics enables us to understand, and thereby manipulate the physical world around us, this language of Zamenhof's is able to manipulate how humans perceive reality. It is no more, and no less, than that. Can you imagine the power which such a language would have? In the hands of a Gandhi or a Martin Luther King, it would create a peace and utopia as has never been seen before. But in the hands of a Stalin, or a Kim Jong-Il, it would create an unopposable hell on earth for humanity. Can you imagine why people in power may want it? And that's why we want it, Mr. Cire. To advance humanity, not enslave it. And we are willing to do anything to prevent this manuscript—and the only man alive apparently capable of deciphering it—from falling into the wrong hands."

"Well, that's the other thing I've been wondering," I said. "About me. Why am I that guy? There's a million linguists in the world, but I'm not one of them. Why me?"

Lamont stood up, as did Peter.

"I'm afraid that's all we have time for, Mr. Cire. You must come with us. Now."

The gun that suddenly appeared in Peter's hand was aimed squarely at Nev.

"The price of refusing, I'm afraid, will be your associate's life," Lamont said.

Nev stood up, arms akimbo. "I think we should go with 'em, boss. I kinda like living."

"I guess so," I said.

"Get the manuscript," Lamont said.

I turned to the safe, opened it, and pulled out the manuscript.

"Got it," I said.

"Now walk in front of us, out of the building," Peter said. "Outside, turn left and start walking down the street."

"Coats?" I asked.

Peter made a face at me. "You kidding me?" he said.

I shrugged. "Had to ask." I looked at Kuraĝa, who had stood up. "Stay," I said. "Somebody will come for you." I patted him as he sat back down.

We walked out of my office and started going down the three steps to the main floor of the building. Nev looked back at me and then she tripped and fell down, face first, her arms in front of her, bracing her fall. I was right behind her and almost fell on top of her, but rolled off onto my shoulder and scrambled around until we got ourselves untangled. I made sure I stayed between her and our visitors for as long as possible.

Peter stood at the top of the steps, his gun still pointed at Nev.

"Damn, sweetie," he said. "You think I was born yesterday? Get up, get in line, and walk out, like I told you,"

If looks could kill, Nev would have dropped him on the spot.

I stood up and rubbed my shoulder. Nev stood up in front of me, her hands in front as if they were manacled and we continued our perp walk out the front door. Nev turned left, stopped suddenly and stuck her foot out behind her, tripping me to the ground. Again.

She continued to turn without pause and brought up her right hand, which now had a pistol in it, and fired. Peter dropped like a stone.

By the time I got back up, she was advancing on Lamont and muttering imprecations in Spanglish.

"Wait, Nev. Hold up," I said. I looked around. The street was empty, the town deserted.

"That your Beemer over there?" I asked Lamont. He nodded without speaking.

"Grab your buddy and drag him into the car. Then stand next to the door," I said. With Nev's gun square on him, Lamont picked up Peter underneath the arms, dragged him to the BMW and fished the keys out of Peter's pocket. Lamont shoved his body in the back seat.

"Good," I said. "Now turn around. Hands on the car."

He followed my directions and I frisked him. As I'd thought, there was nothing on him. Peter had been the muscle of the pair. I took the manuscript, still in its envelope, out of his hands, folded it and shoved it in my back pocket.

I opened the driver's side door. "Get in. Get the hell out of here. Go back and tell your consortium—whoever the hell they are—that neither I, nor the manuscript, are for sale."

I slammed the door. Without looking at me, Lamont started up the car and pulled out. Nev and I watched as he drove off.

"They aren't the bad guys," I said to Nev.

She brushed her wet hair off her face.

"I know," she said. "They talked too damn much."

The wind was blowing the rain right at us.

"But they're bad enough," she added.

The BMW accelerated down the street to the stop sign. Its brake lights went on, but the car didn't slow down. It rolled through the intersection without stopping and started to gain speed on its way toward the curve that led to the bridge. It was going much too fast.

Lamont veered off the high side of the curve and slammed into a telephone pole. Seconds later flames jetted out from the engine as the car exploded.

"Shit!" I said. "They're here."

"What do you mean?" Nev said.

"BMW's don't explode like that from running into a pole. That damn thing was rigged," I said. "Run! Now! Back to the shop!"

We turned and I realized we were too late. A fist slammed into Nev's head, and she fell backward. Hands grabbed me from behind. The first man pulled Nev's gun from her hand and began dragging her by the feet back to the shop.

Behind me, a voice said, "Walk into the shop right behind your friend and don't try anything else," he said, "or I'll break both your arms."

I did as I was told.

MONDAY – CHAPTER 44

I was frog-marched back into the office while watching Nev's head bounce up each step. I couldn't see much of the man dragging her because he wore a rainjacket with the hood up. Still, he radiated a sense of menace.

Kuraĝa had stayed as he had been told, although he was whining and growling.

"Down, Kuraĝa!" I said before he jumped. He sat, but I swear I could see him vibrating.

Nev was laid out face down on the floor. Menace Guy pulled a roll of duct tape from his jacket pocket and taped her ankles together and her wrists behind her back. That was going to make things more difficult. Not because of Nev, but because a man who arrives with duct tape is not a man inclined toward negotiations.

Frog-marcher turned me and shoved me into the chair.

"Ok, asshole, here's the story," he said. "You're getting the manuscript and coming with us. No bullshit. There's no time for that. For every minute you don't give us the manuscript, girlfriend gets something cut off. And we aren't talking about hair."

"Easy, easy," I said. "I've got the manuscript right here."

I reached into my back pocket and handed him the folded envelope. He opened it, pulled out the pages and scanned them. Then he smoothed the fold out of the pages, returned them to the envelope, and shoved it, unfolded, into the back waistband of his pants underneath his jacket.

"One requirement, though," I said. "You want me to go with you easy, she's alive when we walk out the door. Deal?"

"Damn, old man, you're hardly in a position to cut deals," Frog-marcher said.

He looked at his partner, who was a good three inches taller than I. On his cheek was a pale blue tattoo—I couldn't tell of what—done prison-style. Menace Guy nodded and looked back at me.

"Ok, she's good," Frog-marcher said. "Let's go. We get outside, you give us any problems, we shoot you. ok?"

I had got him. I had made it easy for him and he got lazy. There was no way in hell they were going to shoot me. I was the prize, as much as the manuscript, and neither could be delivered as damaged goods.

"Got it," I said and stood up.

"Turn around," he said and he again grabbed me by the wrists and pushed them up toward my shoulders.

I took one last glance at Nev. Her head was moving. We had to get out of there. I walked forward in front of both men.

"Kuraĝa, stay," I said, just to be sure.

We exited the store, and Frog-marcher started turning me to the right. This was my opportunity.

When somebody has you in a hold like that, there are a couple of different ways to get out of it. The easiest, though,—especially when someone is taller and stronger than you—is to use his own strength against him. Being old, and getting more than a little irritated with people shoving me in and out of my own shop, that's what I did.

I exaggerated my turn to the right, which forced Frog-marcher to accelerate his turn behind me and increase the pull on my left arm to get me back under control. As soon as I felt his pull, I immediately reversed direction and backed out toward his right side, using the slack on my left wrist to pull it in front of me. He followed the pull and I ducked and backed out under his right arm.

Now he was in front of me, coming toward me, both hands still holding on. I stepped back and to the side, brought one hand down, the other up, and accelerated his movement past me. He went flying head-first into the shop window, shattering it.

Menace Guy, of course, hadn't been standing around picking his nose, and I turned around just in time to see a billy club swinging toward my head. I stepped back and at the same time grabbed Menace Guy's arm like it was a baseball bat and forced the billy club all the way through its trajectory. Still holding his arm, I stepped in, raised it like a sword and turned in place. Then I swung his arm directly down.

Menace Guy fell on his back, hard, and his head bounced off the sidewalk.

I looked back at Frog-marcher. He was getting up, looking at me, brushing glass off his head. I started toward him. I guess he read my thoughts about what I wanted to do with the broken glass and his face. He turned and ran.

I watched him go up the street until he was out of sight, and then I counted to thirty.

I looked in the opposite direction. A cop car, lights flashing, was pulling in to where the BMW had blown up. There were still flames licking from the chassis, and I heard the wail of a fire engine in the distance.

Only one thing left to do.

I started screaming at the top of my lungs.

MONDAY – CHAPTER 45

When Officer Peterson got there, I was sitting on the steps in the pouring rain, soaked to the bone, rubbing my head like I had gotten hit.

Peterson looked at Menace Guy on the ground, looked at me, mumbled into his lapel mike, and then came over.

"What the fuck, Asa? You okay?" he asked.

"Yeah," I said. "Goddamn looters. He was trying to break into the shop. I, umm, deterred him."

"Jesus," Peterson said. "Town's going fucking crazy. Car ran into a pole down the street. You sure you ok?" he asked again.

"Better than this guy," I said, waving my hand at Menace.

"Well, lemme get some backup here, and some EMS, and then we can go inside and talk."

"Fine," I said. "Mind if I go in and get a coat in the meantime?"

"Sure, go ahead," Peterson said. His eyes flicked back to Menace, who was starting to sit up. "Better you get out of here for the next few minutes anyway."

I strolled inside, moving more jauntily than I felt. My left shoulder hurt like a bastard from falling on it and from all of Froggy's jerking. I grabbed the box cutter off Neveah's desk and went up into the office.

Kuraĝa jumped forward when he saw me and I put my hand on his neck. I knelt beside Nev. She was awake, alert and struggling, but wisely staying silent. I put my finger to my lips and cut the tape.

"Nobody is here, Nev. Especially not you," I whispered in her ear. "Stay here with the dog until I come back. Got it?"

She nodded. I looked at Kurağa, and said "Stay with her." He sat back down, looking at me pleadingly. "I'll be right back," I said.

I grabbed my coat off the hook and went back outside.

Peterson was standing in front of Menace Guy, his hand about an inch away from the pistol on his duty belt. The holster was unsnapped. Menace was sitting in a puddle on the ground, his back against the stone foundation of the building.

"Sure, you'll have your lawyer," Peterson was saying, "but I think you need to see a fucking doctor first."

Peterson looked at me as I came out the door, closing it behind me.

"Gonna take a little bit," he said. "Between the blown-up sedan and a crash on the bridge, town's a little stretched right now. EMS had to call over to Watertown for help."

His eyes snapped back to Menace Guy, who was starting to get up.

"Lie down, face down," he said, "and put your hands behind your back."

Menace complied, and with a practiced hand Peterson put some cuffs on him and sat him back up. He crouched down in front of Menace, his face inches away from him.

"Try anything, and I will beat you like a fucking circus monkey," he said and turned to me. "What the fuck did you do to this guy, anyway?"

I explained to Peterson how I'd been in the shop and heard the window breaking and ran up front and saw this guy grabbing stuff. So I ran out and stopped him.

"We were wrestling, and I guess he slipped on the sidewalk and fell down," I said. "Between you and me, if felt kinda good watching his head bounce off the sidewalk."

"Fuck," Peterson said, "I'm going to pretend I didn't hear that."

An ambulance was wheeling down the street, sirens on. It pulled up in front of the shop.

"I tell you what," Peterson said, "With all the shit going on, I'm a little busy right now. We'll get this guy processed, I gotta go back to the fucking car wreck, and I'll call you tomorrow and you can come down to the barracks and I'll take your statement while we're not standing around in the pouring rain with some asshole."

"Sounds good to me," I said. I stood up as the EMS guys were pulling the stretcher out. I looked back at Peterson. "Have a good evening, officer. Don't work too hard."

Peterson looked at me.

"Shut up," he said and then walked over to the stretcher and the guy lying on the ground.

MONDAY – CHAPTER 46

When I got back to my office, Neveah was sitting on the floor with an open beer in one hand and her other draped over Kuraĝa. I shrugged off my jacket and hung it up. I was still soaked, but at least I looked better than Nev. She'd gotten sucker punched, soaked and then dragged across the ground.

"Your wolf here's not half bad," she said, and took a pull on the beer. "Likes beer."

"Jesus, Nev," I said. "You gave him a beer?"

"He looked like he needed one as much as me, so I shared," she said. "This is our second."

I shook my head. "So you want to know what happened or you just want to sit there and get drunk with my dog?" I asked.

"I kinda killed a guy today, boss," Neveah said. "Imma gonna drink and let you talk. Last thing I knew, we were in front of the shop, and then I wake up all taped up and a fucking wolf licking my face." She put her beer down and rubbed the side of her head gingerly. "Fucking hurts," she said.

I sat down at my desk and reached for a pipe and tobacco. I considered for a second. What did I want right now? Something sweet, I thought. The sweet smell of success. That whole performance had been improv, and there had never been a single point at which I thought I had anything even slightly under control.

Still don't, I reminded myself. Never will.

I reached for a tin of Ugly Chuck's Blend, filled my pipe and lit it. Then I gave Nev the whole story, backing up a little bit because I was pretty sure that she didn't remember the beemer exploding...not after she'd taken a hit like that.

"What the fuck, boss," she said when I was finished. "You calling this a success? Damn, you let that other guy just run away."

"Yup," I said. "He figured, rightly, that getting half the prize was better than none of it, and he headed for the hills."

"With the manuscript," she said.

"Yup," I said. "The wrong one."

"The hell?" Nev said. She thought. "The one that came in the mail today?"

I nodded. "The very same."

There's lots I don't know about Nev, but the one thing I do know is she's fast. Very fast. Even after a concussion and two beers.

"Holy shit. So they think they've got the manuscript and—lemme guess—they thinkin' that maybe they'll get somebody who's not an asshole to figure it out for them, and they'll leave you alone."

I re-lit my pipe. "And the weather is getting so bad out there that this town is going to be locked up tight for the next few days. Between roads flooding and trees down, it's going to get hard to move around. So I've got at least until the end of the hurricane to figure out what to do with the real one."

"Yeah," she said. "And then they'll smell the pages just like you did, and know that it's a fake, and we're fucked again."

"Not so fast, kid," I said. "You smell what I'm smoking right now?"

Nev wrinkled her nose. "Smells like a damn candy bar," she said.

"Yup. And all afternoon, I had those pages out of their sleeves, smoking a Latakia blend, blowing the smoke all over the pages as I examined them. Latakia blends have been around for centuries. That put a stink on those pages, so if they do take a whiff, all they'll get is the smell of woody smoke. Someone who knows what they're doing will still be able to suss out the forgery eventually, but that will take more time."

Nev finished her beer. "So where's the real manuscript, boss?"

"Right here," I said.

I turned around to face my desk. It was huge, a conversion from a pre-Depression era square piano. Along its edges were two layers of small drawers and cubbyholes, not unlike something you would see on an old-school roll-top. This one had been custom made by a German immigrant cabinetmaker living in Ohio and, like most Germans who had lived through the first war, he knew the value of having a place for what you value. So the desk had a few secrets.

I emptied one of the cubbyholes, slid my hand in and felt for the slight give where the wooden latch was. I pushed and felt the top loosen. I pulled out all the cubbies and drawers on that side as a unit. That left a blank piece of wood which looked like a support, and which covered the corner. I gave a slight push on one of the corners of the piece of wood, felt the second latch give, and pushed what was now a door inward on its springs.

I pulled out the manuscript.

"That's some clever," Nev said.

"Now you're the second living person in the world who knows that this exists," I said. "There's some other stuff in here you should know about, as well."

I put the real manuscript on the desk and reached in again. I pulled out a fat roll of bills and showed them to Nev.

"That's fifty thousand in hundred dollar bills," I said. "In case of an emergency."

"Big-ass emergency," Nev said.

I put the roll back in and then pulled out a piece of paper with two lines and numbers on it.

"These are the pass codes to two sources of money: One is a cryptocurrency wallet. The other is an offshore bank account. They also have two usernames, which I'll tell you in a minute. Together, they have about seventeen million in them, give or take. The crypto can be pretty volatile, but I have automatic transfers set up if a fall gets severe."

Nev gave me a look I'd never seen from her before. I wasn't altogether sure what it meant.

"Sure you want me with this?" she said.

"Yeah, I'm sure. Because if anything happens to me, you're taking this money, these pass codes and getting the hell out of Dodge. I have no heirs, Nev. No family. I go up in smoke, all of it will get re-absorbed or stolen."

She shook her head. "I don' want it," she said. "There've been other times in my life I coulda got plenty of money, and I didn't. Just drags you down."

"But that was drug money, no, and you would have been stealing it, right?" It was a guess, but her expression told me that it was a good one.

"Kinda. I don't want this money."

"I know you don't. But you're going to need it. Next time you're on the run, you're not going be so lucky as to run into a shopkeeper in a sleepy little town who doesn't want to know."

She nodded, biting on her lip. After a minute she looked at me with the same direct stare that she had given me when we first met.

"Ok," she said. "I'll take it...but only if I need it."

"Deal," I said.

I told her the usernames and she put her hand over her mouth and started laughing.

MONDAY – CHAPTER 47

After securing the shop and exchanging some words of caution between us—Nev had tried to convince me to take the 9mm home with me—we left for the evening,

I left the jeep in front of the shop— to give anyone looking to pinch me a little misdirection—and walked home. Kuraĝa trotted along at my side.

It was after midnight by the time he and I got there, and the first thing I did was chuck off my soaking wet clothing for something dry. I was exhausted and drained, and both of us were a little hungry so I pulled out some leftover kung pao chicken of uncertain age and sniffed it. It passed the smell test. I split it in half, made some rice to go with it, and shared with Kuraĝa.

As he licked the bowl, I said, "One of these days we gotta get you some dog food or something because pretty soon, my ribs are going to start sticking out like yours."

He looked at me hopefully. I resisted for a minute, but gave in.

"Guess I can make some more rice," I said and shoveled the rest of my plate into his bowl.

I needed sleep. More than that, I needed to find some peace of mind, find my center again. I felt out of balance, out of harmony with the world. Violence may be a part of the balance of this world, but immersion in it for too long draws you further and further into it. It had been too much. I needed to sit.

Kuraĝa followed me as I sat seiza at my altar and went through the candle-lighting ritual. His eyes gleamed in the half-dark of the candlelight, and as I folded my legs underneath me, he stretched his out and lay down with his muzzle on his paws.

I began the process of counting my breaths, letting go, following my breath, then letting my mind settle deeply into nothingness.

I'd like to say I was prepared for her appearance again, but I was still startled. This time, she was not in the river, but on its bank. Behind her, the current rushed into the Cauldron and she stood, head down, her hand clutching her opposite arm below the shoulder.

I stood in front of her, waiting. She didn't move.

"Elle," I said softly. "Elle, I'm looking."

She looked up at me, her face sad. Her hand dropped to her side, and I saw where her arm had been carved, the red raw tissue where her skin should have been.

She clasped her hands in front of her, turned around and walked into the water. Her body was untouched by the current, and she walked toward the middle of the river, descending as she got further out, and then her head was underwater and then she was gone.

I was sitting in front of my altar, candles burning, Kuraĝa stretched out by my side.

One by one, I blew the candles out and stood up, knees creaking. I stepped over to my leather chair, as I had done a few days before, and sat down. The rain was gusting hard and the window rattled. No moon tonight, nor any moonlight through the clouds.

All I knew, all I tried to know, was the present. The past had already happened and could not be changed. Or could it?

Our minds are phenomenal tricksters, and we change and color our memories, shading them in permutations, to fit our present needs. Yet here was the past, rising up out of the water to the present, forcing me to look at it, to experience it, even though it was not even mine.

And what of my past? "Who are you, Asa Cire," I could hear Tanya's voice asking me. "Where did you come from?"

I don't know, Tanya.

I had forgotten my past. Why? Why had I made myself unreachable to myself? That was a useless question, and an endless loop. I could not remember my past without knowing who I was, and I could not know who I was without remembering my past.

On the other hand, what did it matter? Would I behave any differently than I did now? I looked back over my actions the past few days. What would I have done differently, if I had known who I was beyond who I was right now?

Everything I had done had been attuned to the needs of the moment, to keeping Nev and me alive, to staying free of being kidnapped. Would my values have been different? Would I simply have swept my attackers aside with hail from an assault rifle and silenced them and their threat, with little risk?

I shook my head. That didn't make sense whether I valued life more or less. On the other hand, when I had first realized the danger I was in, I should have just taken the manuscript and my money and run and left enough of a trail to keep my friends out of danger, headed for the hills and sequestered myself safely.

Unbidden, a scene came to my mind. A cabin, deep in the woods, deep in snow. Smoke curling out of the chimney. A squeaky step on the porch to announce incautious visitors.

A feeling of safety, of relief, engulfed me. Was this my past, was this something I had come from? No. It didn't feel right. It was only a vision conjured out of fear, out of my desire to once again be let alone.

Once again?

It was not the cabin that was a glimpse of my past. It was the solitude.

TUESDAY – CHAPTER 48

The next morning Kuraĝa and I walked back to the shop. Broken branches were scattered across the road and the wind and rain were so thick now that any dryness beneath my coat was a pretense.

My shoulder wasn't much better than the night before, and when I had woken up, my right hip was stiff, who knew what from? Yesterday had been busy.

While I had made breakfast for us, I had realized how unprepared I was for the worsening weather. I had barely enough food for myself, much less for a large, hungry dog. I looked at Kuraĝa. Even over the past few days, he had begun filling out, his ribs no longer quite so visible, his movements not quite so leaden.

As we walked together toward town, there were no birds chirping in the trees. They were all lying low while the weather passed, and I had to lean against the wind myself to make headway as we dodged through the debris down to West Street. The town still had power, though, so maybe it was time for a run to the grocery store before everything shut down.

I unlocked the shop and looked around. The front of it was soaked where rain had blown in through the window before Nev and I had nailed a deconstructed shipping crate over it. Nev was nowhere to be seen, but the store hadn't been ransacked. That was good news. Perhaps my ruse had actually worked. The window next to the door flexed slightly with the gusts of wind. And we still had power.

I went back to my office, threw the beer bottles in the trash and flicked on the computer. I didn't think my search would take long.

I was right. The woman had left an online trail a mile wide.

A few years after her daughter's murder, Elle Anderson's mother had moved out of town. It wasn't hard to understand why, having to drive every day over the river that had held her daughter's murdered body until it had spitting up the bloated, mutilated corpse.

She had moved to another part of the state and had then married a Marine. Like mother, like daughter, I thought. He'd apparently been stationed at Camp LeJeune because the next time she popped up in the public records was a DUI conviction in Jacksonville. I'd struck gold. That had only been a year ago, I saw. She must be in her fifties by now.

It didn't take long to get her phone number. Her name was Angie. I grabbed the phone off my desk and dialed.

"Hello?" she answered. I heard the years and the cigarettes and the booze in her gravelly voice.

"Angie Anderson?" I asked. "I hope I'm not disturbing you. I'm calling because the investigation into your daughter's death has been re-opened, and if you don't mind, I have a couple of questions for you."

"Anderson?" She laughed, but it sounded more like a gargle. "I haven't used that name in years. Divorced the sunofabitch after I caught him cheating with that fat bitch clerk on the base. Kept the next guy's name, though. Too much trouble to change. Wait a minute."

I heard the clunk as she put the phone on the table, and in the distance I heard her yell, "Stan? Stan! Don't forget to take the garbage out when you leave!" There was silence for a few more seconds and then she picked up the phone again. Then the quiet hiss of her drawing on a cigarette.

"So what's there to know? You guys interviewed me a hundred times already, and what happened to reopen the case?"

"It was assigned to me as a cold case," I said, "and I'm just hoping to close it, if I can."

"You wanna close it, you go arrest Budgie Whatshisface," she said. "I know damn well he did it, and so does everybody else. You guys were too chickenshit to arrest him. Hell, he must have been paying you off. Whadya get, extra donuts?"

"Ma'am, I wasn't here back then, I don't know anything about that. But I was wondering if you could tell me about the tattoo she had."

"You mean the one that Budgie peeled off my daughter's body? That one? I thought you didn't want me to talk about that."

"Well, you can to me," I said. "That's the tattoo I'm talking about, not the other one."

"What are you talking about? There wasn't another one. It was stupid Minnie Mouse. Elle ran off and got it with money that somebody gave her—I don't know what for—and the guy who did it should have been arrested, tattooing a minor like that."

"Was there anything special about it?" I said.

"Anything special? You mean like Minnie bending over in a short skirt showing off her butt, that kind of special? God, you people made me look like such a bad mother, I don't know why I'm talking to you."

"I'm sorry, Angie, that wasn't me. I'm very sorry the other investigators were rude to you."

"Oh, it wasn't just the cops. Everybody in town made me feel like shit. There I was, lost my only child and people were calling me all kinds of names, telling me she was a slut just like me, all kinds of stuff. Why do you think I left town? She made my life hell."

"She did? Who?"

"Elle, you idiot. That's who. God, there were times I wished she had never been born." There was silence, then the snap of a Zippo lighter and another deep inhalation.

"Y'know, I don't know why I'm talking to you. I talked to you all you wanted twenty years ago, and all I got was shit and my life ruined. You know what? You know who killed her, you refused to do anything then, and you won't do anything now. I'm done with that part of my life. I've moved on. Goodbye."

The phone went dead. I put it down, not much more informed than I had been when I started.

TUESDAY – CHAPTER 49

Angie had seemed convinced that Budgie was responsible. On one hand, that may simply be a bereaved mother's obsession with an obvious suspect. On the other, it could be something that the cops hadn't picked up on, or had ignored.

A phone call would be worthless, but paying him another visit wasn't exactly at the top of my fun list, either. At any rate, something had to be done soon, before the hurricane shut everything down.

I had an idea. I picked up my phone and thought for a minute. There were ways to do things, and there were ways to do things. I thumbed up Nev in my address book.

"Wanna make some bonus money?" I asked

"Sure," came the response. "Not like you can't afford it," she said with a laugh.

"I want you to go talk to Budgie today," I said.

"Dafuq?"

"Yeah. I just talked to Elle Anderson's mother, and she seems convinced that he did it. Since he and I have . . . uh . . . a disagreement, I was hoping you might help me out."

"Gonna be hazard pay," she said.

"Just stay directly in front of where he's pointing his gun. You'll be safe," I said.

"So what do you want me to do while I'm dodging bullets, boss? Get a signed confession?"

"That'd be nice."

"Not gonna happen," she said. "Something else?"

I told her my idea.

"Jesus, boss, you're fucking crazy. Also, I'm gonna get killed," she said.

"Probably not," I said. "Plus, when you're done, I'll buy you dinner."

"Only place left open is Chinese, and you bought me that last night," she said. "Aren't you playing that stupid game with your friend tonight anyway?"

Oh, yeah. Charlie and I were supposed to play Go tonight.

"Well, rain check, then. That seafood place after the hurricane."

"Deal," Nev said and hung up.

I had no idea if my plan would work, and there was a very small chance of Nev getting lead poisoning, but I had a lot of faith in that woman. It would take a man a helluva lot better than Budgie to take her down if things went sideways. Well, we'd see.

I made one more phone call to help Nev get things set up, and after a little resistance—easily solved by additional funding—I secured what she needed for today's farce.

That done, I finally turned to my real problem, not the one created for me by a ghost.

TUESDAY – CHAPTER 50

I pulled the manuscript out of its hiding place and pulled the pages out of the envelope. How much time was I going to spend sitting here staring at this, I wondered. And going nowhere.

The one thing that had begun to strike me about the obscure calligraphy on the pages was that, with the exception of the page numbers, every time I looked at them, they seemed a little bit different. One time they looked faintly like Sanskrit, another time like Hebrew. Sometimes they were like classical Mandarin ideographs or slightly Cyrillic letters. Sometimes they might have been Latin letters, but oddly written.

How could I decipher anything, I thought, if I couldn't even figure out what it looked like?

I decided to try an experiment. I pulled out a blank sheet of paper and a fountain pen. I pushed the first manuscript page away from me and placed the blank sheet close, where I could write on it. I was going to try and copy that page, figure by figure.

So as to not create any false assumptions for myself, I decided I wouldn't even look at my copy until I was done. I stared at the manuscript for a minute and put my pen to the blank sheet.

The process took about an hour, and my hand was cramping by the time I was done. It had been a strange process. At times, I sped along, copying character by character, and other times I felt like I was pushing against a stone wall. At one point, it even felt like my hand was on fire, but I kept writing and eventually that sensation faded. I put my pen down, and flexed my fingers back and forth until the stiffness and pain subsided. I wanted to see what I had written, but I had to do it in the right frame of mind, so I took a minute and reached for a pipe.

I debated about the tobacco to put in it, and eventually settled on an old English blend, its origins going back to before World War I. It had been blended specially for a priest who shared it with his friends, and the demand grew until the tobacconist put it on the market. It has been sold steadily ever since, with only minor changes in the recipe to adapt to changing tobaccos, growing and harvesting processes. The blend had been named "Presbyterian." I figured a little religion wouldn't hurt right now.

My pipe lit, I finally looked at my copy of the manuscript.

It was rectangles. A series of rectangles, some larger, some smaller, all in straight lines across the page. Some of the rectangles had smaller rectangles placed inside them, also of varying size.

It. Made. No. Sense.

I stood up. Damn, my shoulder had been made no better by my writing session. Kuraĝa sat up, looking at me. I saw his bowl had no water so I got up, filled it from the sink in the bathroom, and put it down on the floor.

As I bent over, a small book in my bookcase caught my eye. It was the *Tao Te Ching*, the fundamental text of Taoism, with that famous first line in it, "The Tao that can be spoken is not the eternal Tao." Eighty-one short chapters, presumably written by Lao Tsu, explaining—if you can call it that—the central concepts of Taoism. And if anyone were the masters of nonsense, it is the Taoists. Even more than Buddhists, Taoists found supreme expression of their understanding of reality in seemingly nonsensical statements, like that opening line.

Much of what I did, and practiced, had its roots in Taoism. The movements of qigong, the meditation techniques I used, all came from that source. Watered down, simplified, and Happy Mealed, it was often expressed in the West as "go with the flow," but the philosophy was much deeper and richer than that. According to the Taoist perspective, when one was moving in accordance with the movement of the universe, everything was supremely easy. It required little effort to accomplish things, or as Lao Tsu put it, "The Tao is constant in non-action, yet there is nothing it does not do."

I had long ago studied the Tao Te Ching in depth, but had not picked it up in years. I pulled it off the shelf now and flipped it open to a random page.

Thirty spokes share the wheel's hub; It is the center hole that makes it useful. Shape clay into a vessel; It is the space within that makes it useful. Cut doors and windows for a room; It is the holes which make it useful. Therefore profit comes from what is there; Usefulness from what is not there.

"Of course," I said. The dog stopped lapping water from his bowl and looked at me. "I've been looking at the wrong thing." I closed the book and put it back on the shelf.

Then I heard the front door slam as somebody pushed it shut it against the wind.

TUESDAY – CHAPTER 51

The thuds of a large man on the stairs announced Peterson's arrival by the time he had walked into my office. He sat down heavily. His face was sagging. He sniffed.

"Jesus, place stinks," he said. "Where's Nev?"

"I dunno, not my turn to watch her," I said. "And that's some of the world's best English Latakia tobacco you're wrinkling your nose at."

"Latashit is what is smells like," he said. "And what's that goddamn wolf you've got sitting next to you?"

"Kuraĝa's his name," I said. "He's gonna help keep watch over this place from now on."

"Crap, I've seen smaller ponies," Peterson said. "So where's Nev?"

"Did you try her apartment?" I asked.

"Yeah, she's not there. Neighbors saw nothing. No surprise. She's not answering her cell phone."

"What's the urgency, Officer?"

Peterson leaned forward in his chair.

"We gotta talk, Cire, you and me. There's a lot of shit going on that kinda points toward you. I kinda need to know what's going on."

"Like what?"

"Like that Wangy guy. Like being the only place on the block being hit up by 'looters.' Like two guys dying in a car that shouldn't have exploded, and one of them with a slug in him," Peterson said.

"Like I told you, I don't know Wang. And looters like to hit places with valuable stuff, and an antique store is a place with valuable stuff. And I haven't blown up a BMW in years."

Peterson stiffened and his look got hard. Shit, I thought. I wasn't supposed to know the car.

"How'd you know it was a BMW?" he asked. Friendly time was over.

My expression didn't change. "State cop named Peterson told me, that's how," I said. "Looter, remember? Waiting for an ambulance, remember?" I was counting on his fatigue and a jangled memory from too much work.

"Whatever," he said. "But you seem to know a lot of shit you're not supposed to. Like that girl's tattoo."

"What girl's tattoo?" Crikey, Peterson wasn't shooting blanks today.

"That murdered kid, Elle Anderson. You were asking about her the other day. Told me her tattoo had been carved off her. You aren't supposed to know that. Who you been talking to?"

"Why'm I not supposed to know?" I asked.

"Who you been talking to?" Full-on cop stare now.

I reached for my pipe and filled it, taking my time while I thought. I couldn't afford another mistake.

"Lotta people," I said. "Elle Anderson's mother, for one."

"Sober?" he asked.

"Early in the morning. I'm guessing the bottle was mostly full at that point."

"Fucking drunk," he said. "I went looking into the file after talking to you. We were keeping the carved off tattoo on the QT. Thought it might help identify the killer."

"Yeah, well it's been twenty years. A lot of people probably know by now."

"Maybe so," Peterson said, nodding. "So where's Nev?"

I smiled. "Honestly, Officer Peterson, I have no damn clue. None."

"Where does she keep her gun?" he asked.

I thought about the two times I had seen it kind of appear out of nowhere in her hand, and the last time I saw it, stuck in Frog-marcher's jeans, as he ran up the street.

"I'm being completely honest with you here, Officer. I have no idea where she would keep a gun. I don't think she even has one. You want to tell me what the hell is going on with my employee? She's been with me for years and, to be honest, she feels like a daughter to me. So if she's in trouble, I'd like to help."

Peterson's face softened.

"I don't know if she's in trouble or not, but we have to talk to her. You know that woman's got a bit of a past, don't you?"

"I assumed so, but I never asked," I said. "People's pasts aren't my business. Just the things from their past." I waved my hand around the office, shelves crowded with the detritus of the obscure interests of past lives.

"Yeah, well here's a thing from her past," Peterson said. "Resident on Meadow St. called in this morning, found a gun on the sidewalk. Soaking wet, no prints, of course. But the serial number traces back to her ex-husband."

I laughed, in genuine surprise. "Her husband? Really? I had no idea she was even married."

"Yeah. Got divorced not too long after he went upstate for felony possession with intent. Doing a fifteen year bid. He was kind of a thing in the city. NYPD cops who did the raid even had special t-shirts printed up for the event. Even a cop could figure out who probably dropped that gun. But she's got bigger problems than that. We pulled two dead guys out of the burned-up Beemer. Examiner doing the autopsy pulled a slug out of one of them. Says he was probably already dead when that car barbecued him. So I'm just kind of wondering if that slug is going to match up with that gun, which matches up with Neveah Arias, and I want to know what the fuck is going on."

I tamped down my pipe and re-lit it. Thank god for pipes and their eternal need for attention.

"I don't know much, Officer, but I'll tell you what I do know. I know that Nev is an admirable person who has worked for me faithfully and honestly for several years. I have trusted her with my business and my money, and I would not hesitate to trust her with my life." I couldn't get more truthful than that. "As far as I can tell, she doesn't have a record—"

"She's got some juvie stuff, but it's sealed. Nothing since," Peterson said.

"— and whatever she may have done in the past, she hasn't done anything wrong since I've known her." I looked at him, not unkindly. "And I'm pretty sure that's your impression of her as well. Nev's a good woman, Peterson, and you know that as well as I do."

Peterson looked down at the floor.

"I know, Cire, I know, and I agree with you. But she's mixed up in something and might be trouble." He looked up at me. "So if you see her, you tell her to get in touch with me ASAP."

Peterson stood up. "You tell her, whatever she does, not to leave town." He stared at me. "You understand me?"

"I heard you, Officer," I said. "Loud and clear."

He put his state trooper hat on, decided not to try to stare down Kuraĝa, and walked out.

TUESDAY – CHAPTER 52

The black limousine rolled up to the front of the shop sometime after lunch.

I had finished mopping up the mess by the front window and was pulling things from the window display and putting them back on the shelves. The driver's door opened and a short, rotund man wearing a dark suit got out and opened an umbrella. He was soaking wet.

He walked around to the back passenger door and opened it. He held the umbrella over the head of the passenger as she got out, dressed in a long black raincoat with the hood up. She walked into the shop and he followed her in, stopping to shake and close the umbrella first.

The woman pushed her hood back and shrugged the coat off before hanging it on the rack. Kuraĝa, who had been standing at attention, sat on his haunches. His tail wagged, once.

"Holy shit," I said.

It was Nev, her normally curly hair straightened and pulled back tight against her scalp into a bun. She was wearing knee-high boots and a thigh-high skirt that hugged her like a long-lost lover. She had on mascara and eyeliner I'd never seen her wear before. Ruby-red lipstick completed a look that, when combined with the expression on her face, was somewhere between "going clubbing" and "going to kill you."

She smiled.

"Holy shit," I said again.

"Before we get going," she said, "we got a problem, boss."

"We got a lot of problems," I said. "What's this one?"

"Shorty here," she gestured toward the driver, "wants to talk to you."

He stepped up. "Mr. Cire, the limousine sustained some damage," he said. "Tree branch fell on the hood during the course of our trip, and we're going to have to charge you for it."

I walked to the door and looked out. There was a crease clear across the front of the car, deep enough for the rain to have begun collecting in it.

"No problem," I said. "Send me a bill for whatever the insurance doesn't cover."

"Also," he said, "there's going to be an extra charge for cleaning my suit, which sustained some additional wear and tear when I had to move the tree limb off and out of the way."

"Of course," I said. As I walked back from the door, I fingered a couple of bills loose from the roll in my pocket and handed them to him. "Here's two hundred," I said. "That should take care of your personal incidentals."

He nodded and took the bills in his pudgy hand. "You don't need me anymore, right? I gotta get back."

"Of course," I said. "Thank you for the extra effort."

Once the limo driver was gone, I turned to Nev. "How'd it go?"

She laughed. "I gotta get this shit off me," she said, "I'll meet you back in the office."

TUESDAY – CHAPTER 53

"That boy's seen some shit," Nev said.

She had changed to jeans and a long sweatshirt and was sitting on the Skull & Bones chair, but with the makeup still on and her hair pulled back, Nev still looked like a different person. She was absent-mindedly stroking Kuraĝa, sitting next to her.

"Budgie looks like he got run over a couple times," she said.

I smiled. "Yeah," I said. "He does. What'd you find out?"

"I did what you told me to. I came on like I was some shit from the Dominicans. He fell for it. Told him I was looking for a distribution outlet up here, wondering if he could handle it." She laughed. "Time I was done, he was slobbering at the chance. So I quizzed him. He could hardly stop looking at my boobs long enough to answer."

"And?" I said.

"And that boy hardly got the brains to eat breakfast, boss. No way he killed that girl and covered it twenty years."

"You're sure?"

"Shit, yes, I'm sure," she said. "I asked him about it like I wanted him to have done it, you know what I mean? Nope. He ain't got it."

I nodded. "Ok, well, that's it, then," I said. "The cops were right." I thought for a second. "You carrying, Nev?" I asked.

"You know me, don't you?"

"Yeah, ok, I do. You need to give me that gun. Right now." I held out my hand.

"Why, what's up?"

"Just do it, Nev. We're in deep, and I want to get you out."

She reached around behind her back, pulled out the pistol and handed it to me reluctantly. I released the magazine and emptied the chamber, making sure I got my fingerprints everywhere on the gun and the magazine. Then I pulled the bullets out of the magazine itself, also making sure I handled each bullet thoroughly. I opened the safe and put everything in it.

"Is this gun traceable back to your ex-husband, too?" I asked.

Her eyes widened. "No," she said. "No, that was—well, no. It's got no history at all. Never even sold."

"Good," I said. "Here's the thing of it. You've become a 'person of interest' to the police, and you're about one slow day away from being a murder suspect."

"Shit," Nev said.

I spent the next ten minutes telling her what Peterson had told me, wondering as I spoke how much time we had left. I mentioned how explicitly he had suggested she not leave town.

"Whatever goes down, Nev, I think you've got a friend there," I said.

"Lotta good that'll do me," Nev said. She got up without a word, walked to the front of the shop, and the next thing I heard and felt was a bang as something hard slammed against the floor. She walked back in carrying a splintered and bent phone.

"I used that flint axe you have," she said, "I figured you wouldn't mind."

I laughed, thinking of the priceless pipe she'd thrown through the air the first time that I'd met her. I shook my head.

"Jesus," I said. "Ok, so now they can't track you. Now we gotta get you someplace safe."

"Naw, I got that," she said. She stayed standing. "I got a coupla places."

"You're going to need some money," I said and pulled out the roll I'd taken from the safe earlier. "How much?"

"That was a hell of a performance I did today," she said. "It was about three grand."

I counted out thirty hundreds.

"Also, I was planning on giving you a bonus at the end of the year, so I might as well give that to you now," I said. I counted out another thirty and handed her the stack. She folded it, split it and put some in her pants and some down the front of her sweatshirt.

" 'case I catch problems," she said.

"I'm going to need some way of getting in touch with you," I said, "to let you know when everything's cleared up and you can come back."

She looked at me with that direct stare of hers. "Ain't gonna be no cleared up, boss," she said. "Murders don't never clear up."

She was right, of course. And I knew it. I didn't want to admit it.

"I'll get it straightened out, Nev, just give me a little ti—"

"No you won't, boss. You good, but you can't fix everything. You can't fix this, not now, not ever."

"Well, you can't just disappear," I said.

"The fuck I can. I did it before, I can do it better this time."

"So you're going."

"Yup."

"For good."

"Yup."

"Ok." I thought for a second. "Let me give you those pass codes. Any of that money is yours, Nev. You take whatever you need."

"I don't need 'em," she said. "I memorized them when you showed them to me."

Of course she had.

"It's yours," I repeated. She nodded.

I felt my eyes getting wet. What the hell was going on?

"Look, Nev, I just want you to know . . . I . . . you're like a daughter to me. If you ever need anything, I..."

"I got no time for this, boss," she said. Her lip was quivering. She held my gaze for a second, then turned away. She walked over to Kuraĝa and leaned over to pet him. "You be good, Wolf. Look after boss here. He ain't half bad."

She walked out of the office.

I stood for a second, for once in my life not knowing what to do, and got to the door in time to see her putting her coat on and pulling the hood up. Without looking back, she walked out the door and pulled it shut against the wind. A second later she was lost in the weather.

I stood there. I realized tears were streaming down my face. For the second time in a week. Kuraĝa was beside me. I rubbed my face and looked down at him.

"What the hell's wrong with me, dog?" I said.

TUESDAY – CHAPTER 54

By the time I got to the grocery store, I was pretty sure I was the last person in town to think to himself, "Gee, I should stock up for this," because the shelves were empty.

At least in the canned goods section. There was still a little produce left, though. I grabbed some end-of-season corn and beans that had seen better days, some apples, and a few other things that wouldn't go bad too fast if the power blew out.

I had the wood stove for cooking on in a pinch, and town water, so I would be pretty set. Depending on how long it lasted, I had plenty of rice and beans at the house. I've subsisted on less, I thought.

Really? I asked myself. And when was that?

Nothing.

I needed food for the dog, though. He wouldn't be happy with rice and beans, and he still needed to put on weight. I grabbed the biggest bag of dog food on the shelf and chucked it in the cart.

Still thinking of Kurağa, I rounded the corner, headed toward the meat department and nearly collided with a cart coming the other way.

"Excuse me," I said.

The woman pushing the other cart was nobody I had ever seen before. Nemaseck was too large to know everybody, but if you'd lived here long enough, you'd seen just about everybody. I'd never seen her in Nemaseck.

But still, she looked familiar.

And entirely out of place. Like one of the New Yorkers who like to come up in the summertime or have a summer place up here. They're easy to spot, from their clothes to their city-bred haste. But it wasn't that, either.

This woman was tall, even without the high heels she was wearing, and she had a face that on a man I'd call chiseled. Hawk-like. Long salt and pepper hair, looking like she'd just come from the hair stylist. Cool, even, blue eyes that looked at me calmly. I thought I'd seen her before.

"Not a problem," she said. Her voice was clear and cool as a mountain stream and shot right through me like a strum on my spinal cord. But it wasn't that same strum that you get when you see a woman who really should be in your bed, and soon at that. This was different.

"Haven't we met before?" I asked.

She laughed, and it was a gentle rain falling on leaves. "Apparently not," she said. She gestured at my cart. "Big dog, or just stocking up?"

"Big dog," I said. "He'll be a hundred pounds at his peak."

"Oh," she said and the smile left her face. "A puppy?"

"No. A, umm, rescue I picked up recently. He'd been treated poorly and I'm nursing him back to health. By the way, my name's Asa. Asa Cire," I said. I held out my hand.

She looked at it, but did not offer hers.

"Well, Asa Cire, I'm sure you're a good man, but I'm not quite in the habit of introducing myself to men in supermarkets. I'm sure you understand." She smiled again, and it tickled at the back of my brain.

"Perfectly," I said and returned her smile. "It's just that I'm certain that if I don't already know you, I probably should."

She laughed again, gently. "A marvelous pick-up line," she said, "and one that is certainly tempting. But not this time, and not this place, Mr. Cire." She untangled her cart from mine and pushed it forward. "I do hope you weather this coming storm safely," she said as she passed.

I nodded. After she went by, I turned to look at her. As if on cue, she turned her head, and mistaking my interest, smiled and wagged her finger at me.

I could not shake the feeling that I knew this woman, or should.

The only thing left in the meat counter was some ham hocks. I grabbed them and threw them in the cart. I would use them for some bean soup. Put a big batch up to simmer while I was playing Go with Charlie tonight.

Then I remembered. She was the woman who had stopped by my house when I had been chopping wood. Asking about real estate. And how long I lived there. And where I'd lived before Nemaseck.

I was in the spice aisle, getting sage, when the next memory hit me like a train. One moment I was smelling the sage, the next I was on a rocky outcropping on the side of a mountain.

It was dusk, and I was seated, scanning the landscape. My arm ached.

"They'll be coming soon," a voice said. I turned to look at the speaker, a woman with long dark hair woven into a loose braid.

"I know," I said. "But we'll be long gone. We'll get to town, do our business, and we'll be gone again before they even show up."

"Gods help us if they do show up," she said. She handed me a cup of cold tea. It smelled strongly of...

...sage. I dropped the herb into my cart and ran to the front of the store. There was nobody at the sole checkout line. I ran past the ends of the aisles and peered down each. She was long gone.

I went back and gathered my cart. Unloading it, I asked the cashier, "Do you know that woman who was just here?"

She didn't stop scanning to answer. "What woman?" she said. "You, me and Sidney are the only ones here, and to be honest, Mr. Cire, Sid and I are closing the place up as soon as you leave. Weather's getting bad out there."

"Tall woman?" I said. "Long salt and pepper hair?"

"Nope," the cashier said. She held out her hand. "Cash or card?"

TUESDAY – CHAPTER 55

I opened the hatch in the back of the jeep and loaded the groceries, already soaking wet, into the cargo area. Kurağa sat in the front seat, looking eagerly at the food. I climbed in front and put the key in the ignition. Kurağa sniffed at my arm.

"Yeah, that's ham you smell. I'm getting the meat, and you're getting the bones," I said. He settled down in his seat, satisfied, while I pulled out my phone and punched in Charlie's number.

"We still on for tonight?" I asked.

"Your call. You're the one driving," he said. "If you want to chickenshit, I'm good. We'll call it a no-show and I'll take the win."

I snorted. "Like hell," I said. "I'll be there. In the meantime, I got a question."

"Like it can't wait?"

"No," I said. Before his fall, Charlie knew the mountains around here like nobody else. He had located cliffs that most people never knew existed. I described to him the scene from my memory.

"Nope," he said. "Nothing like that around here, at least as of twenty years ago, and something like that isn't going to change. Where did you see this? Postcard or something?"

"Long story," I said. "See you tonight. Oh, one other thing, how are you about dogs?"

"Some are assholes, some aren't," he said. "Why?"

"Well, I kind of have one now. Like to bring him with me."

"Seriously, Asa?" He paused. "Well, whatever. As long as he doesn't bite and doesn't shit on the rug. If he does, I'll shoot him."

"Always the gracious host, Charlie. See you tonight." I hung up.

TUESDAY – CHAPTER 56

Kuraĝa looked thoroughly disappointed when I put the ham hocks into the pot. I reassured him that, yes, in fact, the bones would be all his when I was done cooking. The peas were already in there, and the spices. I had deliberately sniffed the sage again, but no other memories were forthcoming.

I put the flame to simmer, sat down at the kitchen table, and reviewed that brief memory for the hundredth time.

I could no longer deny the fact that, apparently, I wasn't who I thought I was. Or was someone more than I knew myself to be. Maybe I had a brain tumor, I thought, pressing on my gray matter and giving me hallucinations. But that couldn't be it, or at least all of it, because Elle Anderson had been real. So was the manuscript. And so was Nev's departure, I thought sadly. And Tanya's upcoming one.

All I knew was what I didn't know. I didn't know where I had come from. I didn't know what I had been doing, at least before coming to Nemaseck. I didn't know where I was going, and I only vaguely remembered getting here.

On the other hand, I knew that for seven years I had been denying not having a memory. For seven years I had waved off my missing self with stock phrases. "It was a long time ago." "You can't remember everything." I had warded myself against my own lack of knowledge, intentionally so. That was one reason I had never asked Tanya much about her past. I didn't want her asking about mine.

My absent memories were not from something that had happened to me. I hadn't been injured or so traumatized that I had forgotten everything.

I knew, somehow, I had done this to myself. For what reason, I had no clue. I decided to look for one.

I started with where I was and opened every drawer and cabinet in the kitchen, looking for something, a utensil, a pot, a dishrag tucked away somewhere, which had come from my past before.

I turned up nothing.

I searched every room in my house, sorting through everything. Unlike the shop and my office there, my house is very neat, very plain,—sparse you might say—though not unlived-in. The result of my search in the other rooms was similarly unrewarding.

I saved the study for last because it was actually here, I thought, that I would be most likely to find a piece of my lost past. I pulled my books from the shelves and looked behind them. I fanned through the pages of each book in hopes of finding a note that said, "Here, Asa. This is who you are," with words that would explain the whole thing to me in 3D and surround sound.

Nothing.

I looked at my altar. Where was it that I had learned to meditate, I wondered. It was an activity that was core to me, essential to who I was, whoever I was. I had no idea of learning how, or when I started.

I shook my head and reached for a pipe. It was time for a smoke. Charlie wouldn't let me at his place.

Wait. My pipes. I scanned the row of them standing up in their rack. Were all of them new?

I looked singly at each one. For all of them, except one, I could identify from whom or where I had bought it and for how much. Except one. One I had no memory of ever purchasing.

I picked it up from the rack and inspected it. It was briar with a rough, sandblasted finish and a deep curve to it. It was stained dark, but the bowl was darker where my fingers had held it for years. Many years. Longer than I knew. This was the pipe I reserved for smoking my precious Balkan Sobranie, the tobacco one couldn't get anymore. I had bought the last of it from a tobacconist in Hungary a couple of years earlier.

Balkan Sobranie is still made, to be sure, but it is not the same tobacco blend that existed forty years ago. The original Balkan Sobranie had been made from Syrian tobacco, grown in fields that were now a wasteland pockmarked by ordnance. That particular Syrian tobacco no longer existed anywhere on this planet, and other similar tobaccos had been substituted for the blend.

Anyone who had smoked the original could tell the difference immediately. And I had craved that taste so deeply that I had found the only remaining stock of the original and bought it at a hefty price. I had less than one pound left and had been looking the past six months for sources I might have previously overlooked.

Still holding the pipe, I went over to my tobacco cabinet and pulled out a tin. I filled the pipe and compressed the tobacco just enough so that it would stay lit. I sat down in my chair and put a match to the bowl.

I sat there, occasionally inhaling the plumes of smoke around my head, hoping that the smell of the burning tobacco would trigger a memory in the same way that the sage had. It did not. But as I emptied my mind and let the cloud gather around me, I was slowly filled with a montage of feelings.

The feeling of being warm and safe. The feeling of comfort and ease, of being surrounded with people I loved and who I knew loved me.

I slowly realized what the problem with Tanya and I had always been. It was not the difference in our ages. She had been an adult well-formed when I met her, not likely to be overwhelmed by a man senior to her. Little, in fact, was capable of overwhelming Tanya. Nor was it that I loved someone else, a someone still unknown in my unknowable past, as Tanya had thought.

It was that in giving up my past, I had given up my ability to have many emotions. At least emotions deeply felt. I felt trepidation but no fear, concern but no shame. Resolve, but no anger. And no love.

I had forgotten not only the people I had loved, but even how to do so. The steps involved in opening your heart and stepping into that opening in another. I had forgotten, not just who I was, but how to be who I was.

And now that was changing. I was beginning to feel all of that again. It hurt like hell.

TUESDAY – CHAPTER 57

I opened the Jeep door and Kuraĝa hopped in and immediately jumped over to the passenger side. I climbed in after him and felt the jeep rocking gently in the gusts of wind.

The rain no longer bothered to come straight down. It moved sideways and peppered my window. The road in front of my house was littered with small branches, and except for a stretch of main road I suspected most of the way to Charlie's would be like that. I put the car in gear, the wipers on high and I eased forward.

Charlie and I had been playing Go weekly for years, almost since I had met him. Charlie was, if nothing else, a strategist, and loved games of all kind so long as they didn't involve luck. For Charlie, it was skill or nothing. He was no slouch at chess, either, and had online chess games going on at any given time of the day.

But for him, as well as me, there was no better game than Go. Both are ancient. Chess was invented about 1500 years ago—most likely in India—and Go has been played for 4000 years, first in China, and later it was exported to other countries. While both are board games focusing on achieving material gain over an opponent, that's about where the comparison ends.

Chess is played by using pieces of different capabilities moved around the board to capture an opponent's pieces. Go is played with stones, each stoned placed at the intersections of a grid of a much larger board, offering 361 points of play compared to the mere 64 squares in chess. Once a stone is placed on the board, it does not move, and capturing stones is accomplished by surrounding them either singly or in groups,

Success in Go is measured not in the number of pieces captured as in the amount of territory you control on the board. A chess player focuses more on tactics, a Go player more on strategy.

As I had hoped, the road had less debris on the highway north of town,. The downside was higher wind that rocked the jeep and forced me to fight to stay in my lane and on the road. I picked up my speed, but not by much. I fussed that the attention I now needed to keep on my driving was preventing me from preparing for the night's game with Charlie like I usually did on my way over to his house.

Though Charlie played a good game, I usually had to spot him two stones to even the sides. Like chess, a player's Go game reflects his personality, and Charlie was methodical, calculating, and persistent. Given a strong position on the board, he made the most of it and kept pushing for more territory.

That was also Charlie's weakness. Go offers a much wider range of possible moves than chess. On the opening move alone, chess allows for twenty possible moves. Go permits hundreds. There is also a balance to Go as players must consider both the yin and the yang. The opportunities to land a killer blow are limited in Go so a player must be cognizant of the fact that if he gains something at one place on the board, he is going to lose something elsewhere.

One is playing both at the level of influencing his opponent's next moves, but also at looking for a direct attack and defense. Charlie, with his constant attention on attack, often lost sight of his opportunities to influence my future moves. I played a softer, gentler game, and looked more for the connections among my stones than the territory they would capture. In doing so, I found the gaps in his own placements and allowed myself to find a position where he did my work for me.

Past the bridge near the Cauldron, I took a right-hand fork where a smaller road descended and traveled closer to the river. On the other side of the trees, the river had already transcended its bank and was creeping through the woods toward the road. Water swirled around the base of birch trees, loosening their hold in the ground. That flooding and the wind would be bringing some of those trees down soon.

It also meant that there was again more debris on the road. I picked my way through it and through the small streams created by water drainage across the road. To my left the land rose sharply. Somewhere above that, unseen, was the main highway.

In the shotgun seat, Kuraĝa stared intently ahead, shifting back and forth as the jeep bounced over limbs and through potholes. A few miles up, the road diverged away from the river where the immediate river valley widened, and a little past that a dirt driveway cut off to the right. That was Charlie's.

In the darkness of the woods, the fading light was reduced even further and I put on my lights to see better.

Seeing better was the whole point of this trip, in fact. If it had just been to play Go, I would have called the whole evening off.

TUESDAY – CHAPTER 58

I drove up Charlie's dirt driveway, and swung around at the top to leave the jeep facing out.

The headlights swept his property across his large garage, almost a barn, and his wheelchair van parked in front of it. There was a sliver of land behind the house itself and a wooden ramp led from it down to a landing below, where Charlie would go to fish.

Charlie's house was built almost at the river's edge and between the landing and his house, a wood retaining wall held back the soil his house was perched on.

I got out and Kuraĝa jumped over my seat and landed on the wet ground. I went around to the back of the jeep to pull out the groceries I had picked up for Charlie. Holding the sodden bag from the bottom, I walked up the ramp to his front door and we went inside.

Inside, the house was lit up as bright as day and I walked through the small living room. Charlie was in his kitchen. I dumped the bag on his kitchen table.

Charlie eyed me. "Just make yourself at home, why don't you, Asa? Who's the wolf?"

"Kuraĝa," I said. "He's not a wolf, he's a—"

"I know, he's an akita. Looks like a wolf to me."

"Don't be a jerk and he'll be fine," I said. I pulled out a bag of chips from the bag and fished through it for the jar of salsa. "You always have crap to eat here so I brought my own." I left the rest of the bag on the table with the food I'd picked up for Charlie in case he got stuck out there during the storm.

"What's the rest of it for?" Charlie asked.

"Did some shopping. Figured you wouldn't mind if I brought some stuff over, 'case you get blown over out here."

"I do mind, but what the hell, food's food," Charlie said. "Go on in. I'll bring in the coffee."

I walked down the short back hallway that opened up into a large room running the width of the house. A cushioned bench ran across the back wall. Windows looked out over the river, but in the fading light I could barely see the landing, already underwater. The current beyond it rushed by with unusual ferocity.

On one wall were photographs from Charlie's military service and framed medals and commendations. Another wall had pictures of cliffs and mountains and young men in shorts with ropes slung across their shoulders and carabiners hanging from webbed harnesses.

Charlie wheeled himself in with a tray on his lap holding a carafe of coffee and cups.

"You worried about getting flooded?" I asked.

"Naw," Charlie said. "That wall is about six feet high. River comes up that high, we're all screwed. It'll never happen."

He rolled over to the middle of the room where a table holding the Go board was sitting. It was a slab of light colored wood, about five inches thick, resting on round wood feet. The top of the board was criss-crossed by a grid of lines. On one side were two small ceramic bowls containing the playing stones, each stone about the shape of a large lozenge. One bowl contained the black stones, the other white. During play, the stones were placed on the intersections of the lines.

The table looked rectangular from where I stood, but I knew that was so it would present the illusion of being square when Charlie and I were sitting at it. I wandered over to the climbing pictures.

"You climbed some incredible cliffs," I said.

"Sure did," Charlie said and rolled over next to me. "Climbed a lot of them solo, too."

"Who are the climbers in the pictures?"

"Just guys. None of them around any more. A couple died climbing out west, one wandered up to Alaska to be a guide. I dunno what happened to the other two. Just drifted away," he said. "I wasn't paying much attention after my accident."

"Got any pictures of the cliff you fell from?"

"Naw," he said. "That fucker was way out in the backcountry. Took me hours to get there so I didn't have time to stand around playing with a camera. They say there's some old Native American caves back around there, but I didn't see any caves." He laughed, a short, bitter, bark. "Wasn't in any condition to look for 'em afterwards."

"God, that must have been awful," I said. "Lying there, dying, like that."

"I was in shock," Charlie said, "so I don't remember much of it, to be honest. I'd blacked out and then people were all around me rolling me onto a backboard. So pathetic," he said. "I don't know how they found me."

"They were pathetic?"

"Yeah. They should have let me die."

"Well, it wasn't too long after Elle Anderson had been murdered," I said. "Nobody would have wanted the town's star climber to go, too."

"Jesus, Asa, are you still onto that bullshit? She's dead, book's been written, end of story. Let it go for Chrissakes."

"They never found the killer," I said.

"They never will. Who cares? Did you come here to play Go or just bullshit, anyway?" He wheeled over to the table. "I'm white, you're black. Quit yapping and sit down."

TUESDAY – CHAPTER 59

I sat down on front of the board and dipped my hand into the bowl of stones.

"How many you want?" I asked.

"None."

"Really? Getting a little cocky, aren't you?"

"Maybe you're the one getting cocky, Cire. Let's do it." He put his first stone on the board. It was not his usual opening. Charlie almost always opened with a stone on one of the star points equidistant from each side of the board. Such an opening expressed an outward, attacking stance. This time he was immediately looking to stake out some territory in the corner.

Curious as to what he was up to, I placed a stone on a star point near my side. Within a few moves, we had pretty much established our corner positions. I reached out in an attacking move and placed my next stone clear across the board on his side. My purpose was twofold, to keep him from connecting his two corners and to begin establishing a base in the middle.

If he were going for the corners, I'd let him have them. I'd own the middle.

Sure enough, three moves later, we were involved in a brawl on one of my corners. I pulled it to a draw and again went for the middle, figuring that if I played that fight correctly, I'd be able to cut off his corner stones and convert the draw into my territory. Early in the game I wanted to establish boxes of territory—maybe only established by my stones on the corner—but which provided an outer line of defense for the points inside.

I quickly put together a box on the left side, but a few moves later, Charlie had managed to create a bigger, rectangular box around mine. I began trying to figure out how to extend my line outside and connect up with my advancing stones on the other side, and then I saw it.

It had nothing to do with the game.

In my mind I had been drawing the imaginary lines that were the two territories—mine inside his—when I realized I had seen this before. The image corresponded exactly with one of the characters I had drawn when trying to translate the manuscript. Same shape. Same positions. Same ratio of the sides.

I sucked in my breath and reached for my cup of coffee.

Such an outward display of emotion was rarely seen in Go. It was worse than raising an eyebrow when picking up a card in poker. I sat back and looked at the squares again.

Coincidence? Must be.

Charlie, probably thinking my surprise was concern for an unseen threat, permitted himself a faint smile. He thought the focus of my attention was on the board. It wasn't.

In my mind I was recalling the sequence of my translated characters, the squares and rectangles I had written. I could see that one character in my mind's eye, about one third of the way down the page, as well as the characters that followed it.

I put the image out of my mind and put my attention on the board once more. I knew a way out of this, but it would be a little indirect. I placed my next stone in another group, where it posed a threat—but not a strong one—to some of Charlie's stones. I knew that he would think my move was to draw him away from his attempt to enclose my stones. I also knew that he would ignore it. The core of Charlie's playing, instead, was to spot a weakness and attack it.

He did just that with his next stone to further endanger my grouping on the side. At the same time he ended up creating the same configuration that had been the next character in my manuscript—not with those two squares we had been fighting over, but by overlapping them.

I had already decided on my next move. Using the next character in my mind's eye, I placed my stone on the board to recreate the next sequence from the rectangle characters I had written. Charlie paused—it was an entirely incorrect move, from any logical standpoint—and quickly placed his next stone.

We were playing the manuscript.

Or my translation of it. From that point on, each of our moves corresponded spatially to another character, as if we were putting one character on top of the other. The lines grew more complex as more and more characters intersected, but without thought to strategy or tactic, I recreated each succeeding character.

Even more puzzling, so did Charlie's moves.

As the game proceeded, I began estimating the amount of territory we were both accumulating. It was close. At one point I was up by five points, but that advantage disappeared over the next few moves, and then he pulled ahead.

We moved into the end game, and the play went faster, but I continued to stick with the script, no matter how counterintuitive the play felt to me. Eventually I reached the end of the page in my mind, and I put my last stone down. I passed on my next move.

Charlie placed another stone, filling a space he already owned. He wasn't ready to quit.

I passed again. Charlie looked at me and nodded.

"I'll pass," he said.

We scored the board.

I won, by a point.

TUESDAY – CHAPTER 60

Charlie rolled back from the table, visibly angry.

"What the hell was that all about, Cire?"

"Just playing Go," I said.

"Playing like an asshole," Charlie replied.

"I still won."

Charlie rolled forward and swept his hand across the board, scattering the stones over the floor. Kuraĝa, who had been sitting quietly, stood up, his ears pointed forward.

"What the hell, Charlie?"

He looked at me. A cold, hard stare, daring me to drop my eyes, to look away. I didn't.

"You sonofabitch," he said. "You were toying with me. You were jerking my chain the whole damn time, weren't you? Just had to have a laugh on me, didn't you?"

Charlie always seemed on the edge of angry, but this was different. This was a gasket blowing in the armor of control he always had about him. This was dangerous. I was suddenly glad that he was in a wheelchair.

I continued to meet his gaze, calmly.

"Ease up, Charlie," I said. "It's just a game."

"Everything's a fucking game to you, isn't it, Cire? You're always playing around with people, aren't you? All smoke and mirrors. You just fuck with them and fuck with them and then get what you want and leave. 'Here. Here's some money, Charlie. Here, Charlie, you're broke. Why don't you take this food?' Just your way of making yourself better than everyone else. Go to hell, Cire. Get out of here."

I heard a low growl coming from Kuraĝa's throat and I lay my hand on his neck.

"Easy, boy," I said.

I looked back at Charlie. There was a .45, dark and sturdy, in his hand.

"Hey, " I said. "Put that thing away."

His hand didn't move. "Get out of here," he repeated.

I tapped Kuraĝa on the shoulder. "Let's go, Kuraĝa." I stood up and backed out of the room, turned and then hot-footed it out of Charlie's house.

TUESDAY – CHAPTER 61

I opened the door to the jeep, jumped in after Kuraĝa and pulled straight out, glad I didn't have to take any time to turn around.

We were halfway down Charlie's driveway before I fumbled the lights on, and we were pulling out onto the river road when I took my first breath. We turned south, and I began picking my way through puddles and over fallen limbs.

"What the hell was that?" I asked Kuraĝa, still looking like he was ready to lunge at something. He had felt exactly what I had in there, a massive tsunami of anger rolling out of Charlie.

There was no reason Charlie should have been so angry. It was—as I'd told him—just a game of Go. He'd lost plenty of times before. I had, too, though less often than he. What the hell.

As I drove, I thought back over the game in my mind, move by move. I had played a strange game, yes, letting myself be guided by the manuscript. Many of my moves were simply wrong, by any standard, and would have been suicide. Yet I still won.

Just as importantly, I hadn't doubted that I would.

I tried putting myself in Charlie's mind. We had played each other so many times, we each knew the other's preferred strategy. Sometimes I would accurately predict Charlie's next move, and I had no doubt that he often saw mine as well. Even though he had begun tonight's game differently than he normally did, my abrupt departure from my normal routine was no doubt unsettling to him. At the same time, some of my moves looked like bad play, but then I would pull it back, and then put myself in a hole again, and again pull it back.

Thinking about it, I realized I could not, would not, have been able to pull that off under my own direction.

Looking at our game that way, Charlie's reaction was somewhat predictable. He saw me toying with him, of making fun of his best effort. Nobody plans to lose, but tonight, especially, he had been sure of his strength. He didn't even want a handicap. He was planning on a big win. Then, to him, I had essentially made fun of him.

But still. A gun? I mean, Charlie and I were friends, though his reserve made closeness difficult.

But a gun?

It was a common belief that Charlie had pretty bad PTSD. Charlie had once told me, "The Marines don't make good men. They make angry men. And then they cut them loose when they're no longer useful."

Something about that game had triggered that tidal wave of anger, or maybe something else had. Maybe he was more worried about the storm than he let on. Maybe something else was going on that I didn't know about.

I was getting close to where the river road joined up with the highway when I noticed somebody had left me a voicemail. I pulled right to a stop, not really bothering to pull over. Who the hell would be on this road at this time of night?

It was Tanya. "Hi, Asa," she'd said. "I was calling to see if you were going to be at your shop tomorrow afternoon. I wanted to stop by, just for a couple of minutes."

I smiled hearing the sound of her voice.

"I'll be there," I texted back and put the phone down.

I drove on, but didn't pick up much speed because the wind was gusting and pushing the jeep all over the road. Maybe Tanya had decided not to go to the monastery after all, I thought. Maybe she was going to stick around.

I thought about telling her what happened with Charlie. She had never been his biggest fan. In fact, she'd never liked him much at all. When I'd asked her about him once, she shook her head.

"There's something off about that guy," she said. "He's got a thing with women."

"I never noticed," I said.

"Well, you've never seen him with one, have you?" she'd said. "But if you were a woman, you'd notice. It's the way he looks at you. Part loathing, part desire." She shivered. "He's got a screw loose, Asa. I wouldn't be alone with him if you paid me."

It hit me. That time Tanya had showed me the Native American cave, nestled in the bottom of that cliff. Way back in the woods. The way Charlie kept pushing back about Elle, getting angry any time I mentioned her. The knife I had found in the cave, military issue, sitting there cold as death itself. It was Charlie who had told me about the tattoo that had been cut off Elle. The flaying of the dead girl that nobody was supposed to know about.

But Charlie did.

A gust smacked into the jeep, rocking it, and I realized I had come to a dead stop in the road. I put the car back into gear and pulled forward against the wind.

It was Charlie.

Now I had to figure out what to do about it.

WEDNESDAY – CHAPTER 62

Kuraĝa and I walked to the shop the next morning.

We leaned against the wind and picked our way through the debris, and we were both sopping wet by the time we got there. Kuraĝa walked in the door behind me, stood, and shook himself off. Watching a hundred pound dog shake himself dry is nothing less than spectacular. Water sprayed around the shop like a fire hose with a bum nozzle.

"You done, boy?" I asked him when he stopped. He looked at me, rather smugly I thought, and trotted back to the office to settle down on his oriental rug. I followed.

I walked over to the trash can and fished through the Chinese take-out boxes until I found my translation page. I sat down, smoothed out the paper on the desk, and looked at it.

It was nothing like I remembered. Yes, it was all rectangles and boxes and squares and boxes within boxes, but it was not the sequence of shapes that I had played last night, and it certainly wasn't the sequence that I thought I had remembered. It was completely different.

The hell, I thought. What nonsense is this?

I read through it again. These were clearly not the same shapes that had guided my moves the night before.

Just for giggles, I pulled out a portable Go board from my bookcase and began playing a game based entirely on the same way I had interpreted the characters last night. It turned out a nonsense game, full of errors, requiring stones to be placed on intersections already occupied or that crossed into occupied territory. It was madness.

I shoved the board away from me and closed my eyes.

That yielded nothing. I opened them again and grabbed a pipe from the rack on the desk. I filled it with a Virginia-burley blend, something that was undemanding but still had some flavor. After getting it lit, I pulled a few long draws on it and released a plume of smoke from my mouth into the air. I watched the smoke curl and twist and fold in on itself.

That process—the process of filling, tamping, lighting, and drawing—was part of the pleasure derived from pipes. If you filled a pipe too tightly, it felt like you were sucking on a milkshake straw and the pipe would require constant re-lights. Not tight enough and it would burn hot to ashes in a few minutes, losing its flavor and burning your tongue in the process. Just right, and you would have a pleasant time for forty minutes or more and not have to think much about it while you went about your business.

I watched the smoke rise, changing shapes as it moved with whatever air drafts it encountered. That's what this manuscript felt like, I thought. Like smoke.

Every time I looked at it, the characters had a different shape. They changed with whatever invisible currents it felt. Even my own odd re-creation of the first page had changed. What I looked at today was not what I would see tomorrow. The manuscript morphed over time.

Or did it?

What if I were the smoke, and the manuscript the pipe? The manuscript wasn't changing. It was how I saw it each time I looked at it. What had Charlie said during his irrational rant last night? "It's all smoke and mirrors."

Yes, Charlie, you're exactly right. I am just smoke and mirrors, a man with no past and quite possibly no future, throwing up illusions about myself to hide the fact that I am essentially nothing.

No thing.

Suddenly three things happened at once. The door to the shop slammed open, Kuraḡa stood up and barked. I heard the sound of many heavy feet entering the store.

"This is it, boy," I said to the dog. "Bite 'em if you got 'em."

WEDNESDAY – CHAPTER 63

I stepped to the door of my shop and saw Peterson and another state trooper, both wearing raingear, and four men in blue jackets with "Forensics" printed in yellow on the back.

The lab guys had already fanned out into the shop and were starting to pull stuff off of the shelves. I put my hand on Kuraĝa to stop him from lunging forward.

"Asa Cire," Peterson said rather formally, "I have here a warrant giving us legal permission to search your premises and remove any items that we find material to our investigation." He reached in his jacket pocket and held it out. "Would you like to see it?" he asked.

I waved my hand at it. "Put it away," I said. "And good morning to you, Trooper Peterson. Pleasant morning for a duck, isn't it?"

He looked at me for a second, trying to figure out if I had just insulted him.

"We'd appreciate your cooperation in the search, Asa." he said.

"Just as I would appreciate your not making too much of a wreck of things. Can you tell your guys not to break anything valuable? And by that I mean everything in the shop."

"We'll be as careful as we need to be," Peterson said. He was giving away nothing.

I looked at the crew making their way methodically through the untidiness.

"Looks like this might take a while," I said. "Can I offer you and your friend there..."

"This is Trooper Maloney," Peterson said.

"Well, can I offer you and Trooper Maloney some coffee while these men do their work?"

"Sure," Peterson said.

He and Maloney climbed the steps to my office.

WEDNESDAY – CHAPTER 64

Coffee made, Peterson and Maloney's coats and hats now hanging on the rack, I finally sat down.

Maloney barely fit into the chair I'd offered him. He was a big slab of beef, red-cheeked and red-headed, a guy central casting would have sent if I had called down and said, "I need a cop." He was clearly younger than Peterson and, I would have guessed, a guy on the go. The Nemaseck beat was not in his future if he had anything to say about it.

Maloney squeezed between the arms of the chair, squiggling his duty belt through the restriction. Once settled, his big hands tapped a quick beat on the armrests.

I looked at Peterson. "This about Nev?"

He nodded. "She's now officially wanted for questioning." His words were a shrug, as if to say, "I did what I could."

"She's disappeared," Maloney said, playing it gruff, because he seemed to think Peterson was doing the good cop shtick. Maybe he was, for all I knew, but then again, I knew what Peterson thought of Nev.

Peterson nodded at the dog, now sitting next to me, ears pricked forward at attention.

"What the fuck is that?" he said.

"It's a dog. You can call him Dog. I got him for protection, you know, after the whole looter thing."

"That the only reason?" Peterson said, squinting at me.

"No. He also makes a mean pulled pork," I said. "What the hell, Peterson. What's going on?"

Maloney leaned forward, itching to push me a bit, but with one glance Peterson put him back.

"That gun we found? You know it matched the slug in the burned guy in the car, and it's also been linked to two other murders in New York."

"Guess her husband was a busy guy," I said.

"Sure, before he was sent upstate," Peterson said. "But when the guy in the Beemer was killed, Nev's guy was sitting in an AA meeting behind three locked doors and a guard station. We all had a meeting and discussed it and decided that he probably didn't really do that shooting," Peterson said. "But Nev could have."

"So you tossed her apartment, didn't find anything, and then decided to come make a mess of things for a hardworking town merchant," I said. "Sure, makes sense. She kept her secret stash of guns in the bathroom, and we posted a list of the people she wanted to kill in the front window last week."

At that, Maloney popped up like a jack-in-the-box, as I knew he would.

"Look, you want to come down to the station, no problem, we can put you in cuffs and-" he said.

"Shut the fuck up, Maloney," Peterson said. "Cire's a smart-ass. Cuffs will make him worse." He turned back to me. "You are also a person of interest, Asa, but we don't need to make this all hard and ugly."

"No problem, Trooper," I said. "I'm cooperating as best I can. If Nev is a killer, she needs to see justice."

I could almost see Peterson's eyes roll, and I thought for a minute I'd overplayed it. A tech stepped into the office with Nev's laptop.

"We need the password for this computer," he said. Peterson looked at me.

I shrugged. "Damn if I know," I said. "Nev was in charge of keeping the computers secure, not me."

"Ok," the tech said. "We'll take it back to the barracks. It'll take a little bit longer, but we can still get the data off it." He popped back out.

I would have bet him my next paycheck right then that all he would find would be random 1's and 0's. Nev's like that.

"That reminds me, Cire," Peterson said. "We'll need your computer too. I guess you know the password to that one, right?"

I turned around, closed the lid on my laptop, and unplugged it. I handed it to Maloney.

"Here's the *passvorto*," I said and wrote down the fourteen character password on a post-it note. I handed that to Maloney. It wasn't much, but at least I was giving the poor schmuck something to do with his hands.

"What?" Maloney asked.

"That's password in Esperanto."

He looked at me blankly.

My first assessment had been wrong. That kid was dumber than an empty beer bottle.

"So we searched Ms. Arias' apartment," Peterson said, "and we didn't find much. In fact, we didn't find fuck-all. In fact, it didn't even look like anyone lived there. You know anything about that?"

I shrugged again. "I was her employer, not her friend," I said. I saw no reason to go into the whole father-daughter complex that was our relationship. "I don't think I was ever over there."

"Well, we are going to find her," Maloney said, "and when we do, we will apply the full weight of the law against her."

I eyed him up and down. "Well, that would be considerable," I said. "But really? 'Full weight of the law?' You get help figuring out that line, or did you come up with it all by yourself?"

Maloney tried to stand up, no doubt to get a good lean on me, but he got caught on the arms of the chair. While he was struggling his way out, Peterson stood up.

"Christ, Asa," he said. "We were trying to be considerate here."

One of the techs came into my office and began to search it. He was thorough, and not making too much of a mess. Finally he looked at me and spoke.

"Mr. Cire, we need to look into your safe."

"No problem," I said and spun open the lock. There, on the top shelf, was Nev's gun and bullets. Maloney pounced forward.

"What's this?" he said. He slipped on a latex glove and reached for it.

"A gun," I said. "Well, a 9mm to be more accurate. I have a carry permit. Would you like to see it?"

Peterson looked over Maloney's shoulder while he pulled out the gun, the magazine and the bullets and put them in an evidence bag.

"Yes, Asa," Peterson said, "Kept exactly like anyone would keep a gun for protection, the magazine empty and the rounds scattered all over hell and back." He looked at me, then at Maloney. "Feel free to fingerprint them, son, but it's gonna be nothing but Cire all over them. And he does have a permit. I was the guy who signed off on it."

Peterson looked back at me and shook his head. "Goddamn, Asa," he said.

He turned to the team. "Let's get the fuck out of here. We're done with this joint."

After the crowd had left, I scanned the shop. They hadn't made too much of a mess, at least not much more than it had already been in. I looked at Kuraĝa.

"You know what the best part of this was?" I said. "It was the password. Nev set it up that if you typed in one password, you'd get in. Type another one in, and the solid state disc would erase itself and write over the data in a millisecond. You'd still think the computer was booting up before you realized the disk had gone south. I gave them the second one. And all of our data is still tucked away on a server in Switzerland where nobody can get to it but she and I."

I patted Kuraĝa's head.

"I really do miss that gal," I said.

WEDNESDAY – CHAPTER 65

I spent the next couple of hours straightening up and taking an informal inventory to see what else the cops might have taken with them.

All that was missing were a couple of invoices that were printed out for my old-school clients who wanted things like that on paper and, oddly enough, the maul Nev had beat up her phone with.

"Ah," I said to Kuraĝa. "Somebody must have had their head cracked open in that crash. They want to compare impact signatures. Nothing like a good ol' blunt trauma to warm the blood of a cop."

Kuraĝa was busy sniffing around and barely looked up at me.

I climbed the stairs back to my office to continue examining the manuscript and figure out what to do about Charlie.

I was all but certain of his role in Ellle Anderson's death, but I basically had nothing. A couple of coincidences and a bad attitude on a stormy night weren't something you can hang a conviction on, or even an arrest, for that matter.

Any material evidence was long gone by now. Particularly if Charlie actually had done it. He was methodical that way. The knife was a bit of an outlier, though. Why leave it in that cave instead of chucking it in the river? That didn't quite make sense.

I thought for a second and tried to remember what I had done with the knife after I had taken it out of the cave when Tanya and I left. My memory of anything before Nemaseck was lost, but I had little trouble with anything after that.

I hadn't liked that knife at the time—not at all—even long before I knew what it had been used for. I had chucked it into my bin of garden tools, among the clippers and mauls and whatnot. It was probably still there, for all I knew. I hadn't given it much thought since.

A gust of rain-filled wind hit the windows like a hammer and I thought for a second that they would break. At the same time the lamp on my desk flickered. Another gust hit and the lamp went out entirely. We'd lost power.

"Running out of time," I said to nobody in particular.

I rummaged around my shelves until I found a candle and its holder and lit it. Though noon hadn't even arrived yet, it was dark inside the building and I needed that little light to dispel the gloom. I leaned back in my chair. It squeaked. I closed my eyes.

It wasn't too long before she showed up. I had known she would. Ghosts are nothing if not predictable. They're usually somewhere for a single purpose and they hammer away at that purpose with all of their vaporous might, usually mingled with a considerable amount of frustration because their influence in the material world was minimal.

How did I know that? I wondered. I let my breathing settle and my mind empty.

I was standing on the landing above the Cauldron and looking out toward the rapids where the water shoved it's way in. She stood, unmoving in the midst of the current, submerged to her knees. Her arm was red and bleeding where the tattoo had been.

She wasn't looking at me. She was looking at an infant—white as chalk and unmoving—that she cradled in her arms. Tears were running down her face and dripping onto the child.

Slowly, she looked up at me, eyes full of all the pain that a mother can feel. Then, without warning, she was pulled below the waves as if her feet had been grabbed and jerked out from under her.

I fell forward in my chair. I was back in my office. Kuraĝa was growling, deep in his throat, his hackles up, standing next to my chair, looking at nothing.

I rubbed his snout. "It's ok, boy," I said. "Just a ghost. That's all."

Two ghosts, I thought, but one who had never been. I knew why, and I knew why Charlie had killed Elle Anderson.

There was something else that Peterson hadn't bothered to tell me, but it gave me a way, a gate to proving Charlie's guilt.

DNA testing was in its infancy when Elle was murdered, but hers was an open case. They surely would have preserved samples from a murdered, pregnant girl. If I could get a sample of Charlie's DNA to Peterson and it proved paternity, that new information would give the cops enough to go after Charlie. Maybe they could then find the evidence that would convict him. I wondered what the statute of limitations was on statutory rape.

All I had to do was get some of Charlie's DNA. I began considering how I to do that, and I wondered how somebody I had thought was a friend could have turned out to be so evil. I began thinking how to possibly use this with Peterson and leverage a shutdown on the pursuit of Nev. Then my eyelids got heavy and I fell asleep.

That happens sometimes when you're old.

WEDNESDAY – CHAPTER 66

I don't know how long I'd been asleep, but I was jarred awake by the door slamming open again.

Kuraĝa sat up, looked out the office door and then jumped forward and ran out. I followed.

It was Tanya, all wrapped up in raingear. She was kneeling and rubbing Kuraĝa's face with both hands, her face inches from his snout.

"Been a good boy?" she asked him as he licked her. She patted him on the head and stood up.

"What's up with you?" she said and looked me up and down.

"I was napping," I said. "Visit from the cops this morning wore me out and all. They didn't bring any donuts."

"Now what? Do I even want to know?"

"Not sure," I said.

She looked around the shop. "So much stuff here, Asa, so much stuff."

She walked over to a shelf and picked up a white flower that had been carved out of wood and stained white. Even in the dim light, it stood out. The carving had been so delicate that the flower almost looked real.

"I always thought that this flower was so lovely. I don't know why you've never sold it."

"My price was too high," I said. "It's a white peony, called *bai mudan* in Chinese. It was one of my first purchases when I got to Nemaseck, from a wood carver in Maine. He lived way back in the boonies. I visited him, took hours to get there. His studio was filled with flowers he'd carved, all of them looking as realistic as this. Something about this one really grabbed me, and it was the only thing I bought from him. I thought I might buy more, but not long after I was there, I heard his place burned down. He died in the fire."

"So why the high price?" Tanya asked. "One of a kind?"

"Well, it was one-of-a-kind from an unknown artist, so that didn't really set the price," I said. "Fact of the matter is, I never really wanted to sell it. I saw you check it out every time you came here, and I knew you liked it."

She looked at me for a long second, sadness on her normally serene face.

"You trying to make me cry, Asa Cire? Because that's what's going to happen if you keep talking."

I smiled back, my smile as sad as the look on her face.

"No. I'm sorry, Tanya. C'mon back. Take your coat off. I don't really know why you're here. You didn't say in your message."

"I can't stay long, Asa." She said, picking a box up off the floor. "I really only dropped by to give you this."

"A gift? For what?"

"Just open it." She bit her lip.

I set the box down and untangled the flaps without ripping them. I looked inside, and then pulled the contents out. There, wrapped in paper, were the teacups and the pot that Tanya and I had always used after our yoga together.

"I know these," I said. "You're giving them to me, because..."

"Because I'm leaving," Tanya said.

"Yes, but in a month or two, I thought. We have plenty of time for goodbyes after the storm."

"Not really, Asa," Tanya said. "I'm leaving as soon as the hurricane goes through. I got Alexandria Masterson to manage the property and sell it. By tomorrow I'll have everything packed up and ready to go. I've already got buyers for the yoga equipment and my furniture, and what's left will go into a storage unit. I can't bring anything with me to the monastery, you know."

I sat down on the steps to my office. "So this is the goodbye visit, then," I said.

"This is the goodbye visit. Honestly, Asa, I don't know what to say to you. Except that." She pointed to the cups and teapot. "You know, in Buddhism, we are supposed to let go of everything. Let go of our attachments holding us to samsara, to this illusion we live in. And I have. I've been able to let go of everything. I can still work with herbs and health at the monastery, even more so than I've been able to here. So I've let go of everything but you. Everything but you, Asa, I don't know why." Now she was crying. Kuraĝa nuzzled up against her and she wiped her eyes. "But I have to. You know that."

I nodded to her, almost formally.

"I know that, Tanya, as sure as I had known that I would fall in love with you someday. I'm sorry that it was too late. Too, I don't know, too much unsaid. I guess I figured you would always have been around here. That we had all of time."

"We did, Asa. We do." Tanya said. "We have all of time, right in every moment. There is nothing else."

"There is nothing else," I repeated.

We looked at each other, she standing there in her raincoat, me sitting on the steps, and I felt tears running down my face as well.

"Well," I finally,said, "if all we have is the now, let's make this last now happier than just this."

"What do you mean?"

"Let's go to the landing at the Cauldron."

"What?" Tanya said. "Are you kidding?"

"No," I said, smiling. "How many times have we been there, three, six, a million? We both love it there, the water pounding on the rocks, the mist rising up . . . can you imagine what it's like right now?"

"You're nuts," Tanya said.

"That may be," I said, "but look, if this is going to be the last time I see you, I'll be damned if it's standing in this dingy shop with no lights, both of us crying our eyes out. I want something to be the now you remember in the future."

"Asa, in case you haven't noticed, there's a hurricane out there right now. It's about as bad as it's going to get, they say."

"This is nothing, Tanya. Remember that time we were driving up in the mountains, looking for some damn plant you wanted, and the—"

"—and the 'Beware of Falling Rock' sign came true?"

"And all I could do was gun the jeep and hope we got past the rock slide before the last one came down?"

Tanya started laughing. "Right behind us. Right behind us! You wanted to take that rock home as a souvenir!"

"Yeah, like that, Tanya," I said. "Let's go."

I ran up to my office and grabbed my jacket before she changed her mind.

WEDNESDAY – CHAPTER 67

We stepped outside and I slammed the door shut and locked it. I don't know why I bothered.

The entire town was deserted. The stop lights near us were off and it looked like the ones further down the street were sagging, as if the poles were coming down. Her car and mine were the only ones out front. There wasn't another car anywhere along the street.

We ran to the jeep and got in, Kuraĝa jumping into the back and hitting the rear view mirror as he went. I adjusted the mirror and got a look at my face. My gray hair was soaking wet and plastered to the side of my head. My beard was covered with droplets of water. Everything about me looked exhausted, tired and worn.

Except my eyes. My eyes sparkled.

As we rolled up West Street toward the two-lane highway that would take us to the Cauldron, I glanced over at Tanya.

"So you want to know what's going on, or would that make it harder to let go?"

"I suppose you're going to tell me, whether I want to hear it or not, so go ahead," Tanya said.

I dumped everything. Two attempted kidnappings, Nev saving me with an extraordinarily well-aimed bullet, cops, and finally Charlie, and what I believed Elle's ghost had shown me.

"I knew it," she said.

I risked another glance at her. "You knew Charlie killed the girl?" I said.

"No. I mean I knew he was a shitheel. I told you before, he gives me the creeps."

I thought for a minute. "Did you know him back in the day? Back when you and Elle were in school?"

"I knew *of* him, of course. Everybody knew about the war hero who had come back home and had become one of the biggest climbers on the East Coast," she said. "But I didn't know him personally. He would have been seven, eight years older than me. And I kept myself well-distanced from people back then. Ice Queen, remember?"

"I wonder what happened to his family," I said.

"None left, if I remember right," Tanya said. "Dad died before he left. Mom died of uncontrolled diabetes or a heart attack or something like that. Papers always mentioned that in stories about him because the Army wouldn't let him come home. It was back when they were still doing forced deployments, even if your enlistment was up."

"Damn. So he came back to nothing, angry and alone and full of PTSD," I said. "That's the devil's brew right there."

"And twisted. I don't know if he was always that way, but when I met him, I knew something was wrong with him, deep in his core."

"Asa!" Tanya suddenly shouted. "Watch out!"

I saw it, but it was too late. A trash can blew right into the jeep, hit the grill and bounced up. I heard it hit the roof and then saw it tumbling down the road behind me.

"Damn," I said. "Beware of Falling Trash Cans."

Tanya laughed. "Beware of cloth roofs," she said, reaching up and behind her. She stuck her hand through the new rip in the roof and waved it around in the rain. "This will need more than duct tape. And Kuraǧa is going to get soaked."

"Meh," I said. "He doesn't care. And I'll get some extra-wide duct tape and fix it."

"Some things can't be fixed, Asa," she said.

"Like us?" I wrestled against the wind to keep the jeep on the road.

"Like you," Tanya said. "Asa, do you have any idea what happened to you?"

I listened to the wind and the rain – far louder even than my sigh – as it pounded against the jeep.

"I think you might be right, Tanya," I said. "Something's missing. But I wasn't in an accident, I don't have a tumor, I just—I just don't know. Maybe I did it to myself for some reason. I dunno. All of a sudden, I've been getting glimpses of things. Little pieces. Like the other day I thought I saw this woman in the supermarket. Hell, I did see this woman in the supermarket. She was pushing a cart. We talked. Then I walked down to the spice rack and suddenly had this memory of her and I, on a mountain, on an outcropping. We were being chased, I think."

"The love of your life?" Tanya asked. She spoke her words carefully.

"No, nothing like that. More like an associate or a business partner. Not lovers, I'm sure of that." I looked at Tanya. "Still matters, doesn't it?"

"It shouldn't. But it does."

We were both silent for a minute. "What happens if you can't let go, Tanya? What do you do then?"

She bit her lip and looked out at the road ahead.

"I don't know, Asa. I won't...I can't come back here. I don't care if I never see Nemaseck again in my life. I imagine I'll stay at the monastery and meditate, and walk, and cook rice, and talk to plants until that's all that's left. Until everything else is burned away. You know, that's what the Buddha did, Asa. He had a wife and a son, but when it was time for him to find enlightenment, he picked up and left. Left everything behind. And I can't help but wonder if it was the pain of that separation that helped propel him through all he had to go through to find the dharma. Maybe that's the way it will be for me. Maybe that's the way it is for all of us who search for more."

The road up ahead began to curve and beyond was the bridge over the Cauldron. The pull-off for the landing was right around the curve, but we weren't close enough to the river to see it yet.

"We're almost there Tanya," I said. "I wonder what it will look like today."

WEDNESDAY – CHAPTER 68

I pulled the jeep to a stop on the berm of the paved road. I wasn't going to go down a dirt road only to get stuck in the mud and not get out.

The jeep rocked in the wind as we got out. Kuraĝa followed Tanya out the passenger's side and she and I both pulled our coats around us—for what little good it did—and we began walking down the rutted dirt road to the landing below. Kuraĝa ran ahead of us, but not too far. He kept looking back to make sure we were following him.

As we got down to the river's bank, the road leveled out. Ahead of us we could barely make out the landing, a half-circle patch of dirt and gravel at the edge of the river, surrounded by a half-acre grassy field. During good weather people would drive their cars down the dirt road and park them there. On the far side of the turnaround—if you knew where to look—a trail canted up the side of riverbank, the same trail that had begun our trek to the cave.

That summer day, its joy and beauty, seemed so far away now.

"Remember our trip to the cave, Tanya?" I asked.

"I'll never forget it," she said.

"Did you ever go back?"

"No," she said. "Did you?"

"No. And we never went back together."

"I didn't feel right there, Asa," she said. "That cave didn't belong to us. It belonged to another time, other people."

"And other gods," I said.

"You never mentioned it again," Tanya said. "Why not?"

"Well, you didn't either."

She stopped walking and looked at me. "Do you remember what we saw there? That vision we had together?"

"Of course."

"It scared me, Asa," Tanya said.

"Why? How? Did it—"

"Do you know how close our minds had to be to see the same thing? How close our spirits must have been together at that point? I've never..." She broke off for a second, thinking. "Don't take this wrong, Asa, but I've never wanted to be that intimate with anyone. That was the most intimate experience of my life, and to be honest, it made me want to run. Run away. Run anywhere."

The water ran off my beard and onto my chest. It was just following gravity, though, not running away from anything.

"It was a message for us," I said. "For the two of us."

"And it said....?"

"I don't know, Tanya. I've often thought of it, the two of us, standing on the shore of a gray ocean, the wind and the waves. I've always thought that we were supposed to see that. Something intended us to see what we saw. But I've never known what the message was." I shrugged. "Maybe I'm wrong. Maybe there was no message at all. And maybe there is no meaning to this."

"I'm a Buddhist, remember?" Tanya said. "And a Zen Buddhist, at that, None of this has any meaning at all. It's just illusion. Illusions keep us here, keep us from realizing our true nature. There's no meaning to it, Asa. Only the energy that was there and how we interpreted it."

I had no response to that. To me the path of Buddhism always seemed to end in exactly that. No meaning, no reason. Just the lies we tell ourselves.

I turned and started walking toward the river.

As we walked across the short grass, we could see where the river was already escaping its banks. It was almost up to the big rock with its Native American history plaque and warning sign. We got as close as possible to the river bank without getting our feet wet. The gravel was almost all under water.

The river was narrow there, as it funneled into the cauldron, but you couldn't see the far side of the river through the rain. The wind, as well as the current, was kicking up steep waves that rushed about, confused by the conflict of water and air, and then disappeared. Some were breaking against the shore.

We might have been standing on the edge of an ocean, for all you could tell.

To the left of us was the bridge, spanning across the river where the Cauldron began. Below it billowed a water-smoke, a mist rising from the falls clear to the top of the Cauldron, only to be blown to shreds as soon as the wind hit it. The Cauldron roared as the water pounded through it, rushing to get through, pushing at the rocks and the churning water in front of it. Like a panicked crowd at a concert trying to reach the exit when they heard shooting.

I looked at Tanya, gazing across the water.

"What do you think?" I shouted to be heard above the roar of the Cauldron.

"It's beautiful," she said. "And terrifying."

I nodded in agreement.

"I've never seen it like this," she said. "I've never seen anything like this. It's so powerful. But not happy. Not happy at all."

"What do you mean?" I said.

"Mother Earth, she's angry," Tanya said. "She's screaming. She's not screaming for us, or for help. She's screaming at us."

I wondered for a second if Tanya saw the contradiction in her words. How nothing had any meaning at one moment, and yet the earth herself was speaking to us in the next.

"Tanya, I—" I began, but I never finished my sentence because everything began happening at once.

WEDNESDAY – CHAPTER 69

I heard the report of a gun and Kuraĝa, who'd been sitting next to me, jumped up, slammed into my knees and knocked me into Tanya. She and I both fell down in a heap. At the same time, I felt burning in my left buttock.

Tanya struggled to get up.

"Stay down!" I shouted. "Somebody's shooting!" Out of the corner of my eye, I saw Kuraĝa racing across the field toward the woods. Up above me on the bridge, I barely made out the silhouette of a large vehicle, a pickup truck or a van.

There was another report of a gun. Kuraĝa leapt and yelped, but kept making a beeline toward the woods.

Tanya rolled over. "Asa, get behind the rock," she shouted and started running, crouched over. I started to follow her, but when I tried to get up, I felt my hip muscle tear and I fell over. I rolled my way across the ground and when I got to the rock, Tanya reached out and pulled me in.

"Shit, shit, shit," I said. "I've been shot. Shit." The burning in my leg was increasing. I looked at Tanya, her face muddy and creased. "They're on the bridge. We have to find a way to get out of here before they come down."

"We can't." Tanya said. "We'll never make it to the woods in time."

I rolled over and put my butt in the mud. The cool of the earth eased the burning.

"We have to," I said. "We're sitting ducks here."

Lying there, looking at the sky, I got control of my breathing and started to slow it down. I couldn't afford to go into shock. Not now.

Tanya looked at me, worried. "Where'd you get hit, Asa?"

"In the ass," I said.

I saw her lip quiver as she tried to hold in her emotions as I watched Tanya the friend recede, taken over by Tanya the first responder.

"You sure?" she asked.

"I'm sure," I said. "It's burning like hell."

"Roll over. Let me take a look."

"Not yet," I said. "Let's get out of here first."

She looked around, first at the edge of the river, inches away from us, and then at the expanse of grass to her left.

"How?" she said. "You can't even stand up."

"Give me a minute," I said and I closed my eyes.

"Asa!" Tanya said. "Stay awake!"

"Shut up. Let me think," I said.

In my mind's eye, I recreated our predicament as if I were a bird overhead. I pictured the vehicle on the bridge, the landing, the water, and the Cauldron below, steaming with the enormous flow. If only that wind weren't blowing, I thought to myself. Just let the mist from the Cauldron spread over us, like a fog, destroying our visibility.

If only.

Quit wasting time, old man, part of me said. But I ignored it. If I were going to die in the next few minutes, as seemed likely, at least I would die with hope, as imaginary as it may be. My ass was burning like somebody had put a torch to it, but I clung to my vision and concentrated on the breathing in my chest. My heart was pounding. I hoped I wouldn't go into shock.

I knew I had to slow my heart, but I couldn't, and the burning started to change into a numbing cold. Helluva death, I thought, in the mud, half in the river, half out, and Tanya repeating my name over and over . . .

"Asa! Asa! Look!" she said. I opened my eyes. The wind had stilled and the land around us had covered in mist. I couldn't even see the edge of the clearing.

"Let's go!" Tanya said in my ear and stood up. For a second I imagined her face being blown apart by a bullet, but there was only the roar of the water.

"Come on!" she said. "Get up!"

I rolled over onto my hands and knees and tried to push myself up, but my leg gave out underneath me. Tanya grabbed me as I fell back down and looped my arm over her shoulder.

"We can't go back to the jeep," I said. "We'll never make it up that hill, but if we do, they'll be waiting for us."

"That's not where we're going," Tanya said and she half carried me, half dragged me, while I struggled to move on my good leg. We didn't head toward the dirt road, but diagonally away from it, toward the woods.

"Where the hell are we going?" I said.

"To that abandoned shack," Tanya said. "Then we'll figure something out."

We staggered onto the trail, me leaning on Tanya, pulling my bad leg behind me, putting as much weight on it as I dared. "Kuraĝa! Where is he?"

"He ran for the woods when you got shot," she said. "He's good. Better than us, probably."

We angled up the slope along the trail. I helped Tanya with what I had, but the cold and the numbness was creeping down my leg and it eventually became useless. For the last fifty yards up to the shack Tanya was holding me up, her arm wrapped around me, dragging me with her as she stumbled up the trail. She was stronger than she looked, but I knew that already.

She pulled open the door to the shack and half dragged me in, half threw me to the dirt floor inside.

She collapsed next to me.

Wednesday – Chapter 70

In a minute she sat up, but she was still panting.

"Get out of here, Tanya," I said. "Now. They want me, not you. You'll just be collateral damage if you're here when they get here."

"The hell I am," she said. "You're wounded—I don't know how bad—and you'll go into shock and die if I leave you here. I'll be damned if I'll let the man I love die while I just go waltzing off into the woods."

Our eyes locked as we both realized what she'd just said. Then First Responder Tanya took over again.

"You said your leg's gone numb?" she asked. "And you sure as heck can't use it. I'm going to roll you over and see how much damage has been done. Don't pass out."

She pushed me over so I was lying injured side up and pulled on my pants. I barely felt her fingers pushing and prodding in the muscle of my left buttock.

"Doesn't look too bad," she said. "Small caliber, right into your glute. Not too much bleeding. Went in at an angle, though, so it probably missed your pelvic bone. Still in there, no exit wound. Must have hit a nerve, though. That's why you've gone numb."

She was half talking to me, half talking to herself. She dragged her canvas bag over the ground toward her.

"But if it gets septic," she said, "that won't be good. I have to find some way of closing it."

As she spoke, her voice got more distant, as if I were somehow going further away. The numbness was starting to creep up my left side and the beating of my heart got louder and more insistent. Tanya glanced down at my face.

"Asa?" she said. "Asa, stay with me. You're going into shock, Asa, listen to my voice. Stay with me, Asa."

"Something's wrong," I said. "The numbness...it's going up now. Going into my chest," I said.

"You're going into shock," she said. "Stay with me, Asa."

"No, no," I said. "Something's wrong. I'm starting to have trouble breathing."

For a second I thought I saw worry flash across her face, and then it was gone.

"My heart. It's pounding like it wants out."

Tanya put her fingers to my neck and felt my pulse. She put her ear down to my chest and listened to my heart.

"Jesus, Asa," she said. "What's going on?"

It was getting harder to breathe. It felt like a weight was on my chest, forcing the air out. I forced my lungs to inhale. It wasn't enough. I felt like I was suffocating. Somehow, I knew this feeling. I'd felt this before.

"Poison," I managed to say. "I've been poisoned."

My eyes rolled back into my head and I forced them back down. Tanya wavered in my vision.

"Poison? A poison bullet, you mean?"

My mouth moved but I lacked the breath to speak. All I knew was my heart pounding in my chest, louder and faster as I ran out of oxygen.

Tanya sat back on her heels. "Dad was a pharmacist in the army," she said. "One time he told me about the poison bullets they tried to develop. What did they use? Oh, god, what did they use?" She sat back, out of my narrowing vision.

"Fuck," she said. It was the only time I'd ever heard her swear. "Fuck. They used arsenic. They put it in a hollowed out bullet. It would make your heart explode in a minute."

I could hear her scrabbling through her bag. She was in front of me again, holding the foxglove we had picked the other day.

"How much, how much?" she said to herself as she ripped some of the leaves off and rolled them between her palms.

"No time," she said. "Asa, look at me. Look at me. Can you still move your jaw? Can you swallow?"

I opened and closed my mouth.

"Good. I'm going to put this in your mouth. Foxglove. It's what digitalis is made of. Either it will destroy the poison or it will kill you. I don't know which, but without it you'll die anyway. Do you understand me?"

I nodded.

She pried my mouth open and stuck in the rolled up ball of leaves.

"Now, chew. Chew and swallow."

I did my best. I choked a little when I swallowed, but it all went down. My heart still felt like a freight train in my chest.

"Don't you dare die, Asa Cire. Don't you dare die."

My eyes rolled into the back of my head and everything went black.

WEDNESDAY – CHAPTER 71

When I opened my eyes, it was early morning. The light was coming in through the opening in the wall of the old shack where a small window had been.

I lay there for a minute, sensing things. I was still alive. And I was breathing. And my heart was no longer pounding. So far, so good.

The shack was empty. No Tanya. No Kuraĝa.

I didn't hear much from outside, either. All was stillness. I lay there for another minute or two and then very gingerly rolled over. Aside from an ache in my left butt cheek, there wasn't any pain. I clenched my fists and opened them and I wiggled my toes. So far, so good.

I rolled back over and got on all fours. Even better.

Slowly I stood up. I leaned against the wall of the shack to steady myself, but my leg seemed able to bear my weight now. I was far from dry, but my clothes were no longer dripping wet.

With my arm bracing myself against the wall, I took a couple of unsteady steps. Then I stood on my own. I was alive and apparently everything still worked. I exhaled. Yes, everything still worked.

I stepped outside the shack and looked around. It was strangely bright. There was an aura to the world, a glow to it I'd never seen before. I looked up at the sky through the trees. None had leaves on them anymore. The densely packed clouds had started to give way and the wind was nothing that a sailor would have complained about.

I wondered, why did they take Tanya and the dog, and not me? I realized that once Tanya had seen I would be ok, she did the smart thing and had high-tailed it out of there. She probably hooked up with Kuraĝa and they're safe somewhere.

Up the trail, I thought. They must have gone further up and found another place to hide. I wasn't about to yell for them. That would be disaster. I grabbed a thick branch off the ground and using it as a walking stick, began my ascent up the trail.

My mind must have been still fuzzy, though, because at some point I lost the trail and found myself walking through the brush, with no packed dirt beneath my feet. I didn't worry much, though, because I was still ascending to the ridge and I would meet up with the trail again there.

Besides, they were unlikely to have curled up next to the trail. They would have hidden themselves somewhere off of it. I was just as likely to find them here as I would there.

I began to worry when I got to the ridge and found nothing. No trail. No sign of them. Maybe Kuraĝa would hear me and come looking. I kept walking and the woods got much thicker, slowing me down considerably as I picked my way through branches and brush, but there was still that glow, that brightness to everything.

I'd lost track of how far I'd gone when I saw the clearing with the large building in it. I'd never been there before. I would have remembered something as big as that. Maybe it was somebody's house. Maybe Tanya and Kuraĝa had found their way there and were waiting things out. Maybe they'd found help.

I stepped over a few fallen trunks and stepped into the clearing. The building was even larger than I had thought. A path entered the clearing from below and curved up to the broad, wooden steps of a large veranda. The post and beam house was all unpainted wood. The roof, shingled with wood, swooped down from the center in four directions and a square cupola, windowed, sat in the middle at the top.

I stood for a minute on the edge of the clearing, mesmerized by the building. It was beautiful, and in an odd way, it felt welcoming. It also felt empty, uninhabited almost, although there was no decay, no overgrown weeds to be seen. Just empty.

If there were anyone in there, they would know I was there by now, I thought, but nothing stirred. I limped my way to the steps, listening and watching carefully. Using the stick to support myself, I climbed the steps, one by one, and crossed the porch.

I walked around the veranda to the side of the house. There, where I hadn't seen it before, a huge deck extended out, supported by four round beams and open on the three far sides. I leaned the stick against the veranda railing, took the two steps over to the deck without assistance, and stepped on one of the straw mats covering the floor.

WEDNESDAY – CHAPTER 72

Inside my shoes, my toes curled instinctively to find their footing on the mat while I looked around.

A rack filled with wooden jo and wooden practice swords hung against the wall of the house, and the open side of the deck across from me looked off into a deep valley. The floor was dry as a bone, even along the edges where the wind should have blown in the rain.

Without really knowing why—I was operating solely on instinct at this point—I walked over to the rack and picked up one of the jo. It was worn, and sweat had stained it where it had been gripped many times.

I stepped out into the center and took a few swings with it, working out the stiffness in my body, letting the pain and the tension ease away as I moved with surprising fluency through a short kata. I wasn't even short of breath when I finished, and nothing hurt. My hands didn't ache. Even my butt cheek, where I had been shot, didn't hurt. Nothing hurt. I took a deep breath, bowed to the valley far away, and hung the jo back up.

Next to the rack was a wooden door with a small window in it, perhaps for the sensei to look out at their students practicing. I grabbed the hammered iron latch, pushed the door open, and stepped inside.

I stood in a room with a long, rectangular table in the middle with chairs for eight. There was clearly nobody there, but there was not a speck of dust or dirt on the floor or the table. I felt like I was dirtying the place by walking in. To the left was an open doorway and steps that led down into another room.

I went down the stairs and entered the room. It took my breath away.

I was in the back of the house now, and the large square room was open to the peak of the roof with light from the cupola flooding in from above. That wasn't what took my breath away, though.

The room was filled with books, a bookcase on almost every wall, leading all the way up to the roof. A rolling ladder gave access to the upper stacks and a desk sat in front of the far glass wall, near another staircase leading down. I walked along the bookcases, letting my hand drag against the books, to make sure they were real. I read the titles on the bindings, and they appeared to be written in every language, in Sanskrit, and Mandarin, and French and English and languages I had never seen.

Next, the desk drew my attention. It was so incongruous. Where the rest of the woodwork in the house had been smoothed and sanded and shaped, the desk was rough-hewn and not much more than a simple table. It could have been built by a caveman with a stone maul and too much time on his hands. Thick and sturdy and massive, the desk sat there, anchoring the room around it.

On top of it sat the manuscript. The Zamenhof manuscript. Its hundred-year-old pages sat there, uncovered, curling slightly at the corners. I walked over to the desk and sat down.

I picked up the manuscript and thumbed through it. It had the same yellowed pages, with the same numbers—4, 13, 7, 5, 8, 18 and 22—at the bottom. No pages in between. I returned to the first page and began reading it.

It made sense. The characters were no longer smoke in my eyes, changing each time I glanced at them. They were whole. They had meaning. As I read through the manuscript, they made sense.

I sucked in my breath. My gods. This is what it was all about.

I read through the manuscript three times to make sure I had every bit of it memorized, put the pages down, and sat back in the chair to try to make sense of everything I had just learned.

Somewhere outside I heard a dog barking.

Not any dog. Kuraĝa! I could hear him, downstairs, outside!

I ran from the desk, jumped down the nearby stairs and landed at the bottom. I was outside, on the grass, and Kuraĝa stood there barking. He wasn't looking at me. He was staring at a well with a short rock wall around it.

"Kuraǧa!" I yelled.

He ignored me and continued to jump up and down in place, barking at the well.

Oh my god, I thought. Tanya! She's fallen in. I rushed over to the well and leaned over it, looking in. The opening must have been six feet in diameter, but I could not see more than a few feet below ground.

"Tanya!" I shouted. "Tanya, are you ok?"

I heard nothing but Kuraǧa's barking. I had leaned further over to get a better look when I felt Kuraǧa's body slam into me again—just as he had on the river landing—and I tumbled into the well.

WEDNESDAY – CHAPTER 73

I felt like I was falling abnormally slowly at first, tumbling as if I were weightless or in free fall, until I flattened my body out, stomach down, torso slightly lower than my feet.

It was pitch black below me, but the wall of the well next to me was like nothing I had ever seen before. It seemed made of pictures—or windows with moving pictures inside, three dimensional—and I fell slowly past them.

Through the first window I saw the river landing, from above, with a van on the bridge, and Tanya and I huddled behind the rock. Then, in the next window, a bus with my face in one window, looking out at Nemaseck for the first time.

The windows started passing by faster, and although I only caught a glimpse of each, I knew immediately what they showed.

A man, standing in tattered clothes and a fisherman's cap, looking out at the bleak landscape of the gulag. A much younger man, not much more than a boy, standing in fatigues at a desk in a bunker. A young Thai girl, pouring water at the family dinner table. A woman in a dress, on her knees in a garden, pulling up potatoes and throwing them into a wooden bucket.

On and on the scenes went. Gradually the speed of my fall increased and every picture passed in the blink of an eye, at the same time getting dimmer and dimmer while a light from below grew brighter and brighter. The last few windows were almost completely dark. I saw only firelight, and then lightning, and then I fell out of the well into an opening at the top of the sky.

Below me was a wide, open field, covered in snow, with a walled village next to it. I heard a terrible wailing, a howling that was full of grief and anger and despair, and it filled the air around me even as I fell faster, the air whistling by me.

In the last few seconds before I hit, I saw the source of the wailing. A dog, covered in ice and snow, howled its anger and sorrow and unimaginable grief, filling my ears as my body slammed full speed into the ground.

THURSDAY – CHAPTER 74

When I opened my eyes, it was early morning. The light was coming in through the opening in the wall of the old shack where a small window had been.

I was still on my side. Lying next to me, and facing me, was Tanya. I was under a filthy blanket.

"Tanya," I croaked, my throat dry as cotton. "Thank god, you're ok."

She smiled, the tiredest smile I'd ever seen.

"I'm ok? Of course I am. The question is, how are you?"

I shifted. Everything hurt. "Uh. Ok. Not feeling too spry, I guess."

"Spry." She laughed, quietly. "I should guess not. You almost died last night. In fact, you did die, at one point. My dosage was a bit too much, I guess. Your heart slowed and slowed and then stopped. I had to do CPR on you for a few minutes to start it again."

"Thank you," I said.

"You're welcome."

We both looked at each other for a minute.

"Where's Kuraĝa?" I asked.

"He's outside. On guard duty, I guess. He came trotting in at some point in the night—not long after your heart had stopped—and sniffed around you for a minute or two. Then he trotted back outside and started howling. He's been in and out all night, checking on you and making sure we were safe. I'm sure he'll be back in a minute. Now, we've got to find a way to get you out of here and to a hospital. I was thinking—now that I'm sure you're stable—I should go back to the firehouse and get some EMTs and a litter and come back and take you to the hospital."

"No." I shook my head. "Not doing that."

"The hell you aren't."

"The hell I am," I said. "Whoever tried to kill me is still out there. I'd be a sitting duck."

"If they were going to come after us, they would have long before now," Tanya said. "They would have found us last night with the ruckus Kuraǧa was making."

I thought I knew what Kuraǧa had been barking at, but I kept my mouth shut. Too soon for the ravings of a half-dead old man.

"No. I mean at the hospital. Tagged and in a bed connected to tubes of who knows what, I'd be an easy target. I'm not going."

Tanya frowned, took a breath, and let it go.

"Ok, Asa, have it your way. After you stopped trying to die on me, I patched up your wound as best I could. Bullet's still in there, but clearly the arsenic has played itself out. And, yes, I think you're an old idiot."

"At least, thanks to you, I'm an alive old idiot," I said. "Now help me up." I threw the blanket off me.

"Found that in the corner last night," Tanya said. "It's probably got cooties. You're going to want to take a shower when you get home."

With Tanya's help I struggled to my feet and leaned against the wall.

"Outside," I told her, "just to the left of the door, you'll find a branch that got blown off in the wind. It's exactly the right size for a walking stick."

Tanya raised an eyebrow at me, but said nothing and went outside. A minute later she came back holding the stick.

"This it?" she said.

"Yeah." I grabbed the stick and leaned on it.

"How did you know...?" Tanya said.

Kuraǧa trotted in through the door, soaking wet, and shook himself off.

"Good god, that's the thirtieth time that dog's done that," she said, laughing. "I would have stayed drier outside in the rain."

Kuraǧa trotted over to me and sniffed me up and down. I looked at him. His eyes glittered in the morning light. He walked back to the door and sat down.

Again I heard the voice in my head. "*Let's go,*" it said.

Gradually and painfully, Kuraĝa, Tanya and I made our way down the trail. It felt like the rain was letting off a bit, but that may have been my imagination. The wind still blew as if to shake the earth itself.

As we got to the bottom of the trail, where it opened onto the landing, I saw that we were going to have problems. The river had spilled way over its banks during the night and the landing was entirely flooded, all the way to the base of the dirt road and beyond. It wasn't still water, either. The current ripped along with a power I knew would sweep me away in my crippled state.

I stopped. Tanya stopped. Kuraĝa sat down.

"Guess it's not going to be as easy as I thought," I said.

THURSDAY – CHAPTER 75

We were trapped by an unfortunate concatenation of civil engineering and geography.

The side of the dirt road dropped away steeply on a bed of gravel—impossible to climb—and that in turn led into the forty foot cement wall that buttressed the highway on our side. The only way to get back to the road was to bushwack our way through the woods to the cement wall and then make our way along the bottom of it back to where the land leveled back with the roadway.

Tanya agreed that was the only way to go. With Kuraǧa leading, we began picking our way through the woods, now cluttered by branches and downed trees, until we got to the abutment. It was slow going, especially when we had to scramble over tree trunks as high as a fence. I wouldn't let Tanya help me, and at one point she yelled at me in frustration.

"What the hell is wrong with you, Asa?" she shouted at me after I had belly-flopped across one tree and fell onto the ground on the other side of it. "You're going to re-open your wound!"

I got up and squinted at her. It was going to be hard to explain, but I did my best.

"The time for aid is over, Tanya. You, and Nev, and Kuraǧa, you've been carrying me this whole time," I said. "It's time I found my own feet again."

Without a word she turned and followed the waiting Kuraǧa.

We made it to the abutment, but hadn't gone far along it when we were stopped again. A small dam of storm debris had collected on the road high above us, and the collected road water had formed a waterfall in front of us.

It had eroded the ground beneath into a deep trough and it now rushed along in an angry stream.

On the other side of it the land again dropped, instead of continuing to rise, and the cement abutment ended, but the ground beneath it was too steep and wet to dare climb. We would find no purchase to get there.

"Shit," I said.

Kuraĝa drank out of the torrent and then sat on his haunches beside me. Tanya sank to the ground, a soggy pile of exhaustion and despair. I would have sat down too, but my wound hurt too much, and I felt it might just be that I would never get up again.

"Shit," I said again.

I looked overhead at the trees towering above. None were close enough to climb and then jump from them onto the road—even if I could do that, and I couldn't—and what about Kuraĝa?

I wandered about and moved deeper in the woods.

"Where are you going?" Tanya asked.

"Wait," I said. "I'm thinking."

I was only a few steps into the woods when a tree caught my eye, a fully-grown hemlock, half down, and leaning heavily away from the wind. With the soil too sodden to hold its shallow root system, it had partially given in and its windward roots now stuck up in the air.

I had an idea. Since moving to Nemaseck I had cut my own firewood, either working off state land with a permit or that of a generous landowner wanting to thin his forest. It had always been my habit—although at the time I had not known why—to thank a grove of trees before beginning to cut them. I'd thank them for giving me heat and ask them for their permission to take them down. Afterward I'd arrange the limbs and tops that I didn't remove into piles that would provide shelter and food for wildlife.

I had spoken to the forest before, yes, but I had never heard an answer.

Now I knew how to listen, how to listen to the forest itself through the vast network of roots and rhizomes that together direct the biome itself. A weirdly pagan notion, I knew, but one supported by a science that has now discovered the metabolism and signaling mechanisms of the forest.

The other thing about a forest was that it didn't give a damn about what anyone wanted. Its chief care—it's only care—was the maintenance of itself as a whole, an entire living, breathing entity, as one. Humans were of little interest except as a compiled threat, but there were times when a human's goals and the forest's coincided.

This might be one of them, I thought.

I looked at this hemlock, with its sprung roots, and looked around it at its brothers and sisters. I put my hand and head on the tree and began speaking to it in a quiet voice, barely more than a whisper.

Such a conversation takes time. There was nothing to do but wait. There is much to be studied, many factors to be weighed, and many outcomes to be considered of which humans have no understanding.

My part in the discussion finished, I stepped away from the tree.

I felt, more than heard, the ripples of conversation in the air above me and the ground below me. After three or four minutes the leaning tree creaked. I stepped back. A gust of wind came and the tree creaked some more and began leaning over further as more roots pulled out. Another gust hit, and with a great crack the trunk of the tree split and the whole hemlock fell over. Its top smashed onto the guardrail next to the road, and the root system, freed of the weight of the trunk, slammed back onto the ground.

"Asa!" I heard Tanya yell. "Asa, are you ok?"

"I'm fine," I yelled back. "Come here."

A minute later Kuraĝa appeared, followed by Tanya.

"What did you do, Asa? Push the tree over?"

"No, it figured out on it's own that it was better to go now than later," I said. "It made us a ladder in the process."

Kuraĝa had already jumped up on the trunk and was running his way up to the top.

"Tanya?" I said and beckoned her up and on to the tree as if I were escorting her through a door.

She hopped on and I followed her, holding onto the branches, half-walking, half-climbing, until we reached the road and slithered off onto the ground. Through the pelting rain, the Jeep remained parked where we had left it a lifetime ago.

Tanya held out her hand. "Keys, Asa," she said. "I'm driving." I handed her the keys.

She was right. I had no business behind a wheel in this mess.

THURSDAY – CHAPTER 76

Tanya and I were mostly silent as we drove back to town. Tanya was fighting her fatigue. I was painfully squirming around on the seat.

"Stop that," Tanya said at one point. "You're going to rip open that wound I super-glued shut."

"You what?" I said.

"Super-glue. I had some in my bag. Basically the same thing a doctor would use to close a small wound, except it costs less."

Jesus. I had lead and superglue in my butt. Didn't that make me special.

I was also trying to make sense of what I had experienced during the night. I had seen some part of my own past—I was sure of that—but I didn't seem to bring back any other new memories with me. At least not specific ones, like birthday parties or weddings or births. Mostly I only had feelings, or general impressions, or just ideas…like the one that had me talking to the hemlock back in the woods. I didn't quite know what to make of that. At all.

We got closer to town and Tanya slowed to a creep to dodge all the debris and fight the side wind.

"Tanya!" I said. "I remember."

"Remember what?"

"Everything. Or, at least, pieces of everything. It must have been when I was dying last night—you know, when your life flashes before your eyes? Kind of like that, but different."

"So you know where you were before you came to Nemaseck?"

"Sort of. No, not really. I know who I was, though. And who I was before that. I guess I've been around the block a few times."

"Haven't we all," Tanya said. As a Buddhist the idea of rebirth wasn't new to her. "So who were you? A prince, a king? That's what most people say."

"Well . . . not exactly. A Jewish prisoner in the gulag. A young girl in the Philippines. An Irish wife, pulling potatoes."

Tanya laughed. "Wouldn't that be the ticket?" she said, "Asa wearing a skirt and carrying a bucket of potatoes,"

She pulled the jeep into the parking spot next to her car in front of the shop, killed the jeep's engine and handed me the keys.

"You should probably get to someplace safe, Tanya," I said. "They must know who you are. Go home, grab some clothes and leave town."

She waved her hand. "In this weather?" she asked. "Actually, I'm not going home at all."

I furrowed my brow. "Coming to my place then?"

A short, bitter, laugh. "Hardly," Tanya said. "I'm driving to the monastery now. Right from here. I can't take anything with me as a monk anyway, so I'm leaving now." She looked at me. "And I'm never coming back, Asa. I can't do this. I don't know what has happened, but I know I can't stay here. I can't help you with whatever is going on, and I can't watch you die again. I can't, and I won't, and that's where things are going to end up, Asa. You know that as well as I do. So I'm leaving. Right now. I don't care if it takes me three days to drive there."

She opened the door and got out of the jeep. I opened mine and Kuraĝa jumped from the back seat onto my lap and bounded out ahead of me.

"Ouch! Jesus. That hurt," I said.

Tanya and I stood in front of the jeep, facing each other, the wind and rain tearing at our clothes. Her face was streaked with dirt and her black hair was plastered against her head. I couldn't imagine I looked any better, and probably a damn sight worse. We stood there for a moment looking into each other's eyes, and then Tanya turned to go.

'Tanya!" I said.

She stopped and turned as if she didn't want to.

"Will you be studying koans at the monastery?"

"Of course, Asa, why?"

I would have assumed she was beyond "What is the sound of one hand clapping?" but maybe not, I thought.

"Let me give you your first one then," I said. She looked at me blankly.

"Two monks were standing beside a stream," I said. "The first monk said to the second one, 'What is love?' The second one picked up a stone and tossed it into the middle of the stream."

She blinked at me twice and turned away to walk to her car.

"That's my koan for you, Tanya," I said. "I hope you find the answer."

She stopped, her head bowed in thought. She turned around and walked back toward me. As she came close, I saw the faintest of smiles on her face. If I hadn't known her all these years, I would have missed it.

She stopped in front of me, raised her hand, and with her finger tapped me, once, on the chest. Right on the sternum.

Without saying a word she turned around, got in her car and drove off. I stood and watched her.

She didn't look back.

THURSDAY – CHAPTER 77

I watched Tanya's car as she picked her way through the branches on the road until she became lost in the rain. I had finally remembered who the great love of my life was, and she was driving away forever.

I felt Kuraĝa nudge my leg, and I looked down at him.

"Yeah, I know," I said. "I'm hungry and thirsty, too. Let's see if there's anything in the shop."

I limped up the steps and, forgetting to unlock it first, pushed on the door. It opened easily at first, as if the latch had been sprung, and then it stopped dead.

In fact, there was no latch there, only a pile of broken wood, leaning up against the door to keep it shut. I shoved the pile aside with the door and walked into a scene of destruction.

The shelves along the wall were empty. Everything had been thrown onto the floor and then demolished. Everything—absolutely everything—had been beaten into pieces.

The floor was covered with broken pieces of wood, ceramic, jade and metal. The monitor of Nev's computer, left behind by the police, was smashed and lying on its side. An ancient maul lay on the floor, its handle broken and its head shattered. A European Renaissance vase lay in pieces.

It took me a minute, standing there, to absorb the enormity of the vandalism. Even some of the shelves themselves had been broken, smashed into half. The carved wooden flower that Tanya had admired so much lay crushed into pieces on the floor.

I walked, or rather kicked my way through the debris toward my office and the back of the store. I spotted the stem of my Al Pache meerschaum pipe and the ripped pages of a first-edition book. I got to the back and saw the floor was covered in water, still flowing through the ceiling from my office above.

Kurağa followed me as I limped up the steps to my office. The destruction there was no less thorough. Every book in my bookcase had had its cover torn off or its pages ripped out and was lying on the soaking wet floor. The Skull and Bones chair lay on the floor, its legs and back broken off. I looked in the cardboard box in which Tanya had brought the tea set.

Nothing was left but little pieces.

The safe had been drilled open and emptied and the rare manuscripts inside had been ripped into pieces and were now lying in a puddle. My desk—the beautiful desk rendered from a square piano by a German cabinetmaker—had been broken in half and its fat piano legs were in a pile on top of it.

I rushed over to it as quickly as I could and saw that the secret cubby where I had hidden the Zamenhof manuscript had been broken open. Of the manuscript itself, there was nothing anywhere in the office. No ripped pages. Nothing scattered on the floor. It was gone.

I leaned against the wall, shaken not only by the totality of the vandalism, but by the pure rage that had lain behind it. Whoever had done this was not solely looking for something. They wanted to destroy everything associated with me.

I had no doubt, looking again at my broken desk, that they had found what they were looking for.

My throat was parched. I went into the bathroom and found that the sink had been broken into pieces. Only the faucet was left, standing alone on the copper pipes, clinging forlornly to a few fragments of porcelain. The toilet too had been smashed, and water burbled out of the inlet and poured onto the floor. I reached behind what was left of the bowl and turned off the valve.

I looked around and found an old Chinese food container in a pile of rubbish from the overturned trash can. I rinsed it out, threw the rinse water onto the floor, filled it and drank out of a corner of the container. I filled it, drank again, then filled it a third time and offered it to Kurağa. After he had

had his fill, I poured out the remainder on the floor. It didn't matter any more.

Kuraĝa walked over to the far end of the office and settled down on a pile of books above the water level. He watched me as I wandered aimlessly about the office.

Everything that was of any importance to me was now gone. My work, my books, the manuscript, my friends, the woman I loved. Nothing was left.

I needed a bowl of tobacco. Of course all of my mason jars were broken, but I found a couple of small piles of tobacco on what was left of the desk. Sweeping them up together, I picked out as many of the shards of glass I could find, pulled a soaking wet pipe out of my jacket pocket and stuffed the tobacco into it. My lighter, though wet, still worked.

I walked over to the office wall next to Kuraĝa and sat down, leaning my back against the wall. The floor was wet there, too, but what did it matter? It didn't.

My left buttock was burning again. I lit the pipe and smoked the random leftovers I had culled together. It tasted like shit.

I must have sat like that for half an hour, watching the rain come in from the broken windows. When I'd smoked the last of the tobacco, I tapped out the dottle from the bowl onto the floor. It didn't matter anymore.

Kuraĝa, who had hardly taken his eyes off me the whole time, was looking at me expectantly.

"Yeah, I'm hungry too, dog," I said. "Let's go home and see if anything is left there to eat."

I didn't bother to close the door when we left.

THURSDAY – CHAPTER 78

I parked the jeep in front of the house. At least from the outside, everything looked normal.

No broken windows. No pile of broken junk lying on the porch. Kuraǧa and I went inside and to my relief it looked like nobody had been here. It was how I had left it. Whoever it was had gone to the shop first, found the manuscript, acted out their rage, and left.

Kuraǧa pushed in front of me, sniffed this way and that, and came back to give me the all-clear. I limped into the kitchen, dark in the gathering twilight, found a candle and lit it. I poured some water and rice into a pot and started a fire in the stove. I filled a bowl of water and put it on the floor for Kuraǧa.

Without electricity I knew the refrigerator would have already lost much of its coolness and I pulled out the steak I had been hoping to have for dinner and tossed it to a grateful Kuraǧa. I pulled out a hunk of cheese for myself and returned to the living room to wait for the rice to cook.

I didn't want to eat, but I forced down a cup of rice and then sat down on the floor and watched the flames dance through the glass door of the stove. Kuraǧa lay down an arm's length away and sighed.

"Me too, buddy, me too," I said.

Before long my eyelids got heavy, and I fell asleep, sitting there on the floor, feeling like an old man, my chin bowed to my chest.

THURSDAY – CHAPTER 79

It was dark when I awoke and the fire in the stove had dwindled to embers.

I stood up. Every bone in my body ached. I peeled off my clothes, stiff with dried mud and blood, and dropped them on the floor where I stood. I took a long, hot shower.

Afterward I put on a pair of gi pants and a t-shirt and thought about what I should do next. And I thought about who I was. And what I had learned from the Zamenhof manuscript.

Truth be told, I still didn't quite know who I was, but I did know that I was not who I had thought I was. There was a knowledge in me—unlocked by reading the manuscript—that I had hidden from myself for…I don't know how long. Years.

With it came the understanding of the importance of the attacks on me, and a sort of visceral understanding of what I had done to myself. I had hidden myself precisely because of that knowledge, and in doing so had stripped myself of much of my humanity.

Now, somebody out there wanted me dead, deader than dead, dead so that I could never return. Now, it was clear to me that I could no longer hide.

The night I had spent almost dying in the shack—and regaining part of myself in that strange building on that strange mountain—was a clarion call. Anyone with the ears for it would now know where I was and I could only expect the attempts to kill me to come faster, harder, and with less restraint since I no longer had possession of the manuscript.

But the fact of the matter was, I hardly cared. What did I care if I lived or died, or if the knowledge within me died as well? I had nothing in this life left that mattered. Kuraǧa was the exception, perhaps, but I was more than sure that he could take care of himself without me.

I realized I had never had any goals, any ambitions. I had somehow fallen into this life and done what I knew how to do. I learned. I talked to people. I traded in the baubles of this world which others called treasures and passed them through my hands and people gave me money for that. Quite a bit of money, more than I had expected, but again, what did I need of it? What could I possibly spend it on? There was nothing I wanted.

Except one thing. I had discovered the identity of the man who had killed Elle Anderson and something inside me craved justice for this murder. I didn't know why. Perhaps because she was an innocent, and innocents deserve our protection. Maybe that was all I had left to do, and then . . . and then what?

Maybe that was all. Maybe then I could rest. People had died for less.

I sat down in front of my altar. For years I had meditated to melt myself into nothingness, to dissolve the footprint of my personality, because somewhere deep in my unconsciousness I knew that by reducing my psychic footprint, I would make myself harder to find. I don't know when or how that tactic had failed, but, since it had, perhaps I could make better use of this skill.

Shamans from time immemorial had used trances to enter another world or, better put, to see the unseen in this world, to directly encounter the forces and energies that barely register on most people. They brought this knowledge back to use for healing the sick or for advising leaders or for gaining advice and understanding for themselves.

So tonight, instead of drowning myself in the immensity of the eternal, I would do something else. I would seek clarity and understanding. I would try to understand what I should do going forward...or if even I should go forward.

The obvious place to start was to find the ghost of Elle Anderson. She was the only contact I had, although I well knew now that others existed. All transactions are built on relationships, on understanding others' motives and needs, and on giving some of what you had to get something in exchange. It was upon this property of reciprocity that the ancients had built their relationships with the gods. An offering was given so that the deities would listen and respond to their needs.

Not that a god needed the smell of incense, or a bowl of fruit, or a dead animal, but what they did need was humans' recognition of their importance. That belief had been – maybe still was—what they lived on and was how their energy was attracted to us. It was a form of metaphysical commerce, coupled with these other beings' own needs and wants.

"I understand you," an offering said, and, if successful, it was met with a response.

Over time a relationship developed. A god or a fairy or an angel or a demon—whatever you wanted to call them—would develop an affinity for an individual or a group of individuals. The cults worshiping specific beings grew, and the relationship between the two benefited one another.

That was precisely what I lacked. The only such being with whom I had any relationship was the ghost of Elle Anderson. So it was there that I would begin.

My wound was far too fresh and painful for me to sit on my heels, as I was accustomed to. I grabbed a couple of pillows and sat on them cross-legged with my altar in front of me. I leaned forward and lit the candles, closed my eyes, and focused my attention on my breath.

THURSDAY – CHAPTER 80

As my stillness deepened and the time came for intruding visions, instead of waiting to get past them or be succumbed by them, I instead created one.

In my mind's eye, I stood up from the altar and walked out of the house. I wasn't seeing things in the third person, but as I would have had I seen them with my physical eyes. I walked off the porch and then began shifting the environment around me, first the trees, then the shape of the land, and then the river in front of me, until I was standing at the landing above the bridge.

It wasn't raining there, and it wasn't dark, and the river was not flooding. I stood still until I heard the waterfall of the Cauldron and the birds in the trees. If this was to be my point of entry, I would make it as pleasant as possible. I was sick and tired of the damn rain.

I stood there and waited, I don't know how long. Time is a sketchy thing at best, and on a vision quest such as this, time is a currency of little value. I waited, and I realized that I should have taken some steps to protect myself both here and at home. Not everybody was friendly in either of these worlds, and I was a sought quantity among some quarters.

Elle walked out of the river slowly, still holding the baby in her arms. Her transparency was evident in the sunlight and I could faintly see the waves of the river directly behind her. Her face was streaked with tears, her head still bowed, still looking at her child. She stood at the edge of the river as if she were connected to it in some unseen way.

"Elle," I said. There was no response.

"Elle!"

I spoke in a more commanding tone that I was pretty sure I could get away with. She looked up at me, and the sadness in her eyes tore at my heart. What a horrible end for someone so young, so innocent. I felt anger rising in me, anger at the person who had done this to her.

"How would you like it to be done?" I asked in a gentler tone. This would be her true last request. After this her ghost could rest from the justice delivered to break the world's hold on her.

She opened her mouth and was about to speak as the water began boiling behind her. She turned to look and a snake's head broke through the river's surface, a head that was nearly as long as I was tall. It rose high in the air and Elle screamed. Its jaws opened wide and it fell down on her and consumed her.

I stepped back and I wanted to run, but my feet felt glued to the ground. I suddenly heard Kuraĝa barking, madly, wildly. But he wasn't there.

Oh, shit, I thought. I have to get back.

The water boiled again and the snake's head rose high above me, this time to consume me. I could not move.

In my mind I saw Kuraĝa, his lips pulled back into a snarl, his eyes staring. My eyes locked with his and time froze.

Now I was looking out into the room from Kuraĝa's eyes and time was moving again. Everything was distorted, and dim. I could see a man aiming a gun at us. Another man was swinging a baseball bat at my head.

Not a death blow, but not a love tap either. This was real.

Through Kuraĝa's eyes, I made my arm rise, not to block, but to create the opening for a throw from where I was seated. Then Kuraĝa leapt at the attacker with the gun and I could sense his jaws locking onto the man's hand, heard a growl of thunder and then bones crunching and a scream of pain.

Kuraĝa and I, now as one entity, twisted our head and bit through the remaining tendons. The man fell to the floor just in time for Kuraĝa to look once again at the other attacker coming at my body with the bat. Midway through his strike, I pulled him off balance,and he was stumbling forward, staring at his one-handed partner.

Kuraĝa and I could smell the fear on him, and as Kuraĝa leaped forward, I reached through the dog's eyes once more and forced my body to grab the jo leaning next to the altar. I threw it and it passed through the wall while Kuraĝa leapt for the neck of the second attacker.

Suddenly I was back at the river's edge again. I caught the jo as it appeared and hurtled toward me. Time itself had somehow paused while I was split between the worlds.

The snake's open mouth was descending on me and I rammed the jo into its soft upper palate. His head snapped up, I slammed the other end of the jo behind his lower teeth and it locked his jaw open. The snake's head reared back and I heard the jo snap as his jaws dropped back down on me. He was screaming.

I still couldn't move, but I could talk.

"Kuraĝa!" I shouted as loud as I could, "Bark! Bark, Kuraĝa!"

I felt more than heard Kuraĝa's howl, so strong that it vibrated between the worlds, and I let the sound pull me back to him.

I landed prone on the floor of my study, next to the two bloody and lifeless bodies.

THURSDAY – CHAPTER 81

Kuraǧa's howl ended, his bloody snout inches from my face.

I pried myself to my hands and knees. On one side of me lay the man who had held the pistol, his amputated hand lying on the ground, a gaping wound in his throat. On the other side lay my other attacker, eyes open, the only visible damage the teeth punctures on his neck. Kuraǧa had crushed his esophagus, and the man had suffocated to death.

I turned and looked back at Kuraǧa. He looked at me. His tail wagged, twice, as if to say "what a good boy am I," and all the fear flooded out of me. I began laughing.

I don't know how long I kept laughing, but I would have been classified as hysterical by anybody of right mind.

Eventually I went quiet. My ass hurt where the bullet had hit me and I got to my feet, every joint in my body protesting. There was blood all over the floor, all over the altar. Books were scattered about in the pools of blood.

"Another bloody mess," I thought, which almost set me to laughing again, but I had work to do. I was ravenous. Kuraǧa wanted out.

I blew out the candles and he and I walked out of the study together. I latched the door firmly—briefly wondering what I was going to do with those bodies – and I made my way to the kitchen and opened the back door. Kuraǧa bounded out and as soon as he hit the yard, began rolling in the mud.

I lit another fire in the wood stove, put on more rice, and by the time Kuraǧa wanted back in, I had located the last of the steaks. I chucked it to him.

I cooked the rice and I tried to eat it, but it tasted like sand. I gave the rest to Kuraĝa. He apparently thought it tasted just fine and finished it in seconds. I sat and thought and watched Kuraĝa gnaw on his bone.

Problems were piling up, and I needed to sort them out. I grabbed my cell phone. No service and ten percent of my battery left. I turned it off and threw it back on the table.

Were Kuraĝa and I even safe here? As safe as anywhere, I thought—dead guys in the study aside. That attack had been carefully choreographed. Whoever was behind it must have known that I hadn't died the night before, but that something else entirely had happened, so they tried to kill me while I was at my most exposed, my body in one place, my mind in another. They completely underestimated Kuraĝa, though.

It would take them time and planning and opportunity to make another attack. More than one night, I guessed.

I wasn't even sure myself what had happened in that study or on that riverbank, and I didn't have the energy to suss it out now. It was past, anyway.

Right now I was resting on a needlepoint of tension. Tomorrow would bring another attack, and another, until I and Kuraĝa went down. They might want to keep me alive. They might not. They had the manuscript now. Maybe they didn't need me.

I shook my head at the thought. Fuck. They had the manuscript. Knowing what was in it, I knew that nobody should have it, not even—or maybe especially—me. I had no idea of what the results of its exposure might be. I was pretty sure at this point that I wasn't dealing with Good People.

So what could I do? I couldn't run and hide anymore, not with what I knew now. That knowledge couldn't be hidden. It was a target on my back from now on, wherever I would try to hide. Kuraĝa might escape—and well he should—but I doubted he would leave on my say-so.

The only thing I still felt that needed to be done, or even within my ability to do, was to bring justice to Elle. The look on her face, before the snake had come, haunted me. The only worldly way to gain her justice would be to get a sample of Charlie's DNA and hope that the police had preserved their evidence this long.

Or I could take things into my own hands.

I groaned as I got up, grabbed a log, and threw it on the fire. The air was definitely starting to cool, although I usually didn't need a fire for warmth when it was seventy-five degrees out. I was tired. I grabbed a blanket off the couch, threw it over me, and lay down on the floor in front of the flames.

The last thing I saw before I closed my eyes was Kuraĝa, sitting two feet away from me, his ears flicking this way and that as he listened to the sounds of the night.

FRIDAY – CHAPTER 82

I slept late. The rain had eased off by morning, but the stiffness of my joints was worse, if possible, as I struggled to get to my feet.

Kuraĝa looked like he hadn't moved all night, and it was quite possible that he hadn't. He did want to go out, though, and I watched him through the windows as he sniffed his way around the yard and back and forth along the front walk and the porch.

I brewed a pot of tea and retrieved a pipe and some tobacco from the study. I stepped carefully across the corpses. There was already a tinge to the air and they were going to start to smell soon. The least of my problems, I thought, as I closed the study door.

In the serenity of tea and tobacco smoke, I let my eyes wander about the kitchen. I thought about the times Tanya would come over with an armful of groceries and some plants she had found, and we made dinner together, laughing about her latest dating adventures, or me telling some long, drawn-out dog story about my latest acquisition. She never really liked to talk about her work as an EMT or about the people who came to see her for help. She walled that off most of the time. Occasionally, she would talk about an ambulance run that was too painful for her to keep in and that she needed to get out of her head.

Then, out of nowhere, I remembered the time I'd asked Nev if she had any skin cream in her purse. It was winter and my hands were getting really chapped.

She looked at me like I had two heads.

"Do I look like the kind of girl that carries skin cream?" she'd asked. "Hell, do I look like the kind of girl that carries a purse?"

I gave her a tube of skin cream for Christmas that year and she laughed and laughed.

"You trying to make me a white girl, or what?" she'd asked me.

I opened my present from her. It was a strange, flat, u-shaped piece of hammered-out beer cans.

"What the hell," I said.

She reached over and pushed on the center and the one piece became two, at an angle hinged in the middle. She took the pipe out of my mouth, and it nestled right in the holder.

"There," she said. "Won't be getting ashes all over your desk now."

It was my turn to laugh in delight, and she told me that she had picked it up on the island when she had gone there to visit family. I wasn't quite sure what "visit family" meant, and I didn't ask.

That gift, too, had been destroyed by the vandals in the shop. I shook my head and finished my tea and my pipe.

I spent the next several hours cleaning up the house, throwing all of my soaked clothes in the wash, vacuuming and putting everything away, and ignoring the study. By mid-afternoon it was time to go. I changed into a pair of clean jeans and realized I had lost so much weight over the past week that my belt was now useless. I stepped down into the basement to cut a piece of rope.

I was kicking around the pile of tools looking for something to cut the rope to length when I saw the knife, the knife I had brought back from the cave that day long ago. I held it in my hands for a minute as if I could feel the weight of its evil. What the hell. It was a tool.

And what better tool to use, I thought, and lay the rope on the cement floor and slid out the knife from its sheath. The blade was rusted and pitted and any edge it might have once had was long gone. By the time I got the rope cut, it looked like it had been gnawed in two. I threaded the rope through my belt loops, cinched it up, and shoved the knife and sheath into my back pocket.

Kuraĝa knew something was up. At the top of the stairs, he danced around me, ears going all which-way. I grabbed the bag of dog food from under the sink, poured it out into a big salad bowl and set it on the floor. I found a similar-sized bowl, filled it with water, and put it next to the first.

I took a deep breath and kneeled down. I put the prancing Kuraĝa's muzzle between my hands and held his head and looked at him.

"Gotta leave you home for this one, boy," I said. "This isn't a trip you want to take." He sat down. His ears stopped twitching and they pointed at me. "But lots of food and water. I know it's shit, but it'll hold you 'till I get back."

I reached forward and wrapped my arms around his thick neck and nuzzled my face against his.

"Be good, boy," I said. "I'll see you again."

I looked around the living room, everything neat and clean. "Good bye, Kuraĝa," I said and walked toward the door. He ran up next to me and tried to come out too.

"No, Kuraĝa. Sit. Stay," I said and closed the door behind me.

As I limped in the rain toward the jeep, I heard his body slam the door. I started the engine and drove off without looking back. I couldn't.

FRIDAY – CHAPTER 83

The rain was something less than a torrential downpour, but it still hammered down as I drove. The wind was less, too, but it still gusted hard.

The back seat was soaking wet from the gaping hole in the roof, and the front seat was none too dry, either. I listened to the click-click of the wipers. Still nobody else on the road, not even any police cars. Everybody was still holed up.

I turned onto the highway heading north and drove. The gusts of wind kept me under twenty, so I kept the jeep in second gear and trundled along, avoiding the big pieces of debris and driving over the small ones. Twice I had to get out and shove and tug the big branches and a small tree that had fallen all the way across. It was slow progress, but I was in no hurry.

It was starting to hit twilight by the time I got to the bridge across the river. I skirted across to the other side of the road to get under the fallen hemlock that we had climbed. What, was that only yesterday? Two days ago? It seemed ages past. When I got to the center of the bridge, I pulled over and stopped.

I looked out the side window and saw nothing. I got out of the jeep and walked to the edge overlooking the landing. The flooding had gotten worse and the river was way over its banks on both sides. I stood in the rain and the wind—as if Elle might come walking out of the water one more time, or I would see myself and Tanya and Kuraĝa making our way down the trail.

I walked across the road to peer into the cauldron. The mass of water was exploding through the narrows and shooting into the pool below like a water cannon. "The river is angry," I heard Tanya's voice in my head say. Sopping wet now, I walked back to the jeep and climbed in.

On the other side of the bridge, I turned to go down onto the dirt road that paralleled the river on its way toward Charlie's house. It was nearly flooded with the water from the river washing across it, but only a few inches deep yet. I knew it would get deeper over the next day or so as the water would come pouring down from the hills. But that was tomorrow's problem.

I drove along, the dark woods to my left, and the gloom got deeper. I turned on my headlights. creeping now, trying to make sure I didn't go nose deep into some pool. I kept working my way by feel across the washouts from the rain and as I clawed my way up one washed out trough, the jeep's nose up in the air, I felt, rather than heard, a tree coming down.

There was a giant shudder as its neighbors tried to catch it, but then let go, and I jammed on the brakes as the upper trunk slammed across the hood of the jeep. Steam spewed out of the bent metal and I turned off the ignition. The tree rolled back slightly and stopped, wedging itself against the windshield.

I sat there in the sudden dark and listened for more trees that might have gotten knocked loose by this one on its way down. I got ready to jump out the door and go face first into the washout, but nothing else came down.

Still, I sat there. I heard the wind blowing through the branches above and the gurgle of water as it dammed up against the broken jeep.

Finally I got out and stepped calf-deep into cold water pushing its way to the river. I still had a few miles to go, and the only thing to do was to walk it. I looked back. I was in the dark and there was nothing on the road behind me.

I walked around to the rear of the jeep and tried to unzip the back window, but it was stuck. I I grabbed a broken branch from the ground, jammed it into the plastic and ripped it at the seams. My jo was in there, the spare one I always kept there for when Tanya and I wanted to practice weapons. I pulled it out, put one end on the ground, and leaned on it with my full weight. No cracks. The jo would get me there, or near enough, I figured.

I walked around to the passenger side, ducked under the fallen tree trunk and began limping my way up the road with what little light there was left.

FRIDAY – CHAPTER 84

I kept myself to the side of the dirt road furthest from the river where it was mud or shallow water.

Though the clouds were too thick for the moon to shine, the road made a subtle difference in the darkness, and I followed it carefully. My feet told me when I had strayed out of the mud. I would hate to be walking through the woods tonight, I thought. I would get lost in a minute. I had to walk slowly so as not to fall, but also to keep my butt cheek from hurting too much. It was already burning, and I had miles to go.

And miles to think. I had no plan for when I got to Charlie's. I was only going because it needed to be done, and, well, what else was I going to do? I'd figure out the rest when I got there, I hoped.

What I wanted to think about was Tanya, but I couldn't let myself. Her absence made me feel weaker than I already was. And the "if only's" were endless.

I forced myself to think about what I had been avoiding thinking about since that night in the shack, that dream I had had when I died. It was obviously the creation of a mind slowly starving of oxygen, and though it had seemed to go on for hours, it would only have taken seconds while my mind searched desperately for a way to stay alive.

In that dream, I had been alive for many years, hundreds of them, and I had slipped in and out of lives like other people changed their clothes. Though that was what the dream had said, I still had no memories of the days before I came to Nemaseck. I had been a Jew shipped to the Gulag, and before that, an infantryman in the war, and before that, an officer in another war. I was drawn to fighting and chaos and death, yet I never seemed to be caught by death myself. Instead, I weaved in and out of lives, going back in time, to...where? I didn't know.

I faced a wall as impenetrable in my dream as pre-Nemaseck memories were in my real life. Then, like a projectionist changing the reel in an old-time theater, another series of lives started up. These were dimmer, somehow, but they also felt more real, more visceral.

Dry earth in my hands as I pulled the potatoes from the ground, brushed them off, and put them in my pail, a sense of desperation in that mind, thinking of a hungry family. The heart pounding in a Thai girl's chest, and the fear behind her eyes as she was running from some someone, the terror as hands grabbed her and pulled her, screaming, back to—somewhere.

Then other sensations as well, more occluded, more distant, but heavy. Heavy in the way that an overfull sack is. Heavy in the weight of years and pain and suffering.

The Buddhists have a word for that, *dukkha.* It's the first Noble Truth of Buddhism, the first teaching of Gautama when he was finally convinced to bring his truth to humanity. "Life is *dukkha*," he said. But it isn't suffering as we understand it in English. It is the distress of a wheel that isn't round, rolling across a dirt road like this, bumpy, limping along in lives that don't really meet the reality in which they are lived, lives that never reach their destination.

In my dream, I had had no memory of those lives, only the aggregation of their emotions, a sum of eternity in a moment.

And then that great fall from the sky, my last moments presumably before my heart started beating again, Kuraĝa howling in a pain and agony and a loneliness that pierced the heavens and cleaved time in half. I knew that pain. I had felt it.

I felt it right now and I stopped and opened my mouth and screamed at the sky, a scream that I thought would never end.

When it did, I felt the echoes of my wail taken by the wind to the trees and the river and the mountain beyond.

What the hell was I doing, I thought, as the echoes receded and I stood, once again, on a dirt road next to a flooding river. What the hell?

I stood for a minute, probably two or three, feeling the rain running down my face, into my collar, beneath my useless jacket. I need to sit down, I thought, but there was nowhere to sit. There was only the darkness and the slight change in the darkness where the absence of trees let more darkness fall. I grasped my jo harder and trudged on.

FRIDAY – CHAPTER 85

It wasn't much further until I reached the fork in the dirt road. The right one would take me to Charlie's house, and the left would gradually ascend to join the highway.

I nearly missed it, but I sensed a change in the darkness there and I stopped and poked and prodded around like a blind man. I found where the road split. It was no less flooded there, and perhaps was more so.

And then there was the business of the manuscript too, I thought, the Zamenhof manuscript that I had found sitting on the desk in that strange house, a building that felt more familiar to me than any place I had ever been.

When I had sat down at the desk to look at it, I had expected to see the same strange markings, that oddly-changing gibberish that I had seen all the times before. But I hadn't. I saw Esperanto, and the first words formed a title, of sorts. *La Lingvo De La Kvin Elementoj.* The Language of the Five Elements.

I knew what the five elements were. They were the fundamental states of everything, the phases of material existence in Chinese philosophy and science. Water, Fire, Earth, Metal and Wood. Everything in existence was comprised of those basic properties, and each interacted with all the others, both in harmony and opposition. Drawn in a circle, each element led into the next. Water gave growth to Wood, which, when it burned, gave birth to Fire. Fire burned down to ash, giving rise to Earth. Earth, in gravity and compression, gave rise to Metal. And Metal melted into a liquid, becoming Water.

But there was another cycle that linked them as well, a destructive cycle. Water put out Fire. Fire melted Metal. Metal bit through wood like an axe. And Wood broke up the Earth as trees set down their roots.

Everything changed according to these never-ending cycles. Creation gave way to destruction and that made space needed for a new cycle of creation to begin.

This manuscript—I had discovered as I read on—was the language in which these phases communicated with each another in a never-ending conversation that created the material world and that governed the immaterial world, the world of energy and psyche.

This language was simple, so simple that it was incomprehensible, like the shifting of an electron from one valence to another, the linkage of one atom to another in a sharing of energy. That simple.

Science had attempted to create this language. It was called mathematics. But mathematics, as man has explored it, became more and more complex and had strayed further from the basic truths it sought to convey. This language did the opposite. It stripped complexities down to the simple harmony of a wave splashing onto the beach, of the wind whistling through the trees.

There were no pronouns to this language, no tenses to its verbs. Everything happened at once, and everything was everything else at once so there was no need to differentiate one thing from the other or from when anything happened. It all just was, and that which was created, not in and of itself, was created only in its infinite relationships to all else.

I had read that language and understood it.

Could I speak it? I suppose, but what good would be of that? I would only be speaking to myself, on the wind of which I breathed.

On the other hand, isn't that what I had done when I had spoken to the trees and the forest? I shook my head. I was only taking advantage of time and opportunity and the knowledge gained from watching—perhaps for many more years than I'd thought—those ways of nature.

It was that confirmation or denial of this extremely odd notion that I had hoped to find when I had returned to the shop, but the Zamenhof manuscript had been gone and was unlikely to be seen by me again. I remembered the words of Rabbi Thomas only a week—or a lifetime—earlier.

"This language is dangerously powerful," he had said as he handed the manuscript back to me. A judicious man, he had washed his hands of it immediately.

I should have been so wise.

I sensed the break in the woods which was Charlie's driveway. I had to walk back and forth along the road, skirting off to the side several times only to be blocked by brush, before I found the entrance. I turned off the road toward his house.

It was getting late.

FRIDAY – CHAPTER 86

I walked carefully down the driveway, less defined even than the road, and I used the jo as a blind man would a cane.

I came around the curve and saw light coming from a window in the back of the house where Charlie and I played Go. It surprised me for a minute, but I remembered that Charlie lived off the grid. Even on the cloudiest days, Charlie's solar panels stored enough electricity in the batteries to power his house, if he was frugal.

I listened to the roar of the river while I walked silently toward the back of his house. From the window's light that Charlie's landing looked entirely flooded and the river was streaming across his retaining wall. It was holding, as Charlie had said it would.

I stopped and listened to the river for a minute. Its current was the slapping of waves on tree trunks and the angry rumbling of a riverbed too full of itself.

I retraced my steps to the front of the house. With my jo I scratched in the mud a sigil, one of the many symbols for water which I had read in the manuscript. Why, a part of my mind asked. I don't know, I replied. For good luck, I guess. Why not?

Leaning heavily against my jo, I walked up the ramp to his front door and opened it. I made no effort to be quiet now. There was no longer any need for stealth.

"Charlie," I said loudly. "It's Asa. I came to see how you were doing."

I walked across the kitchen and entered the hallway to the back of the house.

"Of course you did, Asa," Charlie said. "Of course you did."

I walked down the hallway to the back room. Charlie had parked his wheelchair in the back corner so he could see me as I walked in. The single lamp lighting the room was off to one side, behind him, and he could watch me without the light interfering.

As I got to the end of the hall, I saw a blanket over his legs and a pistol lying on top of it.

"Stop right there, Asa," Charlie said. "I don't want you getting any closer with that stick of yours."

I stopped. We looked at each other for a minute. His face was tight. His eyes flicked across me, missing nothing.

"Where's your fucking dog?" he asked.

"I left him at home. He's keeping a couple of dead bodies company. Friends of yours, perhaps?"

Charlie shook his head. "I guess there's more than one of us who wants your sorry ass dead," he said.

"I guess. It's been a confusing week."

"I'm so, so, sorry, Asa," Charlie said. "Why don't you have a seat in that chair and tell me all about your troubles?" He waved his gun to my left, pointing to the chair I usually sat in when we played Go.

"I'll stand, thanks," I said.

"Well, at least move out of the doorway so I don't have to drag your dead self out of the way when I make myself dinner," he said. He didn't move his gun this time. It pointed at me, his hand as steady as a rock.

I stepped through the doorway and to my left. I was still cut off from any easy exit, as effectively as if I were sitting in the chair right next to me, exactly as Charlie wanted.

I looked around. There was nothing I to use to my advantage. I certainly couldn't hurl my jo at him as I had at Budgie. Charlie would have had a bullet in me before the jo even left my hand.

My movement to the left had also changed the angle between me, Charlie and the lamp, and it made it more difficult for me to see his movements. Charlie had this all figured out to a T.

"So what's the game plan?" I asked.

"Kill you. Make a sandwich. Go to bed," Charlie said. "Tomorrow, when you're nice and stiff, I'll wrap a rope around you and throw you in the river."

"Oh," I said. "Just like you did with Elle?"

Charlie's teeth clenched. "Fuck you, Cire," he said. "You have no idea."

"I know more than you think I know," I said.

"Really?" Charlie faked a yawn, though not one big enough that his eyes left me for a second. "Do tell."

The muscles in my butt were starting to cramp and the burning pain was starting to get worse. I clamped the jo tighter and tried to lean on it a little more without Charlie noticing.

"I know that she was pregnant with your child," I said.

There was silence for a second. "How'd you find that out?" he said. "Even the cops don't know that."

"Yes. Yes they do, Charlie. They kept it on the QT to help identify the killer when they got close."

"Bullshit," he said. "They wouldn't have been able to keep that quiet, not after all this time."

"Well, they did," I said. "Oh, and by the way, I've got something for you."

I moved my free hand to my side.

"I'm not trying to pull a gun on you Charlie," I said, "We both know that wouldn't work."

He was silent as I reached around to my back pocket and pulled out the knife and held it to my side.

The room filled with an enormous roar as Charlie's gun went off.

FRIDAY – CHAPTER 87

Charlie's bullet struck the knife and knocked it out of my hand.

The shock of it loosened my other hand on the jo, and I fell to the floor. My ears rang from the noise.

"Where did you get that?" Charlie hissed. "Where the fuck?"

"Where you left it, Charlie. In the cave." I rolled over and tried to sit up, but my whole leg was shaking. I couldn't even bring my feet under me. I lay facing Charlie.

"You've been there?" he said. "When?"

"Tanya showed it to me. Years ago. I found the knife in the far corner from the entrance, right where you left it."

"Damn you," he snapped. "How did you know it was mine?"

"I didn't," I said. "Not until I started trying to figure out who killed Elle. In fact, it was you who told me."

Charlie looked at me, his question battling inside to be asked.

"The day I went to pick up the *Arthashastra*," I said. You told me that not only had Elle been sodomized, but her tattoo had been removed as well. I later found out from Peterson that was something else they were keeping the lid on. After that point, it was mostly convincing myself that one of my best friends was an asshole."

Charlie laughed. "Speaking of assholes," he said, "How's yours?"

"Hurts," I said. "The hell. You, an army sniper, shot me in the ass. With a 22. A poison bullet. What the hell, Charlie. I'm sure you had something better at your disposal."

My leg had stopped shaking, but I still didn't trust it enough to try to move. There was nowhere to go, anyway, although I hated the thought of dying lying down on the ground like a lame animal.

"Damn straight I do," Charlie said, "but I wasn't going for the quick kill. I wanted you to feel the pain of a broken pelvis, feel what I feel every goddamned day. And I wanted you to know who killed you and in your last breath, realize that I had finally outmatched you. Would've worked, too, if it weren't for that dog. That pissed me off. Pissed me off so much that I wasted a shot on him instead of taking out your girlfriend and making you suffer just a little bit more."

"Well, you missed with both of them. And Tanya had some foxglove on her, some herbal digitalis, and that kept me alive until the poison was spent," I said. "I still have the bullet in me, though." I brought my leg up under me, and I managed to sit up this time. "Wait. I just realized something. That cliff—that cliff above the cave—that's where you fell, isn't it? You hid the knife in the cave, went climbing, and fell."

"Fell hell," Charlie said. "I let go."

"You tried to kill yourself."

"Biggest mistake I ever made," he said, "but it was that fall that saved my life. Surviving that—man, that was tough. Tougher than anything I'd ever done. I got my shit together after that. And then you came along and decided to fuck everything up."

He shifted the gun in his hand. It was pointed at my head.

"Not going to make the same mistake twice," he said. "This one's going right through your face. You won't even know it. The bullet will hit you, bounce around, and come out before you even hear anything. Any last words, old man?"

There it was. The end of a long life, and I was more than ready for it. The only thing—the only damn thing—was that I had failed to get justice for Elle. Now her ghost was destined to wander around for eternity, bound to the place where she'd been killed, in fear and desperation, the way she had died.

I couldn't let it go like that.

I thought of the sigil I had scratched in the mud outside. In the silence I heard the river running angrily over its banks, as angry as I. I felt the power of its current, the unstoppable power of the water that had carved mountains and caves, that had broken continents in two. I filled my lungs with that thought and began to hum.

Not hum, exactly. Just a vowel and a consonant, like a mantra, only not om, not the sound of peace, but the sound of anger, of giant waves on a beach, the sound of a tsunami as it is about to hit.

My tone merged with the raging current and the waves and I hoped that it was enough, that the energies combined would work in my favor. The Language doesn't give the power of command. I didn't believe any other language would either.

All I had was persuasion and desperation and anger.

"That's it?" Charlie said. He was grinning. "You're going to hum your way to death? Well, have it your way—"

There was a loud crack and the timbers of the retaining wall broke away. The river pounded on the ground behind it and carved away the soil in an instant.

The house began to tilt, not much, but it was enough for Charlie's wheelchair to go rolling backwards. He slammed against the back wall and the wheelchair bucked up. Charlie's head hit the wall.

I grabbed my jo and shoved myself up. The house tilted more, and I hobbled toward the front door as fast as I could and shoved my way out. The ramp had torn loose from the house and I pushed off with the jo and leaped.

I landed in a crumpled heap, pulled myself to my feet and scrambled away. When I'd reached higher ground, I turned to watch the house, screaming now as the foundation gave way, tilt up and back and slide into the river.

I leaned on my jo, watching.

The river began devouring the house like a hungry lion, ripping off pieces of siding and roof, the current now pulling them in, the waves slamming against the ground where it had stood and gouging out great chunks of soil.

The house was then on its roof beams, then it twisted to its side, and finally the current tore it to pieces as it rolled into the main current.

I watched what was left of the house being pulled downstream and I took a breath for the first time in what seemed like ages.

Then the soil gave out beneath my feet and pulled me into the river with it.

FRIDAY – CHAPTER 88

The shock of the water hit me and my head slammed into a piece of framing from Charlie's house.

I bounced off that and my body was spun around into the main current. I tried to get my bearings and struggled to stay afloat.

My head came to the surface and I took a deep breath. I stopped struggling and I sank below the surface again, but I let the current pull me up. I took another breath, and sank, and it was longer this time before I came to the surface.

A piece of Charlie's house, splintered siding, was rushing by me on the current. I grabbed at it, catching a corner as it sped past me, holding onto it with freezing hands.

The current fought me and I tried to pull myself closer to the white siding. I couldn't. It was going too fast, and I was dragging too slow. The siding ripped away from my grip and went spinning down the river. I sank again.

I came back up to the surface as a tree branch was going past. I grabbed it in a bear hug. Water gurgled violently around me, but I hung on.

The water was fresh from the mountains and cold. My feet were already tingly. I was a few miles upstream from the Cauldron, and that, I knew, was my limit. I wouldn't survive a passage through that. No one ever did, even at normal levels.

I chuckled for a second at the image of my body being spit out like a watermelon seed at the top of the falls. Apparently, I'd rather live.

I had to get to the edge of the river somehow, but I didn't see any way that I could. I was already nearly in the middle of the stream and I could only barely make out the banks in the darkness. There'd be no swimming, not here. A huge river like this, while it looks like a single stream of water, is really hundreds of smaller currents, all bound up with each other, each pushing this way and that, one filling the spot left by another, all of them inexorably rushing to the same direction. Abandoning myself to those currents would be death.

No sooner would I let go of the tree branch than the currents would be tugging me this way and that and then suck me under for good.

I tried angling the branch so that the current would push it to one side and eventually push it to the bank, but that didn't work. The eddy created by my body on the downstream side negated any effect that angle had, and the current sucked me back toward the middle.

Nothing to be done about it, I thought. Just ride it out and hope my head hit a rock first so I wouldn't feel the battering to come. I held onto the branch, floated on my back and looked at the sky. There were no stars to look at, no pale moon to light my final minutes on earth, only a darkness that was a different darkness than the earth below. Soon there would only be an empty spot where I was now, a hole to be filled in by the current.

There would be no legacy. Only a shop full of meaningless pieces and a hungry dog. Kuraĝa, I thought, we should have had more time. And with Tanya. And Nev. Even Chloe and Paul, the closest to a male friend I'd had. Too little time with them all.

We were like mayflies rising from the river in spring to fly in the sunlight for a few minutes, to mate, and then to fall back into the river and die. It didn't matter, but at the same time, it did.

Man or mayfly, the span of a lifetime is the same for everything. It's just experienced at a different tempo.

All those lives I'd lived, all for nothing. All those years I had hidden myself, hidden from myself, in echoes of lives I'd created from the currents and eddies of reality, always hiding the knowledge that I'd gained. I was still putting the pieces together, but at least there had been pieces to put together.

The language of the manuscript was a language of power, but in a way no one understood. Not to control, but to communicate. To bring things together, to understand. Like Esperanto. A language the gods used to create worlds, but no mortal could speak it. Except me.

And that wouldn't be for long.

My hands were beginning to get terribly cold now, and when they got numb, I would lose my grip on the branch. I reached around it with my whole arm so I could clamp on a little longer. That changed my angle, and suddenly I could better see upstream.

At first it looked like a moving mountain—at least from my vantage point—but it wasn't. It was the top of a tree, an evergreen, trailing the trunk behind. I couldn't see the entire thing, but maybe, I thought, maybe if I could get to it, I could climb on the trunk and slow down the hypothermia.

With my cold-addled brain, I didn't think about how I could actually grab on and climb up with hands already clumsy, or toward what end. I would still end up at the Cauldron with the rest of the debris.

But it was a chance, another chance, a better chance, and this was all I did, all I'd ever done, swing like a monkey from chance to hope to broken branch, wishing for the best.

I realized, like a wave slapping me in the face, it hadn't always been like this. I could remember before I floated through time on the eddies of lives. An earlier time when I didn't slip through life after life, hiding in the eddies of time's current. I hadn't needed to.

But then I had stolen the Language from the gods, and I had to go into hiding.

Little good that knowledge would do me now, I thought. That evergreen tree, with all its branches, would never catch up to me. I would have to let go of the branch I was holding so that I would slow down and let the tree catch up to me and hope I didn't get sucked under in the time in between.

I let go. The branch, freed of its burden, shot away from me, and I slowed down. The current pulled at me from below, a tremendous undertow I hadn't felt before, and it sucked me under with it. I fought for a minute to get to the surface, but the undertow had me in its grasp and kept pulling me deeper.

Then something changed.

The tree approached and forced the current to move its path. The grasp of the undertow on me slipped and one of the tree branches scraped my head. I grabbed it and pulled it with all my strength and tried to scramble up it to the trunk, but I couldn't.

I let go, and branches slapped me as they went by and I was running out of air and trying to grab something, anything, but I couldn't. Something else grabbed me by the jacket and then I was hurtling along with the tree and whatever had grabbed me was pulling me toward the surface. Then I was above the water, gasping for air.

I was stuck and was hanging from the root of the tree which had caught on my jacket as the trunk rotated and brought me above the surface, well, at least half-above. I was freezing cold and starting to shiver. All I could do was hang there for a minute and breathe.

Then I heard it. The roar of the water in the Cauldron. The river was now moving swiftly, faster than I'd thought. There was not much left for me to do, though. I was still in the middle of the river with no chance to reach the side—not against the currents that fought to keep me there.

Well, I wouldn't die hanging on a tree root, dammit. I reached up and took the weight off my snagged jacket until it freed itself and I put my feet on the root, underneath the water, and stood there, half above, half below, like a sailor at the wheel of a sinking ship.

We continued to speed up as the river began to narrow. I straightened up. The top of the tree, fifty feet downstream from me, hit a rock, slinging the rest of the tree sideways. I held on for dear life as the tree slid around while the current pulled it sideways and rotated it.

I went under, still holding on, and came back up on the downstream side. I could see that I was almost at the edge of the river and then I was slammed up and over, like a crazed Ferris wheel, and pulled down beneath the surface again when all the wild turning ended.

Everything came to a stop. The tree had grounded against the rocks and on the shore. I was upside down and fighting to untangle myself from the roots when I saw below me the face of Elle Anderson. She was smiling at me and she reached out to me with her hand.

This was my welcome home.

I reached out to her, and as her hand touched mine, I felt a cold numbness, colder than any river water, rising up my arm. Her hand turned into a tentacle, and her face distorted and elongated and she became an ugly, slimy beast, pulling me back under the water. I was helpless to resist.

There was a sudden, searing pain on my ankle—as if it were being crushed in a vice—and then I was suddenly yanked away from whatever had me in its grasp. I felt myself being pulled above the water and then flung onto the shore.

Right before I landed, I saw an enormous black bear running off into the woods, its jaws still wet with my blood.

I slammed into the wet sand on the edge of the river and everything went dark for a minute.

I woke up to Kuraĝa licking the mud off the side of my face and pulling me onto my back with his paw. I reached up and grabbed him and held him like eternity, and he barked happily.

I crawled on the sand as far away from the river as I could, and I had Kuraĝa lie down in front of me. I curled up around him, his body warming mine, and there we spent the night, in a sleep as deep as the oceans.

I woke up as the sun was rising. Kuraĝa was sniffing and pawing at the rocks along the shore, looking for a snack, no doubt. The rain had stopped. The clouds were beginning to break up, and in the east I could see streaks of yellow sunlight breaking through the cover.

I was wet, and I was cold, and I was hungry. I looked at the river and at the broken tree that had brought me to my deliverance, and I wondered how it had all happened, how any of this had happened with the rain and the water and the sun, now looking for me through the clouds.

For the first time in hundreds of years, I was glad to be alive.

SATURDAY – CHAPTER 89

Kuraĝa and I were picked up by a line crew out to make repairs, but they promptly turned around and brought us back into town. They offered to take me to the hospital—I did look a little waterlogged, I guess—but I insisted I was fine and they dropped us off at my house.

Cell service was up by then. I called the police and explained to them how my jeep had been destroyed the night before, going to visit a friend, and how someone had vandalized my shop and then broken into my home, only to encounter my guard dog. All told, it took three cop cruisers, one ambulance for the bodies and about four hours to get everything squared away. Peterson wasn't among the crowd. I was told he was finally back home getting some well-earned sleep.

I couldn't wait to take a shower and have some real food, but there was one more thing I had to do.

I sat down with a sheet of paper and a pencil. I thought about the page numbers on the manuscript. They were the one thing that didn't make sense, but as crazy as it might have been, I'd had an idea.

It came to me when I had been reading the *Tao Te Ching* on Tuesday. What makes things useful, Lao Tsu said, was their emptiness. The openness of a doorway or the emptiness of a cup only becomes apparent when there is a door or when there is water to fill the cup with. So too with the page numbers, the only things written in a Latin script that never changed.

I sat down and wrote the page numbers from memory. 4137581822. I added something that would make that series useful. (413)758-1822.

It was a North American telephone number. Of course, the presence of a telephone number on a manuscript written before telephones and on another continent didn't make sense. But a lot of other things didn't make sense now either, so why not?

I dialed the number. It rang, twice, and was answered.

"Asa!" I recognized the voice of the woman I'd seen in the supermarket, the same woman who had visited me as I'd split firewood. "You're alive? Took you long enough to call."

I had no real idea who I was talking to except that it was someone I should know and that she was a friend. I laughed.

"I've been a bit busy, dying and stuff," I said. "But I'm feeling much better now. By the way, who the hell are you?"

It was her turn to laugh.

"Oh, Asa, dear, you *still* aren't quite up to speed, are you? Well, I tell you what. It's awfully difficult to have a conversation like the one we're about to have over the phone, and I can barely hear you anyway, so what do you say you meet me halfway?"

"Halfway where?" I asked.

"You know the place you went to when you found the manuscript? That house on the hill? Meet me there."

"You mean, that night I got shot? That place?"

"Yes. You know how to get there. You did it when you were half-dead. Or really dead. I'll see you in a bit."

She hung up.

I put the phone down and thought for a minute. The last time I had tried this, it hadn't ended up so well. I knew a bit more this time, though, and when I sat down in front of my altar and lit the candles, I made sure Kurağa was next to me.

I put one hand on his shoulder. I closed my eyes. I began watching my breath. When all was still, I found myself on the path up to the empty house. I walked in and down the steps to the library with its towering wall of books and glass wall looking over the valley. I leaned against the desk and waited.

A moment later, the beautiful woman I had seen in the grocery store faded into view, dressed to the nines. She wore a long black dress, her hair was done up in a bun, and diamonds glittered from her necklace. She wasn't merely elegant. She was the essence of elegance, its true definition. And I knew that I'd known her for half of forever.

She looked me up and down, a broad smile growing on her face.

"You didn't wait that long to call," she said. She reached forward, brushed some mud off my face and gave me a kiss on the cheek. "I'm a bit formal for this, I know, but I was in the middle of a soiree when you called. Ambassadors and world leaders and people like that, you know."

I held a long and slow look at her face, as if I'd discovered the spot for a piece of a jigsaw puzzle that I hadn't known where to put.

"I know that I know you," I said. "It's your name I can't recall."

"Oh, Asa, we've known each other for so long and by so many different names," she said. "Call me Mica. That will work. And tell me what happened. I know parts of the story, but a lot of what went on was invisible to me. Quickly though, my guests will be missing me soon."

I don't know how long it took me, and despite Mica's words it didn't matter anyway because time didn't really seem to exist there. I told her everything. Everything. About the manuscript, the ghost of Elle Anderson, finding Kuraĝa, losing Nev and Tanya.

"So someone has the manuscript? The real one, the one you wrote, not the counterfeit I sent you?"

"The real one, Mica."

"That could be a problem," she said. She turned her head away for a minute, as if she were listening to something.

Then I was on that other faraway mountain again, sitting on that rocky outcrop, looking at her face as she listened for our pursuers.

"It was you, wasn't it?" I said. "You helped me steal the Language."

She turned back to me and laughed.

"Me, the others . . . it took a whole town to pull that off," she said. Her smile disappeared. "It led to some terrible times, though. And, to be honest, I still don't know if it was worth it. Only time will answer that."

"Worth what?" I said.

She reached her hand out, and put it on my cheek.

"If I knew, I would tell you. All I can tell you now is to heal. In time, it will all come back to you, I'm sure."

"But —"

"I've got to go, Asa. The American ambassador is about to start mouthing off about coal power again, and I can't let that happen. Not right now"

I could see concern in her eyes.

"Take care of yourself, Asa," she said.

"You too, Mica. You too."

She squeezed my hand, turned and walked into nothingness.

EPILOGUE

We got another six inches of snow last night, bringing the total this winter to around twenty. That's about right for around here.

My morning coffee is black and strong, and Kuraǧa lies beside my chair in front of the wood stove. It's a big stove, plenty big enough to warm this three-room cabin.

Last night's snow brought a morning that is crystal clear in the way that only a winter morning in the mountains can be. If it weren't for the trees surrounding us, I would be able to see across the valley. The snow is untouched except for a few bird markings and what looks to be fox tracks.

We knew the snow was coming, and Kuraǧa and I had made the trek to town two days ago, about twenty miles all told—five of them each way on foot—and had gotten plenty of provisions. It's a bit of a haul. I have to snowshoe about a mile east from the cabin to my property line by an unplowed dirt road.

Then it's downhill on the road to a small parking lot for a trailhead that connects to a two-lane paved road. That's where the new jeep is parked, and from there Kuraǧa and I drive in. I have a small sled that Kuraǧa loves to pull that we load our goods on to bring them home.

It's hard to find me. Intentionally so. I'm not changing names any more, not slipping in and out of lives that I've created to hide from those who are chasing me. They'll find me when they find me.

That decision was made for me the day I remembered who I am.

The insurance company settled—thanks to Nev's impeccable record-keeping—for about three million in damages for the losses in my shop. I put the money into the two hidden accounts. I listed my house and most of my belongings for sale, and through a dummy company I bought this cabin way back in the mountains and off the grid.

Every day I go out for a long walk with Kuraĝa and listen to the wind, and the woods, and the frozen water and the earth beneath me. In the evenings I listen to the sound of the fire in the stove.

That's how you get good at a new language. You listen more than you speak, and the more you listen, the more you understand.

For the most part, the natural world doesn't talk about humans. It talks about different things, things both closer and more distant. Those voices speak of the changes in soil, the growth of a sapling, a rock turning over in the bed of a stream. Some days I think I can even hear the far away ocean speaking of waves and tides and the moon.

My interactions in the world of humanity are more limited. When I go to town, I use one of the small library's computers to take care of what little business I have left. Last month I saw that someone, probably Nev, had taken two million out of one of the accounts. I was glad to see she'd decided to start using her inheritance.

Of Tanya, I know nothing. I assume she made it to the monastery, but beyond that I would not know, nor would I ask. About her, the winds and the woods and the water do not say.

But sometimes in the deep snowy silence of a winter night, I still listen for her voice.

ACKNOWLEDGMENTS

When I left journalism and walked out of the newsroom for the last time, I knew that there was still a novel somewhere in the bottom drawer of my mind. What I didn't know is that it would take twenty-five years to get around to writing it. When I finally pulled open that drawer I was astounded to find Asa, Tanya and Nev already clamoring to get out and have their stories told. Unbeknownst to me, the seeds of this novel had been planted and watered by two extraordinary teachers who have shared their wisdom with me over the years.

For more than two decades, aikido sensei Laura Pavlick, Shihan, has patiently taught me the way of peace when in the midst of violence. The vocabulary of conflict resolution that I have learned from Pavlick Sensei permeates every page of this book. *Doumo arigatou gozaimashita*, Sensei.

With irreverent humor and unflinching insight, Sifu Lao Zhi Chang has embodied Daoist wisdom as he has guided me along that religion's path of internal alchemy. From his teachings come this book's notions of cosmology and immortality, offered to you through the reflection of my own dusty mirror. I am forever grateful to you, Sifu.

While these teachers provided me with the insights for this book, others supported me in matters far more practical.

As the first reader of *Dark River*'s rough draft, my dear friend Bob Corlett explained to me what I had just written and his indefatigable cheerleading kept me going when rejection letters were coming in by the wagonload.

Similarly, my wife Gayle Carr listened to this story over early morning cups of coffee and late night glasses of wine, offering suggestions, pointing out corrections, and reminding me as often as I needed it that I am, in fact, the best writer in the world.

Editor Rob Carr was instrumental in shaping this book in so many ways that it is impossible to list them all. From rough manuscript to final draft, he applied his deft hand and offered me invaluable insight to the book publishing world. If you have enjoyed what you read, Rob is largely to thank, and my gratitude to him is enormous.

Finally, I must thank publisher Reagan Rothe. The world is made richer by his willingness to take on unknown authors and help turn their vision into reality.

NOTE FROM THE AUTHOR

Word-of-mouth is crucial for any author to succeed. If you enjoyed *Dark River*, please leave a review online—anywhere you are able. Even if it's just a sentence or two. It would make all the difference and would be very much appreciated.

Thanks!
Avery

ABOUT THE AUTHOR

Dr. Avery Jenkins is a former award-winning journalist and essayist who took a 25-year break from the writing world to become a chiropractor and acupuncturist. He holds a 2nd degree black belt in the martial art of aikido and is in his final year of training to become a Daoist priest. Dr. Jenkins lives in northwest Connecticut with his wife and two dogs of uncertain temperament.

Thank you so much for reading one of our
Visionary/Metaphysical Fiction novels.
If you enjoyed the experience, please check out our
recommended title for your next great read!

Woman in Red by Krishna Rose

"*Woman in Red - Magdalene Speaks* is a well-researched and believable work of fiction that will challenge believers and atheists with an equally rich interpretive of gospel, history, and culture of two thousand years ago."

–AUTHORS READING

Made in the USA
Middletown, DE
13 March 2021

35470447R00170